No Way to Peace

Tom Milton

NEPPERHAN PRESS, LLC
YONKERS, NY

Published by Nepperhan Press, LLC
P.O. Box 1448, Yonkers, NY 10702
nepperhan@optonline.net
nepperhan.com

PUBLISHER'S NOTE
This is a work of fiction. Names, characters, places, and incidents
are the product of the author's imagination or are used fictitiously,
and any resemblance to actual persons, living or dead, events, or
locales is entirely coincidental.

Printed in the United States of America

Library of Congress Control Number: 2007904422

ISBN 978-0-9794579-0-6

Cover art was licensed from the Image Club
collection of Getty Images, Inc.

For Marie

"There is no way to peace. Peace is the way."

Attributed to: Mahatma Gandhi,
A.J. Muste, and Thich Nhat Hanh

Buenos Aires, 1976

ONE

WHEN HE SAW the two men with their bulky satchels, Stephen assumed they had come to give him the usual type of assignment.

Their operative names were "John O'Connor" and "Bill Lowry," and they had covers as employees of the U.S. Embassy, as he learned when he accidentally met them at a cocktail party given by the ambassador for a junketing senator. Pretending not to know him, John introduced himself as a trade specialist and Bill as an agricultural attaché. On that occasion, as they talked about trade and agriculture, Stephen was impressed by how much they knew about these subjects.

Led by a white-coated *ordenanza*, they crossed the open area of the banking floor and slipped into the conference room, closing the door behind them.

Stephen waited a few minutes, giving them time to check the room for possible bugs, and then he got up and strolled after them. The elegant mahogany desks that occupied the floor were empty now since the account managers were out having lunch with clients and prospects. Lunch was the main event of their day. At lunch, while consuming slabs of beef, the account managers built relationships and made deals.

Entering the conference room, he found John already seated at the table while Bill was methodically waving a detector over the shelves of gilded tomes that contained the nation's convoluted, seldom-observed tax code.

They exchanged greetings. Then John took a piece of yellow paper out of his shirt pocket and handed it to Stephen, saying:

"This is what we need today."

The order, printed neatly in pencil, was for an amount of Uruguayan pesos worth almost a million dollars at the current exchange rate.

"Is that it?" Stephen asked.

"That's it for money," John said. He was a heavy man with a florid complexion and a Boston accent.

Stephen got up and went to the phone and called the foreign exchange department and placed the order while the two agents waited in silence. Returning to the table, he told them: "It'll take about a half hour."

"That's okay," John said. "It'll give us time to talk about the other matter."

"What other matter?" Stephen asked, sitting down.

John glanced at Bill, who was lighting a cigarette. Bill was gaunt, with receding black hair and a poker face. From his way of speaking you could tell that he was from New York and that he had grown up in a tough neighborhood.

"The Montoneros," John said, leaning back in his chair and pausing for effect. He was referring to a group of terrorists who had been waging war since 1970 when they kidnapped and executed General Aramburu. They bombed police stations, military installations, and symbols of foreign capitalism, and they assassinated people whom they regarded as enemies of their socialist vision. They financed their operations by kidnapping business executives and holding them for ransom. "We figure that over the past few years they've collected more than eighty million dollars in ransom money."

"And you don't keep that kind of money under a mattress," Bill observed.

"They must keep it in a bank somewhere," John said. "In dollars of course."

"You wouldn't want to keep it in pesos," Bill said.

"You wouldn't," Stephen agreed. Because of the astronomical inflation the peso lost value faster than you could spend it. That was why the bank paid its employees weekly—so they could spend their money before it lost any more value.

"We've been trying to find out where they're keeping it, but we weren't getting anywhere until a few days ago when we received some new information." John paused again for effect. "It came from a source in Panama, where we have agents poking around. As you know, Panama is the money laundering capital of the world."

"They have a laundry on every corner," Bill said after exhaling a dual stream of smoke, "where you can get your money washed, dried, and folded."

"You can tell he's a bachelor," John said.

"A happy one, unlike you."

"You're only happy because you're high on nicotine."

"It's better than being low on alcohol."

"Our source in Panama," John resumed, "is pointing us toward a bank you know well."

"You mean *our* bank?"

"This man is quick," John said to his colleague.

"He figures things out in no time," Bill said, tapping his cigarette on the ashtray.

"You think our bank is laundering their money?"

"We think it's involved in the process," John said. "Not knowingly, but it's involved. And that's good."

"It is? Why?"

"It gives us a step in the process where we can pick up the trail of the money."

"Okay. So what's the process?"

"Here's how we think it works," John said as if he enjoyed imparting knowledge to ignorant listeners. "They kidnap someone, they get the ransom money in cash, and then they take it out of the country."

"How?" Stephen asked.

"They take it on a plane to Panama."

"On a regular flight?"

"Oh, yeah," John said. "We think they go from here to Brazil on Aerolineas Argentinas, and from there to Panama on one of the Brazilian airlines."

"Unlike the executives they kidnap," Bill said, "they don't waste money on private planes."

"They get on the plane with a bag of cash?"

"Yeah," John said, "like the bags we use."

"We take them everywhere," Bill said.

"But wouldn't they get caught?"

"Naw," John said. "Those airlines don't care what you carry onto the plane, and the couriers don't have to worry about being stopped in Panama."

"If people were stopped from bringing cash into Panama," Bill explained, "the economy would collapse."

"Okay," Stephen said. "They take the cash on a plane to Panama, and then what?"

"They deposit it there in the branch of a Swiss bank," John said, "which transfers it through your Panama branch to a bank in New York called International Bank & Trust."

"I don't know that bank."

"Most people don't. It was started about five years ago by a former political campaign manager who had great connections in Albany. It looks like his purpose was to get a license, start a bank, and then flip it."

"Who owns it now?"

"A man named Marco Safadi."

"I don't know him, but he sounds familiar."

"He's an interesting character," John said. "He's about your age. He was born here during the war—"

"He means World War II," Bill said helpfully.

"He didn't think I meant Vietnam," John snapped. "As I was saying, Safadi grew up in Buenos Aires, and then he disappeared for a while. We know he lived in Israel, but we don't know what he did there. He spent some time in Russia, and then he came back here. He made a pile of money trading commodities and smuggling. One of our sources says he was a big-time operator who knew everyone in customs and could bring in whatever he wanted. About five years ago he bought a local bank and became respectable."

"I could never understand," Bill said, "why bankers are considered respectable."

"They have the money to buy respect."

"Yeah, other people's money."

"Anyway," John continued, "about three years ago he bought International Bank & Trust."

"So he owns a bank here and a bank in New York," Stephen said, putting the pieces together.

"Right. I guess that makes him an international banker."

"What's the name of the bank here?"

"Banco Azulay."

"Now, that bank I know."

"You should know it," John said. "It has a relationship with your bank."

"Apparently a good relationship," Stephen said, having seen Banco Azulay in a recent report on profitable accounts. It was based in Once, the district of Buenos Aires where the garment industry was concentrated.

"This bank was started more than fifty years ago," John said, "by prominent members of the Jewish community, and it's always served that community. A few years ago Safadi began using scare tactics to get its clients and other members of the community to take their money out of the country and put it into his bank in New York."

"What kind of scare tactics?"

"Saying the government could confiscate the assets of Jews."

"Well, that could happen if the military take over."

"Yeah. I know. But Safadi exploits the community's fears to get their money."

"So we don't approve of his marketing tactics," Stephen said. "If their money's in a New York bank, it should be safe."

"It should be. But if it were my money, I wouldn't want it in a bank that's laundering money for terrorists."

"If you know this, why don't you have the New York banking authorities intervene?"

"We don't know it. We only suspect it."

"We need evidence," Bill said.

"What kind of evidence?"

"We need evidence," John said, "that this bank is laundering money, and we need evidence that this money belongs to the Montoneros."

"We only need evidence that the bank is laundering money," Bill said. "The banking authorities don't care who it belongs to."

"We care."

"I know. But we don't have to prove that the money belongs to terrorists in order to have the account frozen."

"Then let's say we would *like* to have evidence that this money belongs to the Montoneros."

"How much of their money," Stephen asked, "do you think they have at International Bank & Trust?"

"We think they have all of it there," John said. "So if we can have their account frozen, we can put them out of business."

"They evidently don't believe in diversification," Bill said.

"And even if it's not all of their money, we can take the wind out of their sails."

"You can tell his family had a yacht."

"Yeah. In South Boston."

"Okay," Stephen said. "So how can I help you?"

"You can get information from your Panama branch that'll

help us track this money," John said. "We'll give you the name of the Swiss bank where we think the cash is being deposited, and you can ask your Panama branch to send you copies of all remittances from that bank over the past three years."

"Don't forget the shipments of arms," Bill said.

"Oh, yeah. We think Safadi is using legitimate imports as a cover for bringing arms into the country for the Montoneros. The shipments are made under letters of credit issued by Banco Azulay and confirmed by your bank. So if you can give us information on all shipments made under their letters of credit, we can stop the arms hidden in these shipments from getting through customs."

"How are they getting through customs now?"

"The usual way," Bill said, rubbing his thumb against his fingers in the universal sign for a bribe.

"Okay. Is there anything else?"

"I think that's enough for you to get started," John said.

At that point they were interrupted by a discreet knock on the door.

It was Salvatori, the head trader, with a canvas sack that he brought into the conference room and set on the table. Salvatori was a handsome man with glossy black hair combed straight back, a virile mustache, and a batch of keys hanging from his belt. "I counted it myself," he said in Spanish that sounded almost like Italian. "It's all there."

"Thanks," Stephen said. He signed the form that Salvatori had placed on the table, having authority to approve up to a million dollars per transaction for deliveries of currency to John and Bill. As required by this special arrangement, both men signed the receipt, and with the signed form in hand the head trader promptly left them.

Bill began to count the money, a bill at a time, as if he were tallying the haul from a bank robbery.

After leaving the two men in the conference room, Stephen returned to his desk and called the credit department and requested the file on Banco Azulay. As he waited for it he remembered how he met John and Bill. It was last July, a few weeks after the Montoneros kidnapped his assistant, Alejandro, a young man with a promising career and the father of three small children. In the eyes of his kidnappers Alejandro had committed the unpardonable sin of working for a foreign bank, and they made him pay for it. They didn't even ask for ransom money, as if implying that his life wasn't worth anything, and they killed him with a bullet in the back of his head, dumping his body at the side of a road outside the city.

The death of Alejandro greatly affected Stephen, not only because he had a close relationship with his assistant but also because as a foreigner *he* should have been the target for the Montoneros, not Alejandro. By then the bank had withdrawn its foreign staff except for Stephen, who volunteered to stay since he didn't have a wife and children to worry about. The vice president in New York, who didn't entirely trust local people to manage the bank, felt that he needed an American there to keep an eye on things, so he agreed to let Stephen stay provided that he kept a low profile.

Stephen was grieving for Alejandro when the two men appeared at the bank in fedora hats and trench coats, looking as if they were from central casting in their roles as CIA agents, with a letter from the chairman of the bank requesting him to deliver currency to them from time to time. He knew they had selected him because of his top security clearance, which the CIA had maintained since his senior year at Princeton when they offered him a job after checking with everyone who had ever known him, including girls he had dated in high school. Two years after he turned down the job they found him in the army and took him out of artillery and moved him into intelligence, which may have spared him from being killed in Vietnam. The experience left him with a complete lack of respect for political leaders since they ignored the information he worked so hard to collect, and they fabricated the information they used to justify their decisions.

In this situation his role would be limited to providing the two agents with money to pay for information about the Montoneros as well as guerrillas in neighboring countries. Since he assumed they would use this information to help the governments in their counter-terrorist activities, he saw the chairman's request as an opportunity for him to play a role in stopping the violence. He needed to do something about it because he felt that he was somehow responsible for Alejandro's death, or that he had somehow failed to prevent it. So with all his misgivings about the CIA and its operations, he finally agreed to help them.

"*Señor*," said an *ordenanza*, whose name was Ignacio. "Here's the file that you requested."

"*Gracias.*" He took the file. "How's your daughter?"

"Oh, she's fine," the man said, brightening. His daughter, who was fifteen, had an emergency appendectomy earlier that week. "She's getting better every day."

Alone at his desk, Stephen sat back and opened the file, which he held in his lap. The pages were attached to both the front and the back covers, with the client's credit lines on the left and correspondence on the right. He noted that the account manager was Tito Arias, who specialized in the textile and garment industries. Arias had been with the bank for more than twenty years, and he had done well. He owned an apartment in Barrio Norte, and he had a second home in Punta del Este, where he was today, having taken Friday off for a long weekend. The vice president in New York believed that Arias was making extra money off the bank, so Stephen periodically asked the internal auditors to take a close look at what he was doing, but they never found anything amiss.

Stephen learned that Banco Azulay had been a client of the bank since the 1930s and that Arias became the account manager shortly after Safadi acquired it. Before that Arias managed the bank's relationship with Safadi, which he had developed years ago as a new business officer in the Once district. Banco Azulay had three approved lines of credit: an overdraft line, a line for confirming its import letters of credit, and a line for foreign exchange. The amounts were appropriate for a bank of its size, and they must have passed the scrutiny of federal bank examiners as well as the internal auditors since there were no negative comments.

It would take much longer to get information about the remittances from the Swiss bank, so Stephen decided to start with the task of getting information about the shipments under letters of credit issued by Banco Azulay.

He called the letter of credit department and talked with Sylvia, the manager. He asked her for copies of all pending letters of credit that the bank had confirmed for Banco Azulay. They were delivered to him about a half hour later, just as the account managers were beginning to return from lunch. It took more than an hour for him to listen to their informal reports of what they had accomplished, with references to food that made him hungry. If he hadn't met with the embassy guys, who always came at lunch hour, he would have been with one of the account managers enjoying a steak with fried potatoes and a carafe of red wine.

When they had settled down at their desks Stephen reviewed the letters of credit, looking for the earliest expiry date. It was February 20, so the shipment had to be on board by then. Depending on its route from Panama, the ship would arrive in Buenos Aires during the first week of March. Since the shipping documents would be presented to his bank's branch in Panama, he would be able to get copies of them to determine the name of the vessel and its expected time of arrival.

By six o'clock the bank was empty. It was Friday, summer, and Stephen had walked around urging managers and employees to go home to their families. He wasn't the top ranking officer, but being the only American—a member of a culture that lived to work—he had the referent power to let people go home early.

Outside, it was still light and still hot, though a faint breeze from the Rio de la Plata provided some relief. The streets were filled with people walking, not rushing as they did in New York but taking their time. He walked to Florida, where cars weren't allowed, and then over to Avenida de Mayo, where he turned and headed toward the Congreso. Its lofty dome was illuminated by the long rays of evening sunlight that traveled from far across the *pampa*.

Avenida de Mayo, which ran for about fifteen blocks between the Congreso and the Casa Rosada, the equivalent of the White House, was the political heart of the city. It was lined with grand old buildings that had ornate facades and cupolas, reminders of a time when Argentina was one of the world's wealthiest countries. The avenue had definitely seen better days, but it still retained an aura of grandeur, and its cafes, bars, and restaurants still buzzed with irrepressible conversations among politicians, journalists, bankers, and businessmen, plotting, conniving, dealing, critiquing, and spinning dreams of wealth and power, with tango music always in the background.

After walking two blocks Stephen turned into the café where he and his friends met every Friday after work. Whoever got there first took over the round table in back where there was room for all of them, though in the summer with vacations they weren't all likely to be there.

Chris and Sofi were at the table. Chris was an American, and he worked for an international nonprofit organization whose mission was to help unemployed people start businesses. He came to Argentina after a tour of duty in Chile with the Peace Corps, and he earned a master's degree in business from the Universidad Católica while working for his current employer. He spoke Spanish so well that he could pass for a native of his adopted country. He was full of enthusiasm, and when he talked about a new project his hands flew all over the place—it was wise to keep your glass safely out of range. Sofi, whom he met while he was still in the Peace Corps, was a social worker who spent her days in the slums that were aptly known as *villas miseria*. She was usually quiet, but you were always aware of her presence, and there was a light in her dark eyes that radiated faith and commitment.

They both got up and exchanged *abrazos* with him. Stephen hadn't seen them for a while since last week he was in New York finalizing his divorce from Leila, and the previous week they were on vacation at Mar del Plata, the beach resort that was most accessible to Buenos Aires.

"Are you all right?" Sofi asked after they sat down.

"I'm fine," he said, appreciating her concern.

"Well, we have some news," she said with a glance at Chris. Her eyes were glistening with joy. "We're going to have a baby."

"You are? That's wonderful!"

"It's due in September," Chris said, beaming.

Knowing how good and loving they were, he felt that the baby was lucky to have them as parents. He noticed that instead of her usual glass of white wine Sofi had in front of her a bottle of Villavicencio water.

A few minutes later Elena arrived with her copious shoulder bag. She was tall and fair, a member of the important Anglo community that still spoke English among themselves though they had resided in Argentina for several generations (at home she was Helen). She was a journalist, covering politics for an English-language newspaper. A well-meaning Anglo client, who thought they would make a perfect couple, introduced Stephen to her a year after Leila had left him. It turned out that Elena wasn't looking for a husband any more than he was looking for a second wife, but they became good friends. Elena had a strong personality that got her into trouble in a culture where males were supposed to be dominant.

After hearing the news about the baby and expressing her joy, Elena turned to him and asked: "How was New York?"

"Efficient," he said. "I'm glad to be back."

"If you'd stayed longer, you might have missed it."

"You mean the *golpe?*"

"It could happen any day now."

As the elected government foundered, people were waiting for the military to come out from behind the scenes and take over. Some people dreaded what would happen, but many people had reached the point where they believed that only the military could end the war.

Stephen, who had come to Argentina when the military were running the country, remembered how incompetent they were. He also remembered how they interfered with the university and perverted the teachings of the church. So he didn't respect the military any more than his friends did, but like them he believed that a *golpe de estado* was inevitable.

"Who do you think will lead the *junta?*" he asked Elena.

"General Videla."

"They say he's a moderate."

Elena snorted. "Moderate? Well, if you compare him with Admiral Massera, you can say he is."

He had heard that Massera was an extremist. Indeed, by those who admired him least the admiral was considered a Nazi. "I assume they'll feel they have a mandate from the people to rid the country of terrorists."

"They'll feel they have a mandate from God."

"Then they won't stop at anything."

"They certainly won't stop at ridding the country of terrorists."

"Terrorists?" said Mario, who had just arrived with his wife Teresa. Mario was a professor of political science at the University of Buenos Aires, and Teresa was an elementary school teacher. "You must be talking about politics."

"What else do we talk about?" Elena said.

"Sometimes we talk about more important things," Stephen said, having risen for *abrazos* with the new arrivals. "Sofi?"

"We're going to have a baby," Sofi said on cue.

There were exclamations and more *abrazos*, and at least for a while no one talked about politics. Then Mario, who had sat down next to Elena, said: "It sounded like you were talking about the military."

"Everyone is," Elena said.

"Everyone's waiting for them to take over, even hoping for them to take over," Mario said. "But whenever they run the country they make things worse."

"So what should they do?" Elena asked.

"They should guarantee a fair election," Mario said.

"In a fair election Perón would win."

"Perón is dead," Teresa said.

"He would still win," Elena said.

"So we'd have a dead man running the country?"

"We have a dead man running it now."

"Well, how do we get rid of him?"

"That's a good question," Mario said. "In fact, it's the only question worth asking about politics in this country."

"We have to get beyond him," Elena said.

"We have to grow up politically," Mario said.

"As children grow up," Teresa said.

"Children who have been abused by their parents," Sofi said.

"We have to break the cycle of abuse," Elena said.

"It can be done," Sofi affirmed. "I've seen it happen."

"I have too," Teresa said. "I've seen students overcome the damage done by their parents."

"Then there's hope for us," Elena said positively.

They all evidently agreed that there was.

They stayed until around eight-thirty, and then they scattered, with the married couples heading home for supper and the two singles sharing a taxi to Barrio Norte. They both got out at the building on Juncal where Elena lived, and they lingered for a while in front of it, talking.

Elena had just turned twenty-six, and by her age most young women in this country were already married, so older people were beginning to shake their heads and wonder if she would end up as a spinster. Like most unmarried women, and most unmarried men for that matter, she lived with her parents, who even though they had three children preferred the city to the suburbs. Her father could walk to work, and her mother had easy access to a wide array of cultural and civic activities that engaged her. On weekends the family could go to the Hurlingham Club, which had a swimming pool, grass tennis courts, a cricket pitch, and a polo field, not to mention its famous Sunday buffet lunch. During the past two years Elena had often invited Stephen to join her family at the club, where they played genteel mixed doubles with her parents while her younger brothers played ruthless singles.

"So you're an eligible bachelor now," Elena teased him. "You better watch out. There're a lot of girls in the market for husbands."

"I've been a bachelor for three years," he reminded her.

"But you weren't legally eligible before."

"Well, maybe we should let people think I'm still married."

"It's too late. They all know."

"They can't all know."

"If one of them knows, then they all know. But don't worry," Elena assured him with an arch smile. "It won't affect our relationship."

"You mean you're still not looking for a husband?"

"If I were, I wouldn't let any of *them* have you."

"That's good. And I'm not looking for a second wife."

"But you could marry again on the rebound."

"No, I couldn't," he protested. "That only happens to men who miss being married."

"Then you can enjoy being a bachelor."

They gave each other a friendly *abrazo* and said goodnight.

Stephen walked to Arenales and then up the street to the apartment building where he lived. The *portero*, an old Spaniard (derogatively referred to as a *gallego*), was standing at the door in the dusk, and he greeted Stephen with the usual formality. Like many others he had fled to Argentina as a refugee of the Spanish Civil War, and he still spoke with a Spanish accent, lisping his zees and soft cees.

There was no mail, so Stephen headed directly for the elevator and went up to the fifth floor. He entered his apartment, groping for the light-switch. After three years he was still affected by the emptiness of the apartment, which had two bedrooms, two baths, a family room, a formal living room, a spacious dining room, a kitchen, a pantry, and a laundry room. He had shipped the last of Leila's things about a year ago when they decided that their separation was permanent, so there was no evidence that anyone else had ever lived there. He used the apartment mainly as a place to sleep, having given up on the idea of cooking for himself—it was so easy and so inexpensive to eat out, and he was now used to eating alone in restaurants.

Stephen had avoided dating even during the past year since legally he had still been married, and the single women he met on social occasions were not the kind who would have relationships with married men. He was now eligible, but he still didn't plan to start dating since these young women, incited by their parents and a culture that looked with askance on a single woman over twenty-five, were seeking husbands, and he had no intention of marrying again.

He slung his jacket over the back of a chair in the living room and headed for the bathroom, where he doused his face and combed his hair. People assumed that he was Argentine, with his dark hair, dark eyes, and olive complexion—the legacy from a Spanish great-grandmother, transmitted through his mother—but when he spoke Spanish, as fluent as he was, they could tell from his accent that he was American.

After freshening up he went out and walked to Plaza San Martín, in the center of which was a statue of the Liberator on a rearing horse with his hand raised and his index finger pointing to the Andes. On a tour of the city after their arrival Stephen and Leila were shown this plaza by a colleague from the bank, an Argentine, who pointed to the statue, imitating the Liberator, and said: "That's San Martín—the nation's first and last hero." A pigeon was sitting on his finger.

Stephen crossed the plaza and headed down Florida. It was dark now, the stores were lit, and people were walking slowly, stopping to look in the windows, mostly at clothes. It was still hot but more bearable now as long as you didn't walk too fast. It was no worse than New York in early August.

He turned on Lavalle and headed for the restaurant where he was meeting Boyd, a client who worked down in Comodoro Rivadavia, the center of the oil region. Boyd was a petroleum engineer with an oil service company, working in an area where a number of Americans remained in the country. For some reason the Montoneros didn't pay much attention to the oil region, while in other countries their counterparts were blowing up pipelines.

Boyd came up to Buenos Aires on weekends whenever he could, and they had dinner about once a month. They always went to La Estancia, which at the front had all kinds of meat grilling over open fires of hard wood. As usual the restaurant was packed, and it took Stephen a while to spot Boyd sitting at a table against the wall.

Boyd got up and shook hands. He was a big man with a buzz cut and jaded blue eyes. A carafe of red wine stood on the table, already half empty. "You look good," Boyd drawled as they sat down, "for someone who has just been stripped of all his assets by a bloodthirsty New York lawyer."

"It wasn't like that," Stephen said, reaching for the wine.

"Then you were lucky. By the time they were finished with me I felt like a plucked chicken." Boyd had left his wife behind when he came to Argentina, expecting to be there only about six months, but his assignment kept getting extended. When his wife finally gave him an ultimatum he decided that he would rather stay in Argentina than return to Oklahoma, so they split up. Among other things that he and Stephen had in common was their unwillingness or inability to leave Argentina.

A waiter came to take their order. Stephen was starved since he hadn't eaten lunch, so he ordered a *parrillada*, a mixed grill with short ribs, sweetbreads, tripe, and two kinds of sausage. Boyd ordered a giant slab of beef, rare.

"I wish they had a place like this in Comodoro."

"I'm surprised they don't. They have meat everywhere."

"They have meat there, but the best is here."

Buenos Aires was not only the nation's capital but also its

financial center and its major port. The meat industry, which exported its products, was based at the Mataderos stockyards on the other side of town.

"So what are you going to do," Boyd asked, "now that you're a free man?"

Stephen shrugged. "Nothing different."

"Oh, come on. You're not a priest."

"I don't want to get involved with anyone."

"You don't have to get involved. You can just have a good time. What's wrong with that?"

"Nothing," Stephen murmured, ending the subject.

The waiter brought a salad of lettuce and tomatoes along with cruets of olive oil and vinegar, which Stephen began to mix in the stainless steel bowl.

"So when are the generals going to take over?" Boyd asked.

"Soon, I hear. It's in the air."

"It won't be too soon. The *peronistas* have made a real mess of things."

"They inherited a mess from the last military government."

"Well, at least that government maintained order."

"That's true." The last military government maintained order by repressing any sign of dissidence. But it wasn't able to reform the economy, and it wasn't able to deal with the legacy of social conflict. So things deteriorated to the point where the military handed the country back to the politicians.

"I read that the Montoneros kidnapped another manager from that Italian company," Boyd said, taking some salad. "Did they ever release him?"

"Yeah. With a bullet in his head."

"Why did they kill him? His company wouldn't pay?"

"I don't know. I guess they felt like killing him."

Boyd shook his head in condemnation of the terrorists. Then after eating some salad he asked: "Why do you stay here?"

"I don't know," Stephen said honestly.

"It's not because you were happily married here."

"No. I lived here while I was married, but not happily. So maybe it's because I don't want to leave the scene of a crime."

"That's heavy, man."

"Well, I wasn't serious." He thought about his mission to stop the killing. "It's because I don't want to leave the country in such a mess."

"Why do you care? It's not your country."

"I don't know why I care, but I do. Why do *you* stay?"

Boyd chewed thoughtfully. "I like my work, the money's good, and I don't have any responsibilities."

Stephen nodded. "That makes sense."

"So maybe we're not crazy."

When the meat arrived, fresh off the grill, they found a good reason for staying.

"You can't get steak like this in Oklahoma."

"Or in New York," Stephen agreed.

After paying the check and tipping the waiter, Boyd said: "Well, now that you're a free man, you have no excuse for not coming with me tonight."

On his weekend visits Boyd always ended the night at a club called Minas, which was reputed to have the most beautiful girls in Buenos Aires. He often urged Stephen to join him, but Stephen always turned him down. Boyd insisted that the girls weren't prostitutes, they were more like geishas, refined and attentive, but Stephen was never in the mood for it.

"I don't think so."

"Oh, come on. Just one time."

Though Stephen still hesitated, the finalization of his divorce relieved him of an inhibition and cleared the way for him to go along and see what Minas was all about.

It was almost midnight when they got there, but things were still quiet at the club. Buenos Aires was an all-night city, as he learned the first time he went to a disco with Leila and others, arriving at midnight and finding it still almost empty.

They were given a table at the edge of the dance floor, the kind of table that would have been reserved for regulars. The girls were standing and sitting at the bar, which abutted the left side of the floor. They had a variety of dress colors, hair colors, and skin colors, though not much variety in age—they all seemed to be in their twenties. On the far side of the smoky room a combo was playing a Latin song.

They ordered drinks. From the red wine at dinner they both advanced to Scotch. And they sat back, facing the dance floor.

"You see?" Boyd said. "It's a nice place."

Stephen relaxed and absorbed the scene. It reminded him of the clubs he had gone to in New York when he was in college, drinking Scotch and breathing smoke and listening to jazz. At the time he wanted to be a writer, and he believed that it was essential to hang out in such places.

The combo had just started playing "*Bésame mucho*" when a girl in a white dress left the bar and glided toward him.

With a smile she extended her hand and asked in English: "Would you like to dance?"

She had neat black hair and coffee-colored skin, and her smile was so honestly inviting that he got up and joined her without a moment's hesitation.

As they started to dance, without talking, she rested her left hand on his shoulder as if it belonged there. They were close enough so that he could feel her warmth against his chest and her breath on his neck. She didn't smell at all like perfume, she smelled like bath soap, fresh and pristine.

They continued dancing, moving slowly around the floor as the piano player sang: "Kiss me, kiss me a lot, as if tonight were the last time."

Whatever it was, the night, the music, the place where he had arrived in his life, he was overcome with emotion, and without even knowing the girl's name he felt as if she were the one he had always wanted.

When the song ended they stopped and stood apart from each other. From the look in her eyes he thought he could tell that she felt something special too, and he gazed at her thankfully, not knowing what to say or what language to use.

She finally said in English: "I'm Cathy."

"I'm Stephen. And I don't know what else to say."

"Then we'll just dance."

They danced for an hour or so without talking until the combo took a break. At that point they joined Boyd and a girl at the table, and prompted by his savvy friend, he ordered a bottle of champagne for Cathy, which she didn't touch.

Around three she went and talked with a silver-haired man behind the bar, and then she stopped and had a brief conversation with another girl, nodding more than once as if she were getting directions. She patted the girl's arm and returned to Stephen, saying: "We can go now."

Without any plan he paid the bill and left with her, looking back over his shoulder and getting a thumbs-up from Boyd, who seemed ready to spend the night there.

Outside, it was cooler, and there were fewer people on the street but the city was still by no means asleep. A taxi pulled up, and a pair of men in uniform with a lot of ribbons and insignias stumbled out.

"Come on," Cathy said, getting into the taxi. "I know a place where we can go."

He followed her and sat beside her while she gave an address to the driver. Like many of the taxis in Buenos Aires it was an old Mercedes, repaired many times and still running well, still relatively comfortable.

About ten minutes later they pulled up at a *hotel alojamiento*, a type of hotel that rented rooms by the hour. Years ago he saw an Argentine film about such a hotel, a hilarious commentary on the mores of *porteños*, as the inhabitants of Buenos Aires were called. It was said that these hotels did more business than the regular hotels.

He paid for five hours in advance, got a key, and went with Cathy in a creaky elevator to the sixth floor. The room was simple, with a queen-size bed, a table, and two chairs. He turned off the harsh overhead light as soon as Cathy turned on a soft lamp on the table.

When she reached out her hands he took them and pulled her gently toward him and kissed her. From the first contact with her mouth it felt as if they were made for each other, and they went as far as a kiss could go.

"Before we go any farther," she said when they stopped to take a breath, "I want to make sure you know what I am. I'm a bar girl, not a prostitute. I'm paid to entertain men at the club, not to sleep with them."

"I understand," he said, though he really didn't.

"I'll be right back," she promised him.

While she was in the bathroom he stood there, not knowing what to do other than wait for her. She reappeared a few minutes later without a stitch of clothes on, strolling toward him in her natural state as if she thought nothing of it.

He drew her toward him, kissing her and clasping his hands around her firm bottom and holding her tight.

She undid his tie and then started unbuttoning his shirt.

Relieved of his clothes, he dropped to his knees and pressed his face against her, wrapping his arms around her.

"*Querido*," she murmured, stroking his hair.

Later in bed, under the sheet, she lay curled up with her face to his chest, an arm draped over his waist, and her knees against his thighs, sleeping peacefully. As he held this girl who smelled like bath soap he was amazed by the fact that though she knew nothing about him, she trusted him enough to go to sleep in his arms. Unequivocally, the language of her body declared that she felt safe with him.

TWO

THEY SLEPT LATE the next day, and on the way out of the hotel he stopped at the desk and paid for the extra hours.

Outside, they were confronted by a bright hot day. The sun was directly overhead and beating down on the busy street, reflecting off the chrome and glass of the passing vehicles in blinding flashes.

"I'll take you home," he offered.

"No, thanks. I'll get a taxi."

He gazed at her in the daylight, struck by how young she looked. She wore no makeup, not even lipstick, but her face didn't need any enhancements. "Are you working tonight?"

"Yes," she said. "I work every night except Sunday."

"Then I'll meet you at the club."

"Okay. You should come around three," she added. "If you buy a bottle of champagne, my boss will let me go."

On an impulse he said: "If you don't have to work on Sunday, we could spend the day together."

"That would be nice."

He signaled for a taxi, and before they parted he hugged her and kissed her softly on the forehead. "I'll see you at three."

"*Si Dios quiere.*" Those were the only words she had spoken to him in Spanish except when they were making love, and they meant: "God willing." For a moment the words left him with the awful feeling that whether or not they saw each other again depended on something beyond their control, but he shook it off, flatly refusing to accept the possibility that God might not be willing.

With a wrench of separation he watched her taxi turn the corner, catching a last glimpse of her neatly brushed black hair. Then he started walking, not knowing where he was but having some sense of direction and heading toward Avenida Santa Fe, which would lead him home.

As he walked he replayed what had happened last night from the moment he saw her coming toward him: her white dress, her inviting smile, her hand on his shoulder, her body against him, her smell of bath soap, the way she strolled out of the bathroom, and all that followed. But what still touched him more than anything was the way she went to sleep in his arms, the way she trusted him with her life.

When he reached the corner of Arenales and Carlos Pellegrini he thought he could still detect on the sidewalk the residue of blood stains from Rodolfo Ortega Peña, a leftist *peronista* politician who was gunned down eighteen months ago by the Argentine Anticommunist Alliance, or Triple A, a right-wing paramilitary group that reported to the minister of welfare, José López Rega. The hit was one of an ongoing series of assassinations by the Triple A.

Approaching his apartment building, he saw the bank car waiting in front of it. The driver was chatting with the *portero*, and the bodyguard was standing by the car alertly.

"Oh, shit," he said to himself, remembering that he was supposed to attend a party at the house of the president of the Argentine subsidiary of a large American corporation, an important client of the bank. He didn't feel like going to the party, but it would kill time, and he had a lot of time to kill before he could see Cathy.

"Señor Wyatt," the driver said, pretending not to notice that Stephen must have been out all night. "Are you ready?"

"I'll be right back," he said, heading into the building.

The *portero* gave him a knowing look.

He took the elevator up to the fifth floor and entered his apartment. Without stopping he went into the master bedroom and shed his clothes. He took a quick shower, and then he dressed informally since the party was an *asado*, a popular form of outdoor entertainment that centered on roasting a variety of meats over an open fire, tended by a master *asador* who made sure that nothing got singed as it did in America.

A few minutes later he got into the back seat of the car. It wasn't a big expensive car, which would have attracted the attention of Montoneros looking to kidnap someone important. It was safer to travel in an unpretentious car and to vary your routes if you were a regular commuter.

As the car pulled forward he leaned back and closed his eyes. They were going to San Isidro, a wealthy northern suburb, and it would take at least a half hour to get there, enough time for a welcome nap.

He opened his eyes as they were turning into the street where the host of the party lived. He had been there before, with Leila in tow, after a heated argument in which she stated her case against having to attend these stupid parties with these stupid people who worked for these stupid companies.

The host, who was dressed in flamboyant golf clothes, greeted him heartily and showed him the way to the bar.

As he waited for a white-coated servant to mix him a gin and tonic, he looked around. There were about twenty people at the party, more men than women. He knew most of the men. He determined that he and an engineer who worked for the host's company were the only Americans.

Standing around the borders of the well-groomed lawn were the bodyguards who accompanied the guests. He counted them and found that there were as many bodyguards as guests. It occurred to him that the host would have to feed them all as well as the drivers, so if you were planning a party for twenty you needed food for about fifty. No wonder there were fewer parties than there used to be.

Taking his drink, he walked over and joined a group of men that included the engineer. They were talking about a recent kidnapping.

"They paid five million for him."

"They did? He's not worth it."

"Well, that's a lot less than they paid for the Exxon guy."

"How much did they pay for him?"

"Fourteen million."

"My company wouldn't pay that for me."

"Your company would pay them to keep you."

"They probably would."

"How much would your bank pay for you?" the engineer asked Stephen.

"Nothing. They have a policy of not paying ransom money."

"Oh, that's what all our companies say."

"I think he's worth at least twenty million."

"And his bank has the money."

"So they could pay twenty million."

"Maybe they could," Stephen said, "but they never would. And why would the Montoneros want to kidnap me if they could get thirty million for you?"

"That reminds me of a story—"

Stephen listened. It was about two men who were running from a bear. One of the men said to the other, we don't have a chance, we can't outrun the bear, and the other man said, I don't have to outrun the bear, I only have to outrun you.

He laughed, though he had heard it before.

Smelling the smoke, he wandered over to the fire, where the *asador* was watching the meat. It wasn't being roasted directly over the coals but at angles, on spits stuck into the ground. He talked with the *asador* and learned that they were going to eat in about a half hour. The man must have sensed his anticipation since he drew a serious knife out of a sheath on the back of his belt and sliced a piece of meat off a carcass and offered it to him on a hunk of bread, saying: "Please try it."

"*Gracias*." He took a bite. "*Riquísimo!* You're a master."

He returned to the group of men, who were still joking about the terrorists. They didn't talk about the manager from the Italian company who had just been killed.

It was after six when he got home, but he still had almost nine hours left to kill.

He tried reading, and he tried watching a soap opera on television, and he tried sleeping, but nothing worked, and the time crept by very slowly. It made him wonder how he passed the time on Saturdays before, and he realized that when you had nothing better to do it was relatively easy to kill time.

Around seven he decided to go to a movie and then have dinner. That would kill at least four hours. So he dressed and went out and walked across Plaza San Martín, where he noticed a pair of young lovers sitting on the steps at the base of the statue and kissing as if tonight were the first time. He headed down Florida toward Lavalle, where there was a concentration of movie theaters. He had no particular movie in mind but he hoped to find one that he probably wouldn't see with Elena, his usual companion at the movies. There were crowds of people on Lavalle, dawdling along and stopping to talk and buying tickets and leaving the theaters in wide-eyed throngs. It was Saturday night, and people were out to have a good time.

He settled on a movie that he knew Elena wouldn't want to see, and he bought a ticket. At the box office they had a board with holes in it for all the seats, and in each hole there was a rolled-up paper ticket. So you could see where you would be sitting, and your seat was reserved.

With the ticket he went back out onto the street. He had a half hour to kill before the movie started, so he found a café and had a double espresso, surrounded by people who were also killing time.

"*Che, viejo. Qué decís?*" a man to his right greeted someone.

"*Claro, claro,*" a woman kept saying.

About five minutes before the show he left the café and headed for the theater. A uniformed usher, a buxom woman, showed him to his seat. Before the movie there was always an *acto vivo*, a live act, which years ago was mandated by law in order to provide employment for local entertainers. Tonight it was a man who played the *charango* and sang folk songs. The *charango* was a stringed instrument made from the back of an armadillo. The man was talented, and his songs evoked the harsh life on the arid highlands of Salta and Jujuy, a different world from Buenos Aires. The culture there was Spanish with a leaven of indigenous, and the language there sounded like Spanish, whereas here it sounded like Italian.

After the live act the lights went on, and women with cases slung from their necks charged down the aisles, hollering: "*Helados, bonbones, caramelos!*"

They sold a lot since people usually ate dinner after the movie and they wanted something to tide them over.

Then came the commercials, followed by the news. The latter always had scenes of dignitaries sitting at long formal tables with plates and glasses and bottles of water, always talking and sometimes gesturing to make a point. You couldn't hear them, you could hear only the voice of the newsman telling you that they reached an agreement, passed a law, or signed a protocol.

Then finally the movie, almost an hour after Stephen took his seat. But that was fine. He had killed another hour.

After the movie he wandered down the street and spotted El Mundo, a very good typical Argentine restaurant where he hadn't eaten in a while. He used to go there with Leila after the movies, so he had been avoiding it. Now, putting himself to a test, he went in and asked for a table.

"For two?" asked the headwaiter, who recognized him. The waiters in such restaurants were pursuing a career, and they stayed in the job until they retired, so they knew their customers.

"No. One, please."

The man adapted and gave him a table against the wall, where he wouldn't be sitting alone in the middle of everyone.

He dined at leisure, starting with hearts of palm, and then a shoulder of lamb with side dishes of roasted potatoes and spinach sautéed in oil and garlic, and ending with a banana pancake. During the dinner he drank a bottle of red wine and a bottle of sparkling mineral water. And not once did he think about Leila.

It was almost midnight when he left the restaurant, but he still had three hours to kill. He walked up Lavalle to 9 de Julio, an immensely wide boulevard that was created by removing a whole line of blocks between Cerrito and Carlos Pellegrini on one side of Avenida de Mayo and between Lima and Irigoyen on the other side. It was supposed to extend all the way across town, but years ago the project was stopped, presumably by members of the Jockey Club, which stood in its path toward Barrio Norte. *Porteños* either loved it or hated it. Those who loved it enjoyed the wide sidewalks where they could sit outside at tables during most of the year and watch people. Those who hated it didn't like risking their lives to cross it.

Stephen stopped and sat at a table and had another espresso, impressed by the number of people on the streets, not only young people but also elderly people, still out at this hour when even in New York most people would be in bed. He was used to it, just as he was used to living in a city on the other side of the world. The Americans whom the bank evacuated for their safety were glad to leave since they hadn't liked it here. They were always complaining about things that were different from home. If they had spent two years in Saigon, they might have appreciated Buenos Aires.

It was after one when he got home, so he had less than two hours to kill. He lay down and closed his eyes, recalling the girl in the white dress.

Minas was only a few blocks from where he lived, so he walked there. The club was packed, but he easily spotted Cathy standing at the bar, wearing what looked like the same dress.

She greeted him warmly and made room at the bar so he could stand next to her.

"Champagne?" he asked her.

"With pleasure," she said, smiling.

While he was paying for the bottle she went and talked with the silver-haired man, who nodded and patted her on the shoulder.

"We can go now," she said, returning.

"He must like you."

"He's a good friend."

He waited at the door while she went into the coatroom and came out with a shoulder bag, ready to go.

Outside, he said: "I have an idea. I live a few blocks from here, so why don't we go to my place?"

"I love your idea," she said with delight.

They started walking.

"Are you tired?" he asked.

"No. I'm fine. I took a nap this afternoon."

"I tried taking a nap," he told her, not holding back. "I tried doing a lot of things. But it was a long, long day."

"It was for me too. I wasn't sure you would come tonight."

"You weren't? But how could you have doubted me?"

"It wasn't you I doubted. It was *me*."

"I don't understand."

"I was afraid I did something wrong," she said after a pause.

"Oh, no," he said, moved. He stopped and turned her until she faced him. "You didn't do anything wrong."

"Good," she said, looking relieved.

He had to use his key to get into the building since the *portero* had gone to bed. Inside his apartment, he led her through the living room and into the main bedroom. He opened the empty side of the closet that Leila had used. "If you have anything to hang up, this space is all yours."

"Thank you," she said. She set down her shoulder bag and removed a yellow dress, which she put on a hanger and smoothed with her hand.

He showed her the bathrooms, and while she was in one of them he straightened the bed. The woman who cleaned the apartment for him came on Fridays and changed the sheets, so the bed was still presentable.

When she returned from the bathroom she was in her natural state. With a joyful laugh she pranced into his arms and pressed her face against his chest.

He held her, rocking her gently back and forth, inhaling the smell of bath soap.

Later she curled up next to him and went to sleep.

In the morning he woke up and found her side of the bed empty. Alarmed, he raised his head and listened. He heard her in the bathroom, relieving herself. She had unabashedly left the door open.

He lay back, waiting for her to return, but after she flushed the toilet some time passed before she sauntered into the bedroom, still naked.

She hopped back into bed and snuggled against him.

"Did you sleep well?" he asked her.

"Oh, yes. I never slept so well in my life."

"Me neither." It was true. He had never felt so much at peace.

"I thought your wife might be away," she said after a long silence, "but there's no sign of a woman here."

"I don't have a wife. I did," he added, "but our marriage didn't work."

"Why not?" she asked.

"I guess we wanted different things from it. She wanted a base of operations, and I wanted—a relationship."

"It sounds like you loved her more than she loved you."

"I did," he said.

"Do you still love her?"

"No. It took a while, but I finally stopped."

"How long ago were you separated?"

"Three years ago."

"Have you seen her since?"

"Only once. A week ago in New York when we finalized our divorce."

"How long were you together?"

"Two years."

With that she seemed satisfied. She rolled toward him and kissed him invitingly. By the time they finished there were no longer any traces of Leila in his mind.

When they got up after sleeping some more they were hungry, but there was no food in the kitchen, so after taking a shower together they dressed and went out. She was wearing the yellow dress, a soft cotton summer dress that made her look even younger than he guessed she was.

As they strolled across Plaza San Martín, emerging from the shade of a *gomero* tree into the sunlight, he finally asked: "How old are you?"

"I'm twenty-two. How old are you?"

"I'm thirty-three."

"Good," she said, presumably referring to the difference in their ages. In her culture men of his age often married women of her age. It was as if they recognized that it took men that much longer to grow up.

They had lunch in a *confitería* on Florida where anglophiles had high tea in the afternoon and literary figures met in the evening. It was a sedate, traditional place, and Cathy seemed at home there. She ordered a sandwich and tea while he had an omelet with bacon and toast and coffee.

They conversed in English. They could have just as easily conversed in Spanish, but they stayed with the language they had started with.

He wanted to know more about her, but his instincts told him to accept her at face value for now and to ask only innocuous questions. From her accent and her skin color he knew she wasn't from Argentina, and he guessed that she was from a country in the Caribbean, but something warned him that asking her where she was from would not be an innocuous question, so after a sip of coffee he asked: "How did you learn to speak English so well?"

"I had an American teacher who took a special interest in me. I was twelve at the time, so don't get the wrong idea," she said wryly. "He was in the Peace Corps, assigned to our school. He saw something in me that I never realized was there, and he opened my mind to possibilities that I never dreamed of. He helped me to start learning English."

"How long was he assigned to your school?"

"Three years. But he stayed in touch with me after he left. He wrote me letters, with lists of books in English that he said I should read. He also got me a job with an American family taking care of their children. I went to their home every day after school, and I spent a lot of time with them, always speaking English."

"How long did you work for them?"

"Five years. The father was working on a project for the UN, and when it ended they all went to another country."

"By then you were twenty, right?"

"Right. I was at the university, studying to be a teacher."

He waited for her to continue but she stopped there as if she had run into a barrier. So after another sip of coffee he asked: "Where did you get the name Cathy?"

"From a book," she said.

"So you changed your name?"

She nodded. "Yes."

"What's your last name?"

"Linton," she said after a pause.

Cathy Linton. It sounded familiar. Then he remembered. "You took the name of the heroine in *Wuthering Heights?*"

"You read it?"

"Of course. It's one of the great masterpieces of English literature."

"That's what my American teacher said. It was at the top of a list he sent me the year I started at the university."

"Cathy Linton," he said, surveying her. "It suits you."

"But I'm nothing like her. She wasn't true to the man she loved."

"You can't blame her. He didn't make it easy."

"It's never easy. But if you really love someone," she said with conviction, "you're true to him."

"That's how it should be," he agreed.

After a long silence she said: "You didn't ask *why* I changed my name."

"I'm sure you had a good reason, and you don't have to tell

me until you're ready. Anyway, whatever your original name was, you'll always be Cathy to me."

"Thank you," she said, covering his hand.

After lunch they strolled down Florida, and like the other women Cathy stopped from time to time and looked in the store windows. He followed her eyes, trying to see what kind of things she liked. He assumed that she was poor, and that she had only a few dresses, including the dress she was wearing now and a black dress for the club that she could alternate with the white. He would have liked to buy her something, but he hesitated, not wanting to offend her by acting like a man who kept a woman, buying her clothes and jewelry and whatever she wanted in return for sex.

When they returned to his apartment he took her into the guestroom, where he had built a bookcase that covered one whole wall. The books on its shelves were mostly in English—a collection of novels and poetry and plays that he had acquired over the years since high school.

"I read that," she said, pointing to *The Great Gatsby*, "and that, and that—"

"You can borrow any of them."

She ran her hand caressingly over the spines of the books. "My American teacher loaned me books. He always encouraged me to read and to keep going to school."

"He sounds like a good man."

"He was. I wanted to be a teacher, just like him, and do for children what he did for me. But now I don't know."

"You don't know if you still want to be a teacher?"

"I don't know if I *can* be a teacher."

"Why can't you?"

Ignoring his question, she touched the spine of *A Separate Peace* and said: "This was on a list, but I never could find it."

"It's excellent. Take it."

"Thank you."

They decided to get some food so that they could have dinner at home. There was a grocery store across from his building that was open on Sundays until seven. The only thing he could cook was spaghetti with tomato sauce, but that was fine with her, so he went out and got what they needed, including a bottle of red wine.

When he returned he found her in the family room, curled up on the sofa with her shoes off, avidly reading the book he had given her. She must have been starved for books, and he wondered what had cut her off from them.

The next morning he had to get up and go to work. As he dressed he told Cathy to stay there as long as she wanted, she only had to close the door behind her when she left and it would lock automatically.

Before leaving he bent over and softly kissed the side of her head, which was nestled in the pillow. "I'll see you at the club tonight."

"At three," she murmured.

"Yes. At three."

He walked to work as he always did, down Arenales to Plaza San Martín, then onto Florida. He passed the newspaper vendor who stood in the same place every day, yelling in a gravelly voice: "*Diario! Crónica! Razón!*"

In the next block he heard familiar music coming from a store. It was the Chalchaleros, a group of four male singers from Salta, who accompanied themselves with guitars and a drum. It was plaintive music, heartfelt and direct, and it triggered the memory of the trip that he and Leila had taken to the northern provinces of Argentina. They were in Salta when he had to turn back because he didn't have any more vacation, but she continued up to Bolivia and into Peru, where she stayed three months studying descendents of the Incas.

With emphasis reinforced by the drum the Chalchaleros sang the refrain: "But my love for you will not die ever, will not die ever, ever."

As always he stopped for a coffee and roll at a place on Diagonal Norte, near the bank, listening idly to the talk around him while he sipped the coffee and munched the roll. It was all about politics and *fútbol*, politics and *fútbol*.

"Boca is going to whip their asses."

"The *peronistas* are washed up."

He wondered why they didn't talk more about the economy. Inflation was out of control. The price of the coffee he was having now was four times what it had been a year ago. Unemployment was high and still rising. Probably one out of five people was out of work, despite what the official figures said. And capital was fleeing the country. In that respect, the Montoneros were acting like prudent money managers.

As he entered the bank he decided to take the information he had collected on Friday and call the bank's Panama branch. He couldn't explain what he wanted in a telex, and even if he could he didn't think it would be secure enough. But the bank had only one secure phone line, which was used for communicating with head office, and it belonged to the general manager. So after picking up his information he would have to go and get permission to use this phone.

He took the elevator up to the third floor and walked through the glass doors into the area where the account managers worked, where clients went if they needed approval to get something done.

The *ordenanza* at the reception desk greeted him, saying: "*Buenos días, señor.*"

"*Buenos días, Ignacio.*"

The account managers were all at their desks, and they didn't seem to notice that he was late. At least they pretended not to notice.

He went to his desk and opened the drawer in which he had placed a folder with the information on the letters of credit. Carrying the folder, he went back out through the glass doors and took the elevator to the second floor, where the offices of the general manager and his staff were located.

"Do you have an appointment?" asked Señora Pérez, the general manager's secretary. Like most secretaries she assumed the rank of her boss, though she stopped short of addressing him with the familiar form of "you" in Spanish.

"No," he said. "I just thought I might catch him before he gets too busy."

"I'll see what I can do."

After he had waited about five minutes she gave him permission to go into the office of the general manager, whose name was Carlos. He had worked together with Carlos when they were both junior officers. They collaborated in preparing the bank's monthly economic letter on Argentina, with Carlos supplying the economic knowledge and him the writing ability. The letter went into a monthly report that the head office sent to its corporate clients, and it was plagiarized by the U.S. Embassy for its report on Argentina.

Carlos was a man of vast appetites, with a love for food, wine, and women but above all a love for knowledge. He had a doctorate in economics from the University of Chicago, and he taught courses at Universidad Católica, which had an excellent business program. Most of the management trainees that the bank recruited were graduates of Católica, and many of them had been taught by Carlos.

When the vice president in New York decided to withdraw the Americans from Argentina he conferred with Stephen, sharing his idea of putting Carlos in charge and asking what

Stephen thought of it. Stephen supported it because Carlos was respected, intelligent, and trustworthy.

"*Che, viejo, qué decís?*" Carlos said, using a local expression that meant "Hey, man, what do you say?"

"It's good to be back," Stephen replied.

A large man in his late thirties with an imposing forehead and horn-rimmed glasses, Carlos had risen to his full height, about six feet four. He gave Stephen a firm handshake, American style, and then he said: "Please sit down."

Stephen sat in one of the chairs in front of the desk, remembering how he sat here as a newly arrived junior officer from New York to be inspected by the general manager, a crusty man who had fought with Patton in World War II and had been with the bank for twenty years. So many things had changed since then.

"It won't be long now," Carlos told him, meaning the *golpe*. "And I can't wait. Do you know who's going to be minister of economy?"

"No. Who?"

"Martínez de Hoz."

"Really?" He hadn't heard that. He had met the man, but didn't know too much about him other than through his relationship with the bank, which for years had given him a line of credit for his stud farm. He was a scion of an old *estanciero* family, and people called him "Joe," a nickname for José of the type that might indicate the extent to which he had dealings with Americans, like "Freddy" for Fernando and "Tommy" for Tomás and "Pete" for Pedro.

"He's going to apply free-market policies," Carlos said, rubbing his hands with enthusiasm, "like they're doing in Chile."

Stephen had closely followed developments in Chile, where Salvador Allende, the first elected socialist in Latin America, was deposed in 1973 by a *junta* led by General Pinochet. The military government there made drastic changes in economic policy, following the model of the Chicago School. For the past two years Stephen had heard about each new development from Carlos, who believed in the model and of course felt that Argentina should have adopted it before Chile. "From what I read, things aren't going so well there."

"Wait and see. The whole world went into recession because of the oil shock, but Chile will be the first Latin American country to pull out of it."

"So we're going to have free trade and a free foreign exchange market?"

"Absolutely. Free markets in every area."

"What about inflation?"

"Inflation is caused by too much money chasing too few goods," Carlos said as if he were quoting from a textbook, "so they'll apply a strict monetarist policy. They'll provide enough money to accommodate growth but no more. Of course they'll have to stop printing money to finance the deficits of the state enterprises."

"You mean they'll let the state enterprises go under?" They were talking about the railroads, the airlines, the ports, the utilities, and even some basic industries that were nationalized by Perón during his first regime.

"No, they'll privatize them."

"Who would want to buy them?"

"With market pricing, they're viable."

"Assuming people can afford to pay higher prices."

"Don't worry. The economy will grow, and everyone will benefit."

Stephen was skeptical, having heard before about the rising tide that lifts all boats. The problem was, there were a lot of boats that the water never reached, and boats that sank when the water did reach them.

Changing the subject, he said: "I'm doing an investigation, and I need to use your phone to call Panama."

"Can you tell me what it's about?"

He trusted Carlos, so he could tell him without going into all the details. "It looks like the Montoneros are using our Panama branch to launder the money they get from kidnappings."

"Where did you get that idea?"

"I got a tip from someone."

"Well, if it's true we have to stop it."

"We will, but to see if it's true, I need information from our manager in Panama."

"Do you want to call him now?"

"I'd like to if I could."

"No problem." Carlos rose from his desk. "I'll ask Señora Pérez to connect you."

Stephen got up, and when Carlos had left, closing the door, he sat behind the general manager's desk. It reminded him that he didn't want to be general manager or any higher position in the bank. He wanted something else, and his mind was wandering when the white phone rang—the previous general manager refused to have a red phone since he thought it was hokey.

He talked with the manager of the Panama branch and explained what he needed. The manager didn't ask why since the request was coming from a colleague over a secure phone line. He agreed to send, via the bank mail pouch, copies of all remittances over the past three years from the Swiss bank that the embassy guys suspected was involved in the money laundering. He also agreed to send copies of the documents for the next shipment under a letter of credit issued by Banco Azulay as well as copies of the documents for subsequent shipments under its letters of credit.

After hanging up the white phone Stephen left the general

manager's office, thanked Carlos, thanked Señora Pérez, and headed back to the third floor, where he spent the rest of the morning doing his regular work, which consisted mainly of reviewing loan proposals from the account managers.

He met Chris for lunch as arranged last Friday before they parted. Chris needed advice on a problem with some businesses that he had helped to start, and Stephen suggested the London Grill since they both liked it.

The meat was roasted over a fire at the front of the restaurant, and the smoke flowed out through an opening and drifted up through the line of clothes that people in the apartment above hung out to dry. If he ever stood next to them on the subway, Stephen was sure he would recognize them as owners of the clothes.

He got a table and waited for Chris, whom he had met about five years ago. Chris had wandered into the bank to cash a personal check, which the teller couldn't do because Chris didn't have an account. They sent Chris up to the third floor, and the *ordenanza* led him to Stephen, who after a brief conversation approved the check. At the time Chris was working in Chile with the Peace Corps, and he had taken the bus from there to Buenos Aires. He had just arrived, and he hadn't yet found a place to stay, so Stephen invited Chris to stay with him. At the time Leila was in Peru so there wouldn't be a problem in his coming home with an unexpected guest.

He showed Chris the city, or what he knew of it, but after seeing the usual sights Chris wanted to see one of the *villas miseria*, the shanty-towns on the outskirts of the city where people lived without electricity, water, or sewers. Though he had seen them from a distance, Stephen had never seen one up close since he didn't have any reason to visit one. But Chris had a reason, a mission, so Stephen accompanied him to a *villa* south of the city. Among other things he noticed that unlike the people who lived in mapped areas of the city, a lot of people in the *villa* had Indian features, presumably having migrated from the northern provinces in search of a better life. But if this was better, the life they had forsaken was unimaginable.

On that visit Chris met a social worker named Sofía, whose grandparents had fled an ancient Greek city in what had been the Ottoman Empire and was now Turkey. Conscious of her heritage and deeply religious, Sofi had committed herself to helping another kind of refugee, and she was the reason why Chris came to Argentina after his tour of duty in Chile.

"Sorry I'm late," Chris said, suddenly appearing. "I got stuck in a *colectivo*."

The *colectivos*, which looked like American school buses except that they were painted bright colors with intricate designs, covered the city in a complex network. You had to be a genius to figure out the system, so most people settled for knowing which line would take them from home to work and back. You only had to know its number.

"No problem," Stephen said.

They ordered *vacío*, a cut of beef for which the restaurant was famous, with *papas fritas* and a carafe of red wine.

"How's Sofi?"

"Oh, she's fine. A little whoopsy now and then."

"Will she keep working?"

"Until the last week. I couldn't stop her," Chris added.

"I wouldn't try."

Chris smiled, and then he said: "My problem is this. I've helped all these people start grocery stores, and they're not making enough profit."

"You mean to live on?"

"That's right. The cost of staples is so high that it doesn't leave them much of a margin, and they can't raise their prices beyond a certain point."

"Can you give me an example?"

"Yeah. Potatoes. The people who grow them make less than a penny a pound, and the stores make less than two cents a pound. Almost all the markup goes to the middlemen."

"So why don't they cut out the middlemen?"

"They can't. They don't have enough buying power to break the chain."

Stephen thought for a moment. "How many stores have you helped to start?"

"I don't know. I guess about twenty."

"Wouldn't that be enough to form a cooperative?"

"Yeah. Maybe," Chris said, intrigued. "And if it's not, I could get some other stores to join them."

As they talked about the idea Chris's hands started flying around, and Stephen had to move the carafe out of the way.

"It's a great idea," Chris said, enthused. "Now, why didn't I think of it?"

"Because you're too close to the problem."

"I guess I am. Do you have any problems that you're too close to?"

"Not now, but I did."

Chris nodded, evidently understanding that Stephen meant his marriage to Leila.

At that point the meat arrived, and they reached for their utensils.

Back at his desk, he noticed that Tito Arias was the only account manager present, and he decided it would be a good opportunity to find out what Arias was up to. His approach would have to be indirect since he didn't want to arouse any suspicions, and he really didn't know what he was looking for.

Stephen decided to ask Arias what was happening in the *extrabancario* market, a market for loans outside of the banking system that existed because of the ceilings that the government imposed on the interest rates that banks could pay on deposits or receive on loans. If you had a million pesos, and you could earn only ten percent interest by depositing your money in a bank when the rate of inflation was more than four hundred percent, you would be crazy to leave your money in a bank, though a lot of small savers, having no alternative, did just that. Instead, you could lend your money directly to a company for ninety days at a rate that more than compensated for inflation, and you could do that with no risk since your loan was covered by a bank guarantee. In that respect, it was as if you had your money in a bank.

This was a profitable business for the bank, which collected a fee from the borrower for finding the money, a fee from the lender for placing the money, and a fee for providing the guarantee. In fact, it was better than taking deposits and making loans since the bank had no assets or liabilities on its books. It only had the guarantee, which was a contingent liability. Though the *extrabancario* market had been created to get around the regulations, it was legal, and the government got its share of the profit by collecting a tax on the guarantees.

As usual Arias was wearing a suit that looked as if it were imported from Italy, with a shirt and tie that completed the look. His face, which verged on being pretty, was perfectly tanned. His voice was in an upper register, and when he was excited it actually squeaked, as it did when he talked about landing a new client or bedding a new girl. He was in his forties, but he looked much younger, and he kept himself in good shape, working out in a gym.

Stephen greeted him informally. *"Qué tal?"*

"Bien. Y vos?"

"Bien."

Arias remained seated at his desk, and Stephen took the chair beside the desk where clients sat while talking with the account manager. He glimpsed a gold cufflink on the arm that was resting on the desk.

"How was your weekend?" Stephen asked.

"It was great. We had perfect weather. Not too much wind."

Having spent the weekends in a rented condo at Punta del Este with Leila during their first summer in Argentina, he knew what Arias was talking about. The *playa brava*, on the ocean side, was sometimes uncomfortably windy.

"What's happening in the *extrabancario* market?"

Arias shrugged. "It's slow now. Everyone's away. But it'll pick up in a few weeks when people start coming back from vacation."

"What's the current rate?"

"Fifty-five percent for ninety days."

"How much is that per annum?"

"Four hundred seventy-seven percent, compounded," Arias replied as if he had a calculator in his head.

"It's going up?"

"Oh, yes. With all the uncertainty there are fewer people who want to lend money in pesos."

"What are they doing as an alternative?"

"Buying dollars and keeping them in a safe place."

"You mean under their mattresses?"

Arias smiled. "If you kept that kind of money under your mattress, you'd have a bad back in the morning."

"So they keep their money in New York?"

"Mostly. There's some in London and some in Switzerland, but mostly it's in New York. They trust Americans."

"They must have found a way around the limits on remittances," Stephen said, referring to the arcane regulations that successive governments imposed in order to stop money from fleeing the country.

"There are many ways around the limits," Arias said as if he knew them all.

"The only two ways I can think of," Stephen ventured, "are taking money out of the country in a bag and having a friend at the Central Bank."

"The bag doesn't work as well as it used to. They search you at the airports in New York and Miami, looking for drug money, and if they catch you—" Arias drew his forefinger across his throat. "It's easier to buy a dollar check in the black market and mail it to your account in New York."

"I can see how that would work for a few thousand dollars, but what if you have a few million dollars?"

"It would still work. But if you have that kind of money, you can afford to have a friend at the Central Bank."

Corruption had always been a problem, but many people believed that the present government was breaking all records in this area, so it was easy to imagine getting a large remittance approved in return for a payoff. Yet it was a stretch to imagine the terrorists using this method. "So what methods are your clients using?"

"They're buying checks in the black market."

Of course it was illegal to buy and sell dollars in the black market, but the government allowed people to do that for the same reason that it allowed people to buy and sell sex. "Are they taking a lot of money out?"

"As much as they can. They're afraid of what a military government will do to them," Arias added impassively.

"You mean they're afraid of the military's anti-Semitism?"

"The right-wing *peronistas* are bad enough, but the military are over the edge. I mean, some of them admire Hitler."

Stephen nodded. "Yes. I know."

"So you can't blame my clients for taking their money out of the country."

"No. I can't." And he couldn't blame Arias for helping them, if that was all he was doing. "*Bueno. Gracias.*"

"*De nada.*"

Back at his desk, while pushing papers, he pushed the pieces of information around in his mind. Safadi was taking deposits from the Jewish community and helping them get their money out of the country. Arias was helping them get a decent rate on peso loans inside the country. According to the embassy guys, Safadi was using his transactions with the Jewish community as a cover for transactions with the Montoneros. Was Arias doing the same thing? Was there a connection between Arias and Safadi beyond the banking relationship?

Later, when the rest of the account managers had returned from lunch, Stephen went across the hall to where the operating departments were located. He approached the desk of the woman who managed the operations of the bank's guarantees. Her name was Rosa, and though she was only in her late twenties she had been with the bank a long time, and she was a trusted employee. Her boss, who oversaw several departments, gave Rosa the ultimate compliment by describing her as *muy seria*, meaning very professional.

Stephen greeted her formally. "*Como está, señora?*"

"*Muy bien. Y usted, señor?*"

"*Bien.* I'm working on the budget, doing a forecast of revenues, and I need some information on our guarantee business."

"How can I help you?"

"Can you give me a list of the individuals and companies who have made loans with our guarantee? I need the names and the amounts of the loans."

"Of course. How far back would you like to go?"

"A year will be enough for this purpose."

"No problem. Would you also like the names of the borrowers?"

"That's not necessary."

"Okay. I can have the information for you by tomorrow morning. Is that soon enough?"

"That's fine," he said. *"Gracias."*

With that information, together with the names he would get from the Panama branch, he could see if there were any matches. If there were, then he would have evidence that Safadi and Arias were doing transactions with the same individuals or companies. By itself it wouldn't prove anything, but it could point him in the right direction.

That evening, instead of going home after work, he walked across Plaza San Martín and followed Maipú down the hill along with the regiment of commuters who lived in the northern suburbs. As he descended to the train station he could see the British Tower with its clock, which told him that he could make the 5:32 train to Belgrano.

On the second Monday of every month, unless one of them had a conflict, he went to see Vittoria, the widow of Alejandro. With support from her family and the bank, which provided a pension in dollars, she was able to stay in the house that she and Alejandro bought four years ago after their second child was born. They had met as students at Católica, where Alejandro completed his degree with tuition assistance from the bank. He married early for a male Argentine, and he already had three children at an age when his peers were only beginning to think about the possibility of getting married. He was twenty-nine when the Montoneros killed him.

In a stream of mostly men in suits he entered the cavernous train station. He paused to look up at the board where the trains were listed, and then he headed for the platform. The railroad system, the largest in South America, was a disaster. Built by the British more than a hundred years ago, the system hadn't been maintained since Perón bought it and nationalized it. People said that he paid too much for it, and that if he had waited he could have gotten it for nothing. The railroads accounted for half of the government's detrimentally large fiscal deficit, which it financed by printing money.

The train was late as usual, but it took him to Belgrano with less trouble than if he had driven. He had stuck with his initial decision not to buy a car since even the public transportation was more efficient than driving and keeping a car in the city, and on the few occasions when he needed to drive somewhere the bank car would take him, with a bodyguard.

It was a good walk from the train station to the house on a quiet leafy street where Vittoria lived. It was still light, and he imagined the contentment of the men he saw coming home to their families.

Vittoria greeted him at the door. She was tall and slender, with her light hair tied back, exposing her finely sculptured face. An attractive woman, she was only twenty-seven, but with three young children she had almost no chance of getting married again. Not that she was looking for another husband—it was less than eight months since she lost Alejandro, and as Stephen knew from the evenings he spent with her, she still grieved for Alejandro, still missed him, still loved him.

Two of the children appeared from the family room where they were playing, and he bent down and kissed them. Claudia was five, and Olivia was four. The youngest, Aleja, had just turned two and was toddling around within reach of her mother. The older two called him *Tío*, which meant uncle.

They returned to their play while he went into the kitchen to make drinks for Vittoria and himself. They always unwound with Scotch on the rocks before sitting down to dinner. They sat at the counter in the kitchen so that she could keep an eye on what was cooking. She had already fed the children, which left her relatively free to relax, as long as there wasn't a crisis with one of them.

"My mother's driving me crazy," Vittoria said after taking a healthy swig of Scotch. "She keeps trying to make me get out of the house and socialize."

"How often do you get out?"

"A few times a week. I go out to shop for food while she watches the children, and I take them to the club with her to go swimming."

"That's not enough for her?"

"No. It's not. She wants me to get back into circulation."

"How could you even if you wanted to?"

"She says she'll watch the children any time. If she had her way, I'd always be out socializing, and she'd be raising my children."

"She wants to help you."

"If she does, then she should try to understand," Vittoria said with a rising emotion that charged her voice and filled her eyes. "I want to be at home with my children. I do *not* want to be out socializing and looking for another husband."

"Have you explained this to her?"

"Over and over."

"What does she say?"

"She says that when I finally wake up it'll be too late."

"And how does that make you feel?"

"It makes me feel like she wants me to feel," Vittoria said, her face contorted. "*Cagada de miedo.*"

"Scared shitless," he translated in his mind.

"I hate her for making me feel that way. And while I hate her I think about those *boludos de mierda* who killed Alejandro, and I want to kill them. *I pray that the military will kill every last one of them.*" Her eyes were overflowing now. "Can you imagine praying for such a thing?"

"I can, and I don't blame you."

"Well, I blame myself. And then I pray that God will take away my hatred, not for my sake but for the sake of my children."

"Does that help?"

With a grimace she said: "It stops me from hating my mother."

He sipped his drink, not knowing what to say.

THREE

AFTER A WEEK of meeting Cathy at three in the morning every day he admitted that he couldn't keep going like this. He was dragging himself into the bank, and once he was almost an hour late. He also admitted that he didn't like her job of entertaining men, though it was how he had met her.

As they were lying in bed on Sunday he said: "You know, if you moved in with me you wouldn't have to pay for your apartment."

"Are you asking me to move in?"

"Yes." He waited anxiously for her reply.

"I share the apartment with another girl, so I would have to find someone to replace me. I wouldn't stick her with having to pay all the rent."

"You could leave and keep paying your share of the rent until you found someone."

"I could," she said thoughtfully. Facing him across the pillow, she searched his eyes as if for further encouragement.

"I want to live with you," he told her, gazing straight back at her. "And I could help you move today."

She smiled. "All right. I don't have much, so it'll be easy."

He rested on that for a while, and then he said: "It would also be better if you didn't have to work all night."

"I know, but I need the money."

"You could get another kind of job."

"I don't know anyone here."

"Well, I know people."

"If you could help me, I would rather work during the day."

"Do you have a work permit?"

"I have a *cédula*."

"You do? But you're not from Argentina."

"How could you tell?" she teased him.

"I could tell from your accent."

"Not from the way I look?

"Yeah. That too." He felt that the time had come to ask: "Where are you from?"

"Colombia. But I don't say that to anyone but you."

"What do you say?"

"I say I'm from Venezuela."

"What about your name?"

"My father's an American oil engineer whose company sent him to Caracas, where he met my mother."

"What are you doing in Argentina?"

"I don't like Caracas, so I thought I would try living here for a while."

"How did you get a *cédula*?"

"My father arranged it. He spent time here doing a project for the national oil company, so he has contacts."

"That's a good story. I would have believed it."

"Well, that's what I say if anyone asks me where I'm from."

"How long have you been here?"

"About two weeks."

"So you just started working at Minas?"

She nodded. "Yes. I met you my first week there."

"Have you tried to get another job?"

"No. I haven't. I don't know anyone here, and I don't have any qualifications."

"You have an education."

"But I don't have a degree."

"Well, I'll see what I can do." He believed that with the help of his friends he could find her another job.

Later, returning from the bathroom, she got her *cédula* out of her bag and showed it to him. The name was "Catalina Linton," and the picture was definitely her, but according to the date of birth she was only twenty.

"You said you were twenty-two."

"I am. I wanted my age to be different on the *cédula*."

"So it would be harder to trace you?"

"Yes." She paused as if she were considering whether to tell him more, but then she said: "It's not a good picture."

"It doesn't do justice to you," he agreed.

That afternoon they took a taxi to her apartment, which was on the other side of town in a poor neighborhood. As she had said, she didn't have much—only clothes and cosmetics, which easily fit into a small suitcase. He had already seen her three dresses: white, black, and yellow.

A half hour later they were back in his apartment, and she was settled.

On Monday he called Elena and told her about Cathy, giving the cover story of her background and saying he had met her at a party. "She's looking for a job," he said, "and I thought maybe you could help her."

"Is she a resident?"

"She has a *cédula*."

"What experience does she have?"

"Not much." He didn't want to mention her experience as a bar girl, and he didn't want to lie to Elena any more than he already had. "But she's good with people, she loves books, and she speaks English fluently."

"Well, let's see. I know someone who might have a position in her bookstore. It wouldn't pay much, but it's a job."

"It sounds perfect."

"I'll see what I can do." Elena paused, perhaps wondering about the extent of his interest in this girl. "Is there anything else I should know?"

"Yes. We're living together."

"You're what?" Elena said as if she might not have understood over the phone.

"We're living together."

"*Qué maravilla!* When did this happen?"

"Recently." He could tell that though Elena was surprised, she was glad for him.

"I can't wait to meet her."

"I'll bring her with me this Friday," he promised, realizing that if he was at all serious about Cathy he would introduce her to his friends.

Two days later Cathy started her new job. She had offered to stay at the club until the owner found a new girl, but that hadn't taken long, and her replacement moved into her apartment, relieving her of the obligation to pay her share of the rent. Of course the job at the bookstore didn't pay as much as her job at Minas, but since she didn't have to pay rent now, she came out ahead.

In addition to meeting her basic needs, Cathy needed enough income so that she could send money to her mother in Colombia. Every month she bought a check for two hundred dollars in the black market, which she mailed to a company in Panama that belonged to a trusted friend, which transferred the money to a bank in Cali, where her mother went and picked it up. For some reason she was making sure that the money couldn't be traced to her.

He was at his desk reviewing a loan proposal when a wizened man came into the bank demanding to see Arias. It was Friday, so Arias was at Punta del Este, taking his usual long weekend.

Ignacio, the *ordenanza*, explained to the man that Señor Arias was out of town, but the man insisted on seeing someone.

Stephen got up and walked over and greeted him, saying: "How can I help you?"

"I made a loan," the man said crossly, "with the guarantee of your bank. The borrower defaulted, so I want my money. And I want it now."

"Please come over and sit down."

The man followed him and sat in the chair next to his desk.

"Do you have the guarantee with you?" Stephen asked.

"Yes." The man reached into the inside pocket of his rumpled jacket and pulled out a folded paper, which he opened and smoothed on the desk. "It says that if the borrower fails to pay at maturity, you'll pay me on demand."

"Let me see it," Stephen said, taking the paper. It was indeed the bank's guarantee, signed by Arias. The amount of the guarantee in pesos was the equivalent of two hundred thousand dollars, plus interest at the rate of fifty-two percent for ninety days. And the due date was February 15, five days ago. "I just need to check it," he told the man, reaching for the phone. He called Rosa and asked her to verify the guarantee.

"What's the number?" Rosa asked.

He told her and waited.

After a long silence she said: "I don't see that number in my logbook. What's the name of the lender?"

He told her.

"I don't see that name."

"You don't have a record of it?"

"No. I don't. Are you sure it's our guarantee?"

"It's our form, and Arias signed it."

"Does it have a seal?"

"Yes," he said, noting the seal to the right of the signature.

"Well, let me double check," Rosa said tensely. "I'll call you back right away."

"Okay," he said, wondering.

"What's the matter?" the man asked as if he smelled trouble.

"Nothing, nothing. It's just a formality."

A few minutes later Rosa called him back and told him: "I have no record of this guarantee."

"Are you sure?"

"I'm positive."

"Okay. Thanks." Since he trusted Rosa, the only conclusion he could draw was that Arias had somehow fabricated the guarantee, perhaps with this man's knowledge, so he decided to put him off. "We're missing some information that only Señor Arias can give us. So why don't you come back on Monday."

"I want my money now," the man insisted, raising his voice.

"If everything's in order, we'll pay you on Monday."

"Are you denying that this is your bank's guarantee?" the man bellowed, slapping the paper.

"I'm only saying that we're missing some information."

"That's not my problem."

"I know. It's ours. So we have to resolve it."

"Well, if I don't get my money now, I'm going to call the president of your bank and complain about you."

Ignoring the threat, Stephen picked up the guarantee and said: "I need to make a copy of this."

The man lunged for the guarantee, trying to grab it, but Stephen kept it away from him.

"Give it back to me!"

"I will. Don't worry." He signaled Ignacio, who came over and took the guarantee to be copied.

The man seemed to deliberate between waiting and running after the *ordenanza*, evidently deciding to wait when he noticed the guard near the door.

"Here," Stephen said, handing the guarantee back to him after Ignacio had returned with a copy.

The man snatched it and rose abruptly to his feet, saying: "I'll be back on Monday."

"I'll see you then," Stephen said affably.

He watched the man go, and then he went across the hall to see Rosa. She was at her desk examining her logbook and looking upset.

"Do you have any clue what happened?" he asked her.

"That number is out of sequence," she told him.

"What do you mean?"

"It's way beyond where we are now."

"Well, how could that happen?"

"It could happen if someone went into the storeroom and got the form from a box we won't be using for a while."

"The storeroom is locked."

"I know, but people have keys."

"Does Arias have a key?"

"He's not supposed to."

"He could have borrowed a key from someone."

"I didn't lend it to him," she said unshakably.

"I know you didn't. I'm not blaming you."

"*Gracias*. But I can't help feeling responsible."

"You couldn't have noticed that a form was missing."

"I know I couldn't have. But all the same—"

"I understand. You're a professional."

She nodded at him appreciatively.

"If this transaction had been legitimate," he said, "we would have booked our usual fees."

"We didn't book any fees."

"Did we pay the tax?"

"No. We didn't."

"So we know what happened, don't we."

"Yes. But we don't know how many of these guarantees are outstanding."

"Let's go and find the box where he got this one."

They went to the storeroom and easily found it. The box had been opened, even though it was down in the pile. And there were fifty missing forms, including the one that the man had just brought into the bank.

"*Carajo,*" he muttered. "This could be a disaster."

"You mean if all the borrowers defaulted."

"The bank could lose a lot of money."

"But isn't he a good loan officer?"

"He is," Stephen said. "And it certainly wouldn't have been in his interest for any of the borrowers to default. In fact, as long as no one defaulted we might have never found out what he was doing."

"Then maybe this is the only bad loan."

"I hope so," he said, closing the box.

He returned to his desk, planning to confront Arias on Monday. He realized that he didn't have much bargaining power since he needed information on all the unrecorded loans that Arias had arranged, and Arias was the only person who could give it to him.

After work he met Cathy at the bookstore, which was on Maipú not far from the bank, and they walked over to Avenida de Mayo. She was wearing her yellow dress, and she didn't seem nervous about meeting his friends, though she had asked a lot of questions about them.

When they got to the café they found Chris and Sofi there as well as Paco, a young priest who worked in the *villas* and had been introduced to the group by Sofi. With his flowing brown hair, full beard, and compassionate eyes he could have modeled for a painting of Jesus. He was dressed in black with a clerical collar that didn't stop women from falling in love with him.

They welcomed Cathy without any questions and resumed talking about a poor family that Sofi and Paco were working with. As Cathy listened, it was clear from her expression that she could relate to what they were saying.

"The mother cleans houses," Sofi told her. "It takes her more than an hour by bus to get into the city, and she has no time to spend with her children."

"How many children does she have?" Stephen asked.

"Five, with another on the way."

"Where's the father?"

"You mean the fathers. They're not around."

"So she's raising the children by herself?"

"A lot of these mothers raise the children by themselves."

"If this woman could start her own business in the neighborhood," Chris said, "she could make more money and spend more time with her children."

"What kind of business?" Sofi asked.

"I don't know. What do they need in the neighborhood?"

"They need a store."

"Then maybe she could open a store. Oh, speaking of stores," Chris said to Stephen, "I'm making progress on your idea of forming a cooperative."

"Good. If you help this woman open a store, you'll have another member."

At that moment Elena arrived. After being introduced to Cathy she sat next to her and engaged her in a conversation, asking how her job was going at the bookstore. It looked like Elena was going to take Cathy under her wing.

When Mario and Teresa arrived he introduced them to Cathy and gave them the cover story about her background.

"You're Venezuelan?" Mario asked.

"Yes," Cathy said as if she were proud of it.

"Well, we're Italian."

"I'm Greek," Sofi said.

"I'm Spanish," Paco said.

"And I'm English," Elena said.

"They're making fun of people," Stephen explained, "who aren't proud of being Argentines. If you ask these people what they are, they never say they're Argentine, they say they're whatever their grandparents were."

"Their great-grandparents," Mario said.

"The Anglos are the worst," Elena admitted. "My father still talks about going *back* to England as if he used to live there. His great-grandfather came here from England to build the railroads, and he never went back. We've lived here for five generations."

"My father talks about going back to Italy," Mario said. "He never lived there."

"My father doesn't talk about going back to Greece," Sofi said. "It's Turkey now where his father came from."

"My father didn't talk about going back to Spain," Paco said. "He knew that Franco would have killed him."

"Franco was the model for our generals," Mario said, which inevitably led to a discussion about politics.

They talked about the story that Elena had written about the number of people who had been killed in the war since early January. The violence was escalating as the right-wing death squads responded to the Montoneros, targeting left-wing politicians and sympathizers. The war had become a blood feud, with each side retaliating against the other, widening its range of victims indiscriminately.

After listening for a while Paco got their attention by saying: "The only way to stop the killing is to stop the killing."

"You're right, my friend," Mario agreed. "But that'll never happen."

"It *will* happen when we have social justice in this world, when we lift the poor and free the oppressed, when we create a society in which all human beings have an equal opportunity to realize their potential."

From their different perspectives they shared this vision of a better world. But they were mindful of the fact that the Montoneros started as a group of Catholic students with the same vision and later adopted the strategy of an influential Colombian priest, Camilo Torres, who after trying a nonviolent approach eventually joined a guerrilla army and died in combat. He had famously said: "If Jesus were alive today, he would be a guerrilla."

When they left the café Stephen and Cathy shared a taxi with Elena, and they all got out at the building where she lived. They exchanged *abrazos* with Elena, and then he took Cathy to dinner at a nearby restaurant where he had been eating by himself at least twice a week. It was called Ligure, and it had a daily menu, written in longhand and copied on a mimeograph. The waiters all knew him, and the one who led them to a table looked happy to see him with someone.

After they had ordered Cathy said: "When they were talking about that woman in the *villa miseria* I felt like they were talking about my mother."

"How many children did she have?"

"Seven. But one died when he was a baby."

"Are you the oldest?"

"How did you know?"

"I just guessed."

"I helped my mother raise her children. But I also wanted a better life. I wanted to get a degree from the university."

"You could get one here."

"I guess I could, now that I have a normal job."

Still trying to fill in blanks, he asked: "What did you do in Colombia after the American family left?"

"I got a job at a club like Minas."

"Did you work the same hours as you did at Minas?"

"Yes. And that was the problem. I was at the university, and I never had enough time to study. So I got a job with a Colombian family taking care of their children, and I worked fewer hours at the club. The father hired me because he wanted his children to learn English. He paid me very well, so I could help my mother. Everything was fine." Again she stopped and after a pause she changed the subject. "Your friends talked about politics, about the military, about the terrorists. Can you explain what's happening here?"

"I can try," he said. "It goes back to Perón—"

"The man they keep talking about."

"Yeah. Perón was an army colonel, a member of the group that overthrew the civilian government in 1943. In the military government he became head of the labor department, and in that position he built a strong base of support among the unions. He married a woman named Eva Duarte, who helped him become immensely popular with workers and women. With their support he was elected president in 1946. His program was to empower the working class and industrialize Argentina. But he nationalized a lot of industries, which hurt the economy. Still, he was re-elected in 1951. A year later Eva died of cancer, and after that he lost it. He got into trouble with the Catholic Church, which excommunicated him in 1955, and later that year the military overthrew him."

"Was he a bad president?"

"Well, he wasn't what the country needed at the time. When he came to power there were major problems. There were conflicts between landowners and peasants, between capitalists and workers, between landowners and capitalists. What the country needed was a political process in which these conflicts could be resolved. It needed an economic program that would not only redistribute wealth but would also create more wealth. Instead, it got a destructive form of populism that made the whole country poorer, and with less to go around the conflicts intensified and became violent."

"So the military took over."

"Yeah. They ran the country for a while. One of the generals who led the *golpe* became president. His name was Aramburu. But they made things worse, so they decided to hold elections. That was in 1958."

"Who won the elections?"

"A man named Frondizi. Under laws passed by the military, the *peronistas* weren't allowed to run for office, so there was a deal in which Perón agreed to tell his followers to vote for Frondizi in return for an eventual change in the laws that would allow the *peronistas* to run. Frondizi allowed them to run in the elections for provincial governors, and when they won most of those elections the military intervened and installed an interim president. The *peronistas* still weren't allowed to run in the next presidential election, so most of them either didn't vote or voted in blank. A man named Illia from another party was elected without a majority of the votes. He wasn't such a bad president, but he antagonized the military by allowing the *peronistas* to run in legislative elections, which they won decisively. So the military took over again. That was in 1966."

"Were you here then?"

"No. I was in Vietnam then, but that's another story." He sipped some wine. "While the military were in power, a group of Catholic students organized a socialist wing of the *peronista* party. They were followers of a charismatic priest who was fervently committed to helping the poor. He believed in a nonviolent approach, but they eventually broke with him and adopted the approach of a Colombian priest who decided that violence was the only way. They called themselves the Montoneros. They believed that they were the true *peronistas*, and to prove themselves they kidnapped Aramburu and executed him. That was in 1970."

"Was that when this war began?"

"You could say that, but the Montoneros wouldn't agree. They'd say it began when the police, presumably under orders from the military, executed a number of *peronista* leaders in a garbage dump. It was known as the León Suárez Massacre. That was in 1956."

"I understand. And the military would say it began with something Perón did."

"If you followed all the causes and effects, you'd go back to the story of Cain and Abel."

She nodded with a look of sorrow.

"When the military took over in 1966," he resumed, "they had a program to reform the economy. But it didn't work. So after trying to run the country for seven years they had elections, and this time the *peronistas* were allowed to run."

"Where was Perón at this time?"

"He was still in exile, living in Spain. He wasn't allowed to run, but his supporters were and they got elected. That was in March of 1973."

"You really know this stuff."

"I've been writing reports on it for years."

"You explain it well."

"That's only because I don't have people on my right and left disagreeing with me." Indeed, there probably wasn't a single Argentine who would agree with his version of this history. "Anyway, the new government invited Perón to return, and in June of 1973 he did return."

"How long had he been gone?"

"Almost eighteen years. The Montoneros, who were hoping that he would create a socialist paradise in Argentina, were at the airport to welcome him, but by then he had moved to the right of his party and he no longer had any use for them. I think at heart he was always a fascist. Anyway, members of a right-wing death squad, which his personal secretary had organized, were at the airport, positioned as snipers, and they opened fire on the Montoneros, killing and wounding hundreds of them. It was known as the Ezeiza Massacre."

"Another massacre."

"From then on the Montoneros were at war not only with the military but also with the right-wing *peronistas*, who finally expelled them from the party."

"What were the military doing then?"

"Watching and waiting and operating behind the scenes. When Perón died in July of 1974 they began to take control. By the end of last year they made the president approve a plan that divided the country into five war zones and gave them special powers to fight the terrorists."

"If they already have these powers," Cathy said, "why would they need to overthrow the government?"

"They want complete control," he said, "and by letting things get worse as they're doing now, they make people want to give them control."

"I understand."

"But they haven't wasted any time. The right-wing death squad that massacred the Montoneros at the airport has been doing a lot of dirty work for them, killing left-wing politicians and union leaders. They're called the Argentine Anticommunist Alliance, or the Triple A. And they have the blessing of the military, though the military would never admit it."

After a long silence she said: "It sounds as bad as Colombia. We have left-wing guerillas, and right-wing death squads, and the military, all of them killing each other."

"It's similar," he agreed.

"And it's always men, it's never women."

"These groups have female members, but you're right. It's a male thing."

"What's the matter with them?"

"I don't know. You'll have to ask a psychologist."

"Well, from what I learned in psychology it's because their mothers didn't love them enough."

"Yeah, blame it on the mothers."

"Of course that's ridiculous."

"It is," he agreed. "You might as well say it's because these guys can't get it up."

"Get it up? Oh." She laughed, comprehending. "I think that's a better explanation."

The next day he met Cathy at the bookstore, which like many shops closed at noon on Saturdays. The store was owned by the mother of one of Elena's friends, who had gone to college in England and stayed there.

When he arrived Cathy was helping to close the store, and from the way the owner treated her he could tell that she liked Cathy, who at least in age could have been her daughter.

Stephen browsed among the fiction until they were ready to leave. The store specialized in English and American books, but it also had a good selection of books in Spanish. He found a book of stories by Julio Cortázar and bought it.

They left and walked over to Santa Fe, where they had lunch in a *confitería*. During lunch she told him about meeting a girl who was going to the university. She had learned from the girl that fall classes were about to begin but there was still time to register. She was thinking of taking one course to see how it went. He encouraged her to try it. She needed to get more information from the School of Philosophy and Letters, which offered the program she needed to become a teacher.

After lunch they strolled over to Arenales and up the street to the food market. They had decided to eat more meals at home, instead of going out all the time, and they were both learning to cook since Cathy didn't have much more experience in the kitchen than he did. She had learned some basic dishes from her mother, such as rice and beans, but the family whose children she had taken care of had a cook, so she hadn't learned anything there. She had bought *The Joy of Cooking* at the bookstore with her employee discount, and they were eagerly learning from it, working together and sharing the tasks of preparing a meal.

The market was an open space with a high ceiling under which there were rows of individual stalls purveying meat, fish, vegetables, dairy, and other items. There were two butchers, and they preferred one of them because he was more helpful, having no doubt guessed that they were novices. The other butcher acted as if he didn't want to waste time answering their questions.

"The easiest way to prepare these," their butcher explained as he wrapped two steaks in brown paper, "is to put them in a hot cast-iron frying pan and cook them about five minutes on one side and then about three minutes on the other side, depending on how rare you want them."

"I like mine medium," Cathy told him.

"*A punto?* Well, then cook it a few more minutes."

They bought potatoes, green beans, lettuce, and tomatoes from the vegetable man, and then they headed home.

When they had put away the groceries they started kissing in the kitchen. They ended up in the bedroom, and when they woke up they were both starved. They cooked the steaks following the butcher's directions, and they fried the potatoes using a recipe from the cookbook. They already knew how to make a salad.

They spent the rest of the evening reading, stretched out in the family room with their heads under the lamps at opposite ends of the sofa and their feet alongside each other's chests. She was reading *Tender is the Night,* and he was reading *Todos los fuegos el fuego,* but there were distractions.

At one point she tickled his foot.

He reciprocated.

She giggled, squirming.

"Now I know your weak spot," he laughed.

"I have a lot of weak spots," she admitted readily.

"I haven't noticed any."

"That's because you're too nice."

"Too nice? They always say that about us."

"What do you mean?"

"They always say that Midwesterners are too nice."

"Are you from the Midwest?"

"Yeah. I'm from St. Paul, Minnesota."

"That's where Fitzgerald was from."

"I grew up about three blocks from where he lived."

"Did you know him?"

"No. I'm not that old. But my father knew him."

"What did your father say about him?"

"He said he was a drunk."

"So why did you leave Minnesota?"

"If you ever spent a winter there you'd understand why."

"But why did you come to Argentina? You could have gone other places."

"The bank had an open position here, and I spoke Spanish, so they sent me here."

"How did you learn Spanish?"

"I learned it from migrant workers in California," he told her, referring to an episode of his life that the CIA evidently didn't know about.

"Migrant workers? What were you doing with them?"

"Helping them to organize a union."

"How old were you?"

"Twenty. I took a year off from college because I wanted to get involved in what was happening. That was the Sixties," he explained, "and a lot was happening. I went to Mississippi to join the marches for civil rights, and then I went to California to help the migrant workers."

"You were doing what your friends here are doing."

"Yeah. And deep down I haven't changed. I still want to be involved in what's happening."

"You mean you want to make a better world."

"I want to do my part," he said.

"Aren't you doing that as a banker?"

"At times I am. But most of the time I'm just helping companies make more money."

"So you would rather be something else."

"Eventually I would. I was going to be a teacher, but then the war in Vietnam came along, and I had to get involved in that. I should have learned from that experience," he added, "not to get involved in wars."

"Are you involved in this one?"

"We're all involved."

"I guess we are."

"If you'd known there was a war here, would you have come to Argentina?"

"I didn't have a choice." She looked as if she might tell him more, but then she asked: "What about you?"

"I knew what was happening here."

"And you came here anyway?"

"Well, there really aren't any peaceful places in the world."

"I guess there aren't." She reached for his hand and clasped it. "Except here."

On Monday morning he sat at his desk preparing to confront Arias. He decided that the most effective approach would be to threaten to call the police and accuse Arias of committing a crime against the bank. Based on his memory of an incident that had occurred during his first year in Argentina, he believed that Arias would succumb to such a threat. It had happened while he was on vault duty, which junior officers had to perform for one week every month. When the bank closed you had to stay and make sure that every teller reconciled his account and put his cash-box into the vault. One evening a teller had a shortage in cash that at the exchange rate then was equal to slightly more than eight hundred dollars. The bank was required by its insurance policy to report any shortage over five hundred dollars to the police, which should have been a routine matter. But the police arrested the teller and threw him into jail, even though the bank hadn't made any accusation against him. In fact, the man had served the bank for more than ten years and was highly regarded. Still, they kept him in jail for almost seven months without his having been charged with anything. They released him only when the bank proved that the missing money was stolen by a man who delivered cash that day for a client—the man was caught trying to do the same thing with another delivery, and he confessed to the prior crime.

As soon as Arias finished his coffee Stephen got up and walked over to him. "Could you join me for a minute in the conference room?"

"Sure," Arias said nonchalantly.

When they sat down, with the door closed, Stephen said: "We have a mystery that I'd like to clear up, and I think you can help me."

"If I can, I'd be glad too."

He unfolded the copy of the guarantee that the wizened man had brought to the bank on Friday, and he placed it in front of Arias. "Do you recognize this?"

"Sure. It's a guarantee."

"Do you see the number?"

"Yes. What about it?"

"It's not in the logbook."

"What do you mean?"

"We have no record of it."

"Well, Rosa must have forgotten to enter it."

"No. She didn't. She couldn't have. Because this number is out of sequence."

"I don't understand," Arias said, acting perplexed. "I got it from her."

"I think you got it from a box in the storeroom."

"Why would I have done that?"

"To make some money on the side. There were no fees booked by the bank for this transaction."

"She must have forgotten to book them."

"I don't think so."

"You can't prove anything," Arias said smugly.

"I don't have to. I just have to call the police and make an accusation against you. They'll put you in jail, and they'll keep you there for a long time before they give you a trial."

"You wouldn't do that," Arias said, his voice rising. "It would hurt the reputation of the bank."

"The bank would survive."

Arias looked as if he were assessing the credibility of the threat and evaluating his alternatives. He finally said: "Okay, okay. What do you want from me?"

"I want information on all the loans under guarantees that weren't recorded," Stephen told him. "Lenders, borrowers, amounts, and maturities."

"If I give you that, will you let me go?"

"I also want to know the owners of any companies that made loans."

For the first time Arias looked worried. "Why do you want to know that?"

"I want to have a complete record."

"Well, I may not have that information."

"You don't know who you're dealing with?"

"The companies were referred to me."

"Then I want to know who referred them to you."

Arias stalled, evidently looking for a way out.

"I want this information by the end of the day. I've instructed the guards," Stephen added, rising from the table, "not to let you out of the bank until I say so."

"*Gringazo*," Arias hissed.

It took Arias a few hours to prepare the list, which Stephen reviewed carefully. There were twenty-three loans, including the one from the man who brought the scam to his attention. Two other loans were from individuals, and the rest were all from three companies, the owners of which Arias hadn't identified.

"You don't know who owns these companies?" Stephen asked, believing that Arias did know.

"No. I don't," Arias insisted.

"You said they were referred to you. Who referred them?"

Arias hesitated, and he finally said: "Marco Safadi."

"All three companies?"

"Yes. All three."

"Then please note that next to each company."

Arias glowered as he went down the list, noting that the companies had been referred to him by Marco Safadi. "There. Now, is that all?"

"That's all."

Arias stood up, saying: "You don't have to worry about these loans. They'll all be good."

"What about this one?" Stephen asked, holding up the copy of the guarantee.

"It's been paid already. That *boludo* was trying to collect his money twice."

"He was? You're kidding. Can you prove it?"

"Yes. I have the receipt." Arias took a piece of paper out of his pocket and handed it to Stephen. "He knew I was away, so he came here and tried to collect from you. If I'd been here, he wouldn't have tried it."

"And I wouldn't have found out what you were doing."

"That's right. You're a lucky *gringo*."

"Okay. You're free to go. But I might want to talk with you further."

"Any time," Arias said, heading for the door.

Stephen remained in the conference room, thinking about what he should do. Among other things he would have to make a report to head office and let them know what had happened. They would probably send a team of auditors to Buenos Aires. They might blame him for letting it happen, or they might give him credit for catching it. That would depend on whether or not the bank lost money.

Of greater interest to him was the evidence of a connection between Arias and Safadi. Since the companies listed as lenders had been referred by Safadi, they were clients of his either from the Jewish community or from somewhere else. If the embassy guys were right about Safadi, then these companies could be owned by the Montoneros, who were using them to keep some of their money in the country. If so, then they were investing this money in the *extrabancario* market on the advice of Safadi, who had referred them to his buddy Arias.

That afternoon he met with Carlos and a lawyer from the firm that represented the bank in Argentina. The lawyer was a partner who specialized in white-collar crime, including embezzlement and accounting fraud. His face was crabbed as if he had a permanent case of dyspepsia. His name was Ferrer.

They were in the general manager's office, with the door

closed, and as Stephen explained what Arias had done Ferrer took notes on a small pad as if he were writing out a prescription to deal with the problem.

"*Bueno*," Ferrer said, laying down his pen. "Are you confident that this man gave you a complete list of the guarantees?"

"As much as I can be," Stephen said. "There were fifty guarantee forms missing. There are twenty-three loans on his list, and he gave me twenty-seven blank forms that he hadn't used."

"That accounts for the missing forms."

"So unless he gave us wrong information on any of the loans, I think we have an accurate picture."

"We can easily find out if he gave us any wrong information," Carlos said.

Ferrer nodded. "You just have to check with the lenders and the borrowers. Have you done that?"

"Not yet. But we will," Stephen said.

Ferrer cleared his throat. "Well, you could claim that he wasn't authorized to sign these guarantees, and you could refuse to honor them."

"We could, but what would that do to our reputation?"

"Lenders wouldn't trust your guarantees."

"And that would put us out of business in the *extrabancario* market," Carlos said.

"Besides," Stephen said, "he signed a lot of legitimate guarantees. So how could we argue that he was authorized to sign some but not others?"

"You could argue," Ferrer said, "that he didn't follow your internal procedures. But it wouldn't get you very far."

"Will you give us a written opinion," Carlos asked, "that we have to honor these guarantees?"

Ferrer nodded. "If that's what you want."

"That's what we want."

Stephen agreed. They didn't want some lawyer in New York,

who didn't understand their business, suggesting that the bank could somehow get out of fulfilling its obligations under these guarantees. And having an opinion from the local lawyer would also help with the auditors.

"Is that it?" Ferrer asked.

"There's something else," Stephen said. "Almost all the unrecorded loans were made by three companies, and we'd like to know who owns them."

Ferrer frowned, looking puzzled. "I can see why you'd want to know who owns the borrowers, but why do you care who owns the lenders?"

"We want to know who we're dealing with."

"A few years ago," Carlos explained, "one of these loans went bad, and the lender turned out to be the Vatican Bank."

Stephen remembered having to deal with it. Four men in church regalia complete with hats had faced him down in the conference room to make sure that the bank didn't renege on its guarantee. He had felt as if they were holding his immortal soul as collateral against repayment of their loan.

"Did they give you a hard time?" Ferrer asked, smiling.

"They got their money," Stephen said.

"All right. Can you give me the names of the companies?"

He handed the lawyer a piece of paper on which he had printed in block letters the names of the three companies.

Ferrer examined it. "I don't recognize any of these names, but we can track them down. How soon do you need the information?"

"By the end of the week."

Stephen stayed late at the bank that evening preparing a report for the vice president using a secretary's typewriter. Without question typing was one of the most useful things he had learned to do. He mastered the touch system at the age of eight on an old Remington that his father had brought home from his office. He had needed the machine to write a story about a dog. The story won first prize in a third-grade writing contest, and he had been writing on a typewriter ever since. By now his handwriting was so bad that there were times when even he couldn't read it. Trying to read a grocery list that he made for a family party, his mother said that with such bad handwriting he should have been a doctor.

He had never wanted to be a doctor, though he had considered a variety of other professions that responded to the call of "Princeton in the Nation's Service." Along with the offer from the CIA he received offers from the State Department and the Peace Corps, but he finally decided to pursue a career in teaching, so after completing his bachelor's degree he enrolled at Columbia with the idea of getting a master's degree in English and teaching in a New York City high school. After getting his master's he followed the advice of his faculty mentor and continued working toward a doctorate in English until one morning when he faced himself in the mirror and found that he could no longer accept the fact that he was being deferred from the draft while less fortunate men his age were being sent to Vietnam. So he enlisted in the army.

When he was discharged three years later, after serving an extended tour of duty in Vietnam, he still wanted to be a teacher, but he believed that with more experience in the world he would have more to offer his students, so at that point he looked for a job that would give him more international experience. No longer wanting to work for the government, he interviewed with corporations and banks that had overseas operations, and he accepted the offer from the bank because it promised to send him overseas after one year of training. During that year he met Leila, who had taken a number of field trips to Latin America while earning her doctorate in anthropology, and when he was assigned to Buenos Aires she said yes, she would marry him, evidently believing that it would be an ideal base of operations for her research. Unfortunately, it was far from the places where you could study indigenous peoples practicing their cultures, and within a few months of their arrival Leila started taking field trips, which kept them apart for longer and longer periods of time as she went to northern Argentina, Bolivia, and Peru.

As he walked home he cleared his mind of bad memories and current intrigues, looking forward to an evening with Cathy. He found her in the kitchen with the dinner almost ready. Knowing he would be late that evening, she had gone ahead and cooked without him. She was wearing a green apron, which not only contrasted nicely with her yellow dress but also brought out the green in her eyes. She greeted him with a warm kiss, which he returned tenderly.

The next afternoon he was at his desk helping one of the account managers with a loan proposal when he received a phone call from Elena, who said: "I'm calling from the lobby of the bank. Can you come down?"

"Sure." He could tell from her voice that something terrible had happened.

He found her in the lobby, stricken, and she motioned for him to go out with her. She led him across the busy street to an open area where they could escape from the crowded narrow sidewalk.

Facing him, she said: "They killed Chris."

"What?" He felt as if he had been kicked in the stomach.

"The Montoneros killed him."

"No." He couldn't believe it. "Why?"

"For spreading ideas of capitalism. At least that's what they said in the note they pinned to his body."

"Oh, Jesus. Where's Sofi?"

"She's with her family."

"Those assholes," he hissed, roiled with anger and pity and sorrow. "How did you hear about it?"

"A police report. We get them every day."

"How did they do it?"

"They took him yesterday as he was going home from work. His body was found early this morning. They shot him in the back of the head."

"That's how they killed Alejandro."

"I know." She put her hand gently on his shoulder.

"What the hell do they think they're doing?"

"They think they're ridding the country of capitalism."

"Well, if they really believed in socialism, they'd try to prove it's a better system in a peaceful way."

"They must believe they wouldn't have a chance that way."

"They never tried. They launched their movement by killing Aramburu."

"I know," she said.

"Whatever vision they might have had, it doesn't justify killing Chris, or killing Alejandro, or killing anyone."

"They must believe it does."

"Then God *damn* them. They killed a good man, a good friend, a good husband—"

"Who would have been a good father."

Overwhelmed, they put their arms around each other and held each other, seeking and giving comfort at the same time, mixing their tears.

By the time he returned to the bank it was time to leave anyway, so he shoved his papers into his desk and headed out. He walked briskly to the bookstore, cursing the people who had killed his friend. He wanted to kill them, and he imagined what he would do if he ran into them with a weapon.

When he got to the bookstore Cathy was helping a customer,

so he waited for her, pretending to browse, but he could only think about what had happened to Chris and how it would affect Sofi.

"What's wrong?" Cathy asked, approaching him.

"Can you leave now?"

"Sure." She went and talked with the owner of the store, and then she rejoined him.

Outside, he told her what had happened.

"Oh, no," she moaned. "Why?"

"He was spreading ideas of capitalism."

"I don't understand."

"I explained it to you."

"You explained why the two sides are killing each other, but you never said they're killing innocent people."

"I thought you understood that in wars they always kill innocent people."

"I guess I should have understood that."

"In this war they've killed a lot of innocent people."

"People like Chris?"

"Yes, people like Chris. They killed my assistant, Alejandro."

"Your assistant? Why?"

"He was working for a foreign bank."

She stared at him, alarmed. "Then they could kill you."

"They could," he admitted. "But I'm not visible."

"Was your assistant visible?"

He shook his head. "I wouldn't have thought so, but for some reason he became a target."

"Then you could become a target."

He shrugged. "I guess I could."

She looked as if she suddenly had a new appreciation of him and a new responsibility. In a different tone of voice she asked: "Why do you stay here?"

It was the same question that Boyd had asked, and he gave

her the same answer. "Because I don't want to leave this country in such a mess."

"But it's not your country."

"So it's not my responsibility?"

"Well, I don't see what you can do here."

He was tempted to reveal how he was trying to stop the killing, but he didn't want to involve her, so he only said: "There're things I can do."

"Whatever they are, you could do them somewhere else."

"So I should just run away from here and forget that those assholes murdered my friend?"

"No, but—"

"I should just let them keep killing people?"

"I'm not saying that."

"Then what are you saying?"

"I'm only saying I care about you," she said unflinchingly.

"I'm sorry," he said, abashed by her candor. "I shouldn't take it out on you. I'm full of poison."

"Poison?"

"Yeah, poison. It makes me want to kill those assholes. *It makes me want to kill them.*"

"What good would that do?"

"It wouldn't do any good at all, but that's how I feel."

"Well, Chris wouldn't want you to do that."

"I know. And I hate myself for feeling this way."

With a frown of concern she asked: "Is that how you felt after they killed your assistant?"

"Yeah. But I got over it."

"How did you get over it?"

"By trying to help his widow."

"Then you should try to help Sofi."

"I intend to. But right now—" He shuddered as if he could feel the poison spreading within him.

"Right now, instead of wanting vengeance," she told him, "you should want what we can give each other."

Humbly, he went into her arms.

Chris's friends were all at the funeral, and so were a lot of people who looked like members of Sofi's extended family as well as people Chris had helped to start businesses and people Sofi had helped in the *villa*.

Stephen sat in a pew with Cathy, Elena, Mario, and Teresa, isolated by the feeling that he was somehow responsible for Chris's death, or that he had somehow failed to prevent it. This was exactly how he had felt after they killed Alejandro, and he had sought relief from the feeling by trying to help Vittoria and by trying to stop the Montoneros from killing people. But he had repressed the primitive urge that surfaced when he heard that the Montoneros had killed Chris, and now he confronted the ugly fact that deep down he still wanted to kill them, he still wanted vengeance. He hadn't gotten over it by trying to help Vittoria, and he wouldn't get over it by trying to help Sofi. The only way to stop wanting vengeance was to start wanting something else.

He found Cathy's hand and held it.

Though it was a Greek orthodox service, the priest let Paco say a few words.

"This is the prayer of St. Francis," Paco said. "It expresses the spirit of our brother Christopher."

Stephen closed his eyes, anticipating the familiar words.

"Lord, make me an instrument of your peace. Where there is hatred, let me sow love; where there is injury, pardon."

Encouraged by the prayer, he started wanting the alternative that Cathy offered him.

"Where there is doubt, faith; where there is despair, hope; where there is darkness, light; where there is sadness, joy. O Divine Master, grant that I may not so much seek to be consoled, as to console; to be understood, as to understand; to be loved, as to love. For it is in giving that we receive; it is in pardoning that we are pardoned; and it is in dying that we are born to eternal life."

"Amen," he murmured.

FOUR

HE WAS STILL committed to working with the embassy guys, but his motive had changed from the time when he first met them. Now, instead of sublimating a lust for vengeance, he only wanted to stop the killing. He believed that by doing his part to intercept their shipments of arms and shut off their flow of money, he could help to induce the Montoneros to make peace with their enemies and pursue their noble vision of social justice in nonviolent ways. So he waited anxiously for the information from Panama.

It arrived the following Monday morning in a large manila envelope that had been sent in the bank's mail pouch. The envelope contained shipping documents as well as a list of the remittances that the Swiss bank had made through the Panama branch over the past three years.

The ship had sailed from Panama on February 19 and was due to arrive in Buenos Aires on March 3, which gave them only two days to make arrangements to expose the contents of the shipment. That wasn't much time, but before calling the embassy guys he wanted to examine the list of remittances, compare it with the lists of loans in the *extrabancario* market, and see if he could find connections between them.

For privacy he took the lists into the conference room, closed the door, and sat down at the table. From the list of remittances he could see that every transaction looked as if it had originated with the Swiss bank, which asked the Panama branch to transfer money to International Bank & Trust, instructing them to credit some of the money to the account of an individual and some to the account of a company called Esmeralda S.A. If the embassy guys were right, then the Swiss bank had combined the funds remitted by an individual from Argentina with cash deposited by the Montoneros, so after the amount was taken out for Esmeralda the individual ultimately received the amount he had sent from Argentina.

Stephen could imagine how it worked. Miguel Levi, who has made a small fortune in manufacturing women's clothing, has lunch with Safadi, the owner and president of the bank that serves their community. Safadi warns him that if the military take over they might initiate another round of anti-Semitism and confiscate the assets of Jews, as happened in Nazi Germany. Safadi offers to help him get money out of the country and put it in a safe place, and Miguel gratefully accepts the offer, entrusting Banco Azulay with a million dollars to transfer to New York. Safadi sends the money to the Swiss bank in Panama, where a courier from the Montoneros has recently deposited a million dollars in cash. The Swiss bank combines the money and remits two million dollars through the Panama branch of Stephen's bank, instructing them to transfer it to International Bank & Trust, a million for the account of Miguel Levi and a million for the account of Esmeralda. Miguel now has in a New York bank account the million dollars he gave to Safadi, so he's happy, and he never knows that he has been used to launder money for the Montoneros.

Some of the individuals on the list of remittances were also on Rosa's list of recorded loans, which meant that they were keeping some of their money in the country. But the companies on Arias' list of unrecorded loans did not appear on the list of remittances, so they evidently weren't being used for taking dollars out of the country. But it made sense. The companies weren't needed for that purpose since the Montoneros had a better method—bags of cash.

There was no apparent connection between the loans made by these companies and the transfers to Esmeralda, but the two operations did have one important thing in common: neither the loans nor the transfers could be easily traced to their origin. And there must have been a reason for that.

To share his findings Stephen called the embassy, and within an hour the guys arrived with their satchels. After placing an order for Bolivian pesos he brought them up to date.

"So it looks like they have two laundering operations," John said. "One for dollars and one for pesos. And it looks like Arias was only involved in the peso laundering."

"Safadi didn't need him for the dollar laundering," Bill said.

"Are you going to prosecute him?" John asked.

"Our head office doesn't want to," Stephen said. "They're afraid that if the word gets out that these guarantees weren't legitimate, it could hurt our reputation in the market."

"So he'll get away with it."

"He might not if he knows too much," Bill remarked.

"Do we have enough evidence," Stephen asked, "to prove that they're laundering money?"

Bill shook his head. "We only have some information on one step of a process that looks like money laundering. We're assuming that the money going to Esmeralda is coming from cash deposited in the Swiss bank, but we don't know that, and the Swiss bank will never tell us where it's coming from."

"Well, what if we could prove that it's going to the account of a company owned by the Montoneros?"

"That would be helpful. But you're not going to find that the shares of this company were issued to them."

"You're going to find that they were issued to a lawyer who's fronting for them," John said.

"But that might lead us somewhere," Stephen said.

"It might. It's worth pursuing."

"I already asked our lawyer to find out who owns the companies that made the loans."

"What about Esmeralda?"

"I just learned about it this morning."

"If it's a Panamanian company, it'll be a harder nut to crack. They have secrecy in Panama. It's like Switzerland."

"It's not like Switzerland," Bill said. "It's a hell hole."

"There must be a way to find out who owns Esmeralda," Stephen said, refocusing them.

"There are public records even in Panama," John said, "but they probably won't tell you anything."

"I could ask our lawyer there to help me."

"Yeah, he could help you find the records."

Stephen reflected. "If we could tie these operations to Safadi, would that be enough for the banking authorities to intervene?"

"On what grounds?" John asked.

"That the owner of International Bank & Trust is involved in a process that looks like money laundering."

John considered, and then he asked Bill: "What do you think?"

"That might be enough," Bill said. "But how could we tie these operations to Safadi?"

"If he's advising the Montoneros," Stephen said, "he must have been involved in setting up their companies."

"He would have used a lawyer for that," John said.

"Then maybe we can tie the lawyer to him."

"I don't have a better idea," Bill said.

"I don't either," John said.

"Now, what about the shipment?" Stephen said. "The ship is due to arrive on Wednesday. How are you going to handle it?"

"You don't need to know that," John said.

"Oh, tell him," Bill said. "He's dying of curiosity."

"We have contacts in the military. We'll tell them we think they should check the cargo of this ship."

"If it's that simple," Stephen said, "then why don't they check the cargo of every ship?"

"It's not that simple. You have to remember that every time a ship arrives an envelope changes hands."

"The grease that keeps the wheels turning," Bill said.

"So if they checked the cargo of every ship," John said, "the wheels would stop."

At that point the head trader arrived with a bag of currency.

After they had gone, with their satchels loaded with Bolivian pesos, Stephen went down to the general manager's office. Carlos wasn't there, but he somehow managed to talk Señora Pérez into letting him use the white phone. He called the Panama branch manager and asked him to find out who owned Esmeralda S.A., assuming it was a Panamanian company.

Cathy decided to resume her studies toward a degree that would qualify her to be a teacher, and since Teresa taught in a public school, Cathy got her advice on the program that she should apply to. She vacillated between the extremes of going full time or taking one course to see how things went, and she finally opted for the latter, with the intention of taking more courses the next semester.

Stephen met her in the evening after her first class at the School of Philosophy and Letters, and they had dinner at El Mundo. She talked with excitement about the course, which would get her back onto the path toward her dream. She liked the subject, she liked the professor, she liked her classmates, she liked everything about it.

That night, as they lay in bed talking, she said: "I wish I could transfer the credits I earned at the university in Cali."

"Why can't you?"

"Because it would give them a way to find me."

"Who?" he asked, alarmed.

"The people who want to kill me."

He waited, knowing he wouldn't have to coax her into telling him more.

"I'm going to tell you why I left Colombia. I started to tell you many times, but I couldn't bear to talk about it. I still don't know if I can, but I'll try." She lay on her side with her head on his chest and a hand on his arm.

He held her protectively as she told her story.

At the club where she was working as a bar girl she met a man, an older man, who took a strong interest in her. She danced with him and talked with him, but that was as far as things went. He always treated her with respect. He was evidently a successful businessman. He dressed well and tipped well after buying the most expensive champagne. He seemed to know a lot of people and have a lot of good connections.

One evening, after he had seen her several times, he asked her if she would like to make some extra money. Suspicious, she said no, thank you, she didn't need it. He laughed, telling her it wasn't what she thought. He was looking for someone to take care of his children. It mattered to him that unlike the other girls he might hire, she was educated and spoke English.

Reconsidering, she asked him how many children he had, how old they were, and where he lived. His answers were satisfactory. And when he told her how much he would pay her she agreed to work for him on a trial basis.

She went to his house, which was very impressive. It was in a neighborhood where wealthy people lived, and like the other houses in the area it was surrounded by a high wall, so you couldn't see it from the street. She met his wife, who was a lot younger than he was, a pretty woman, a nice woman who wanted everyone to be happy. She especially wanted her children to be happy, and she welcomed Cathy as someone who could help her make them happy.

"She said I was a godsend," Cathy said, *"una bendición.* It made me feel good."

Her experience in helping to raise her mother's children was obviously helpful, but now she was in a different situation. These children, who had all the advantages that her mother's children didn't have, needed discipline, which their mother didn't seem to understand. So there were problems until the children and their mother realized that discipline and love were not mutually exclusive but actually reinforced each other.

She hardly saw the father, who was fully immersed in his business and stopped coming to the club as if he had found what he was looking for, or else he went to another club, not wanting her to know what he was up to since she was like a member of his family. But he paid her weekly, in cash, and he always gave her a bonus.

Everything was fine. She was doing well at the university, and she was giving a lot of money to her mother, enabling her to stay at home more with her children. And she was becoming attached to the children she was taking care of.

Then late one evening, as she was doing her homework in the back room where she slept, she heard a commotion down in the courtyard around which the house was built. She heard men's voices shouting orders, and immediately she knew there was something wrong, terribly wrong.

Turning off her light, she sat still at her desk and listened.

Amid the shouting she heard the sound of heavy footsteps coming up the stairs and going into the children's rooms, then going down with scuffling and screaming. She was impelled to get up and rush to the aid of the children, but her instinct for survival held her back. She waited, holding her breath and listening.

When it sounded like they were all in the courtyard she tiptoed down the hall and peered over the railing of the balcony.

Below were the father, the mother, and the three children, huddled together and held at gunpoint by three men. They wore no masks or even hats, so she got a good look at their faces. The apparent leader was shouting at the father, accusing him of being a traitor.

Then, after informing him that they would make an example of him, the leader opened fire with an automatic weapon, spraying the father from head to toe. As the father collapsed on the tiled patio the other two men opened fire, riddling the mother and the three children, who toppled and lay in contorted positions in a pool of blood.

After spraying the pile of bodies for good measure the three men left the house and got into a waiting car.

She didn't move until she heard the car roar off.

Using the phone in the master bedroom, she called the police and told them what had happened. She didn't give them her name, and she didn't stay until they arrived. She left the house and started walking, heading in the general direction of her *barrio* and looking over her shoulder frequently to make sure that no one was following her.

When she reported for work at the club the following evening the owner took her into his office and explained that she was in great danger. The man she had worked for was a major supplier for a drug lord, and he had been killed for defecting to another drug lord. The word had gone out that there was a witness to the killing, so the killers were looking for her. And since she couldn't rely on the police to protect her, she had to leave the country right away.

Luckily, they didn't have a picture of her, and they didn't yet know her name. But they would eventually find out that she had been taking care of the children, so she had to change her name.

"You know the rest," she said. "The owner of the club got me a *cédula* and a passport, and I left the country as an Argentine girl named Catalina Linton."

"The Colombian girl disappeared."

"Like so many other people these days."

"Are you sure there's no way they can find you?"

"The only person who knows where I am is the owner of the club in Cali. And he would never tell them."

"Even if they tortured him?"

"Whatever they did to him," Cathy said confidently, "he would never tell them."

"How do you know?"

"I just know."

"What about the money you send to your mother?"

"It can't be traced. It goes through a Panamanian company that belongs to the owner of the club."

"What about the bank that transfers the money?"

"It's a Swiss bank. And they won't ever tell anyone where the money's coming from."

"Well, then I don't see how they can find you. That money could be coming from anywhere."

"They'll never find me," she assured him.

It wasn't like her to be so confident, so she must have believed that they would never find her. At least she wanted him to believe it.

The ship arrived on March 3 as scheduled. A team of agents inspected the cargo and found arms. They arrested the ship's captain, who argued that he wasn't responsible for the cargo. They arrested the importer, who claimed that he knew nothing about the arms, he had ordered only knitting machines, and he could prove it. They questioned Safadi, whose lawyer correctly argued that according to the uniform commercial code that governed international trade, his bank wasn't responsible for merchandise shipped under its letters of credit. The captain, the importer, and Safadi were released.

"It looks like Safadi uses imports of machinery by the garment industry as a cover for shipments of arms," John said as they assessed the situation, "just as he uses remittances from this same community as a cover for transfers of funds collected as ransom money."

"And they think he's helping them," Bill said.

"If they only knew."

"Well, we stopped one shipment," Stephen said. "But what if they start using another cover?"

"They'll keep using this cover for a while," Bill said. "They need information about legitimate shipments so that they can hide the arms in them, and they can't get this information from another bank."

"But if the police keep stopping them, won't they catch on?"

"They will eventually. But at least for a while they'll believe that they can buy the police."

"So why can't they?"

"Because the agents who stopped this shipment," Bill explained, "weren't police. They were military."

"Oh," Stephen said, beginning to understand. "Then we can do better on the next shipment."

"How do you mean?" John asked.

"Well, after the goods are cleared through customs, the arms have to be separated from the shipment before it reaches the importer. So next time the police, or the military, should let the shipment go through customs and follow it to where the arms are separated."

"They should," Bill agreed. "We'll suggest that to them. When's the next shipment?"

"On March 17."

"St. Patrick's Day," John said.

"That gives us enough time," Bill said.

"Meanwhile," John said, "have you found out anything about the owners of Esmeralda?"

"I'm waiting to hear from our Panama branch."

"Well, maybe you should go there."

"Maybe I should." The bank would probably let him go. There was always a reason to visit another branch of the bank. But he didn't want to leave Cathy, and he didn't know if she would want to go with him.

"If you do, you should get back before St. Patrick's Day."

"So I won't miss the parade?"

"No. So you won't miss the boat. They don't have a parade here," John said dolefully.

That evening, as he and Cathy were having dinner, he mentioned the possibility of his going to Panama.

"Panama? Why?"

He told her about Safadi, without mentioning the embassy guys since he had sworn to keep the relationship a secret.

"So this man," she said with a frown, "is working for the Montoneros, taking their money out of the country and bringing arms into the country."

"That's what I think."

"Then why don't you report him to the police?"

"I don't have enough evidence."

"And you can get evidence in Panama?"

"I hope so."

She glared at him across the table. "Well, I don't like your being involved in this. And I *really* don't like the fact that you didn't tell me about it sooner."

"I didn't want to involve you."

"Whatever you do involves me."

"You're right. I'm sorry."

She was silent for a while, and then she asked: "Why are you doing this?"

"I want to stop the Montoneros from killing people."

"Are you sure you're not doing it for vengeance?"

"Yes. I stopped wanting vengeance."

"When did that happen?"

"When I started wanting something else."

She looked as if she understood, but she still asked: "What do you want now?"

"I want what we can give each other."

She nodded. "All right. But I still don't like your being involved in this."

"I'm not killing anyone, and I'm not getting anyone killed."

"You could get yourself killed."

"I'm at risk anyway just by being here."

"I know," she said as if she could never forget it. "But you're putting yourself more at risk."

"Well, only for a while. And if I can stop the Montoneros, I won't be at risk anymore."

"Do you really believe you can stop them?"

"I believe I can."

"All right. When are we going?"

"To Panama?" he said, appreciating her support. "As soon as possible. I just don't want you to miss a class."

The next day he met with Carlos and explained why he needed to go to Panama.

Carlos listened, and then with obvious concern he said: "So you think Arias was investing money for the Montoneros?"

"It looks that way."

"Then we should have him arrested."

"If we do, it'll tip them off that we know who the money belongs to, and they'll move it to a bank where we might not be able to find it."

"We could freeze the account."

"We don't have enough evidence to do that."

"And you can get the evidence you need by going to Panama?"

"I hope so."

"All right. For now we'll leave Arias in the game."

"We can always have him arrested later."

Carlos nodded. "When do you want to go?"

"Next Wednesday. I can take an evening flight to Miami and get a flight to Panama from there."

"What date is that?"

"March 10."

"I'll ask Señora Pérez to book it."

"I'll need two tickets," Stephen said.

Carlos raised his eyebrows. "May I ask why?"

"I'd like to take a friend along."

Since they were speaking Spanish, Carlos knew the gender of the friend. With a subtle smile he said: "*Una amiga?*"

"Well, she's more than a friend."

"I figured she was. It sounds like you have *una novia.*"

"That's a better word." It meant girlfriend.

"It's about time," Carlos said approvingly. "You've been living like a priest for—how long?"

"Three years."

"It's definitely about time."

"I'll pay for her ticket."

Carlos shook his head. "Don't worry about it. We can say she's helping you in your investigation."

On Friday he met Boyd for lunch at La Estancia. They hadn't seen each other since the night Boyd had talked him into going to Minas.

"So why can't you go out on Friday evenings now?" Boyd asked after they had ordered. "Did your wife come back?"

"Oh, no," he said, dispelling the thought. "You remember the girl I met at Minas the night we went there?"

"Yeah. I remember her. Don't tell me."

"We're living together."

"Congratulations. She's a beautiful girl, and she had eyes for you. The minute she saw you she came right over."

"You observed that?"

"Yeah. I saw her decide that you were the one."

"You did?" Stephen asked skeptically.

"I guess you don't realize that women always make those decisions. Men have nothing to say about it."

"Even if you're right, we can always say no."

"Say no to a beautiful girl? Maybe you can, but I can't."

Stephen wondered if he could say no. People had told him that he wasn't very good at it. But was it something he wanted to be good at?

Changing the subject, Boyd asked: "When are they going to pull the plug on this government?"

"Everyone says it's going to be soon."

"Well, it won't be soon enough. The country's on the verge of collapse. It's not even pumping enough oil to meet its needs."

"I hadn't heard that."

"They don't admit it, that's why. You know, they have more people working for the state oil company than all the majors put together?"

"I hadn't heard that either."

"It's true. With all those people, and all those reserves, they can't produce as much oil as a piss-ant company in Oklahoma."

"They say that a military government will privatize the state oil company."

"If they have any brains they will. They should privatize all the state enterprises—the oil company, the railroads, the ports, the airlines, the electric company, and the telephone company, just for starters."

"I wonder if they really will."

"If they have balls they will."

"They have balls," Stephen said, "but I don't know if they have brains."

"It takes both. So I hope they have brains."

"It does take both. But it takes something more to do the right thing."

"What do you mean?"

"It takes heart."

"Oh, that's the same as balls," Boyd said.

At that moment their food arrived, and they stopped talking long enough to dig into it. As they said in New York, the short ribs were to die for.

That evening after work he met Cathy at the bookstore and they walked to the café on Avenida de Mayo. It would be the second time they got together without Chris, and the first time they had been despondent.

He was surprised to find Sofi there.

"I have my family," Sofi told him as they exchanged a delicate *abrazo*, "but I also need my friends."

"Are you working?"

"Yes. I went back this week."

He nodded. "Good."

"Please sit next to me. I have something I want to ask you."

He sat with Sofi on one side and Cathy on the other.

Mario and Paco were talking about the "emergency plan" that the government had announced earlier that week. The plan raised wages but also raised the prices of public services and fuel by much more. There had been protests in the streets, and tension was rising. The government seemed to have no idea how hard it was for people to survive in an economy that was imploding.

"They pretend they're helping the poor," Paco said sadly, "but they're only hurting the poor."

"They're paving the way for the military," Mario said. "They're making people believe that only the military can solve the country's problems."

"The military will make things worse," Paco said.

"They always do," Mario agreed.

Elena joined them, bending over to kiss Sofi and then sitting down next to Cathy.

At that point Sofi broached her subject with Stephen. She told him that the organization that had sponsored Chris had decided not to send another American to Argentina. They were trying to recruit someone locally, but meanwhile the people Chris had helped to start businesses had no one to turn to. "So I was wondering if you would help them, at least until someone takes the job."

"Of course," he told her, glad that there was something he could do for her.

"I know you're busy, but maybe these businesses could become clients of your bank."

"Don't worry. I don't have to justify it."

"*Gracias*," she said, touching his arm. "I think the top priority is to help the storeowners who are trying to form a cooperative and buy potatoes at a better price."

"I'll start with that. How are you doing?"

"I'm surviving," Sofi told him gamely. "Thank God I have my work. It keeps me from feeling sorry for myself."

He couldn't imagine Sofi feeling sorry for herself.

"You know, every day I think about Chris. I think about what we did together, and I think about what we might have done. But then I think about our baby, and I think about what I can do to help people in the *villa*, and I know I have something to live for, so I keep going. I try to do my part."

"I'll try to do mine," he promised her.

On Monday morning he started working on the potato project. He needed to learn more about potatoes, so he asked a trainee, a young man who was studying business at Católica, to do some research on the industry. He then called a client who might be able to help him, and he scheduled a lunch meeting that day. He had helped the company expand its business by taking a risk on it. The company had a very large order from Italy for garlic but it needed financing to buy the crop. He showed the owners how to use an export letter of credit to get financing from the bank, and he enabled them to make their first big shipment.

The two owners, Sanchez and Moretti, were at the restaurant when he arrived. They complemented each other well: Sanchez, with his square jaw and sober eyes, projected an image of seriousness while Moretti was the bubbly one, the one who did the selling. They both got up and greeted him.

"*Los reyes de ajo*," he hailed them. "The kings of garlic."

"The king of bankers," Moretti replied.

"How's the harvest?"

"Beautiful. Remember that field of purple flowers?"

"Oh, yes." He had gone with them to visit a field of garlic in Mendoza Province, and the sight had confirmed Moretti's poetic descriptions.

"Well, it's heads of garlic now. Big, beautiful, bulbous heads."

"We have a lot of orders," Sanchez said.

"We've become known for our quality," Moretti said.

"That's great," Stephen said. This was the satisfaction you got from being a banker: taking a risk on a business and seeing it succeed. The other side of course was seeing it fail. The vice president in New York, who was old enough to be his father, had explained to him on his first day of work that if you never made a bad loan you wouldn't be a good banker. Two years later, with this in mind, he called the vice president and triumphantly informed him of his first bad loan. Instead of congratulating him the vice president immediately asked him how much money the bank could lose.

When they had ordered Stephen said: "I'm working with about thirty grocery stores who all together buy large quantities of potatoes. And I'm wondering if they could buy directly from the producers."

"That's what we do," Moretti said. "We always buy direct. But we don't know much about potatoes."

"I know a little," Sanchez said.

"Tell me what you know."

"Well, it's a long chain of distribution, and there are two places where you don't want to be—the production end and the retail end."

Stephen understood. "You do better in the middle."

"That's right. Depending on where you are in the middle. It's a long chain."

"But if you go with a big order to the producers and offer to pay them more than they're getting, then both ends would be better, wouldn't they?"

"They would if you could pull that off."

"What are the obstacles?"

"The main obstacle is financing. You need money to guarantee payment to the producers."

"That's the obstacle," Moretti said, "that you enabled us to overcome."

"Do you think I could do the same thing with potatoes?"

"If you have money you can do anything."

Since it was the second Monday of the month he went to Belgrano to have dinner with Vittoria. He had considered asking Vittoria if he could bring Cathy with him, but he had decided that it wasn't a good idea yet.

He had explained to Cathy why he was seeing Vittoria, and

since she knew what had happened to Alejandro, she understood. Instead of sitting at home alone she was going to the movies with Elena, who had taken her to lunch a few times. Elena had adopted Cathy as the younger sister she had always wanted.

As soon as he entered Vittoria's house the two older girls came running to him, wanting him to look at the pictures they had drawn with their crayons. He sat down on the sofa between them, viewing the pictures one at a time and trying to alternate between Claudia and Olivia, who were vying for his attention.

"They miss having a father," Vittoria said after the girls had returned to the family room to draw more pictures.

"I can see that." He got up from the sofa and followed her into the kitchen.

As he started making their drinks she said: "We're a house full of women. Wait until Aleja turns thirteen. *Dios mío!*"

He joined her at the counter, asking: "How are things with your mother?"

"Fine. My father took her to Italy, so she's out of my hair."

"For how long?"

"Three weeks. Though she might stay longer," Vittoria added hopefully. "She has relatives there."

"Where in Italy?"

"Tuscany."

"Does your father still have relatives there?"

"Not that he knows of. The other branch of his family went to America. They're in California."

"Maybe they're making wine there." Her father, who came from a family of vintners in Mendoza, was in the business of distributing wine, so maybe wine ran in the family.

"Maybe," she said. "I love my father. I think he understood what my mother was doing to me, so he took her away to give me some relief."

"Has it helped?"

"Oh, yes. I'm not praying that the military will kill all the Montoneros. But I'm still hoping they will," she added. "And I'm still trying to convince myself that I want them killed so they'll stop killing people."

"You're not succeeding?"

She gazed at him bleakly. "No. Because it's not true. I want them killed because they killed Alejandro."

"You want vengeance."

"Yes. And I know I shouldn't."

"Why shouldn't you?"

"Because only God can have vengeance."

"Vengeance is mine," he murmured in English. "I will repay, says the Lord."

"What did you say?"

"What you just said, only in English."

"Then you know how I feel wanting vengeance?"

"I know how *I* felt wanting vengeance. It was like being filled with a deadly poison that found its way to every corner of my heart and mind."

"Do you still want vengeance?"

"Not anymore."

"How did you stop?"

"I started wanting something else."

She nodded slowly as if this might be the answer she was looking for.

The next morning he had a meeting with the young man whom Chris had selected to lead the effort to form a cooperative. He was in a suit, which he wore uncomfortably, and his eyes darted around as Ignacio, the *ordenanza,* led him across the floor. He had high cheekbones, which suggested an Indian ancestor. His name was Jorge.

"Please sit down," Stephen said after they shook hands.

"*Gracias*," Jorge said formally.

"How's business?"

"Not bad."

"Do you have the papers?" Stephen was referring to the forms they needed to establish the cooperative as a legal entity and the forms they needed to open a bank account.

"Yes. They're here." Jorge opened a large manila envelope and took out the papers, which he handed over.

Stephen examined them, making sure that they were all signed in the right places as well as stamped. He was paying his respects to the culture of bureaucracy, which they had developed to a high level in this country.

"Is everything all right?"

Stephen nodded. "Do you have a deposit?"

"Yes," Jorge said, digging into a pocket of his pants and withdrawing a wad of currency, which he handed over.

Stephen counted the money once and then again. It was the peso equivalent of five hundred dollars. He signaled to Ignacio, whom he instructed to take the papers and the money to the head teller on the main floor.

Jorge watched the man go as if he might have seen the last of his money.

"He'll bring a receipt," Stephen reassured him. "So let's talk about potatoes."

Jorge listened attentively as Stephen recounted what he had learned. While potatoes were cultivated in several areas of the country, the most important area was the southeast of Buenos Aires Province, which supplied the city, so they would focus their efforts there. The objective was to buy directly from producers to get around the series of markups that were applied in the long chain of distribution. They had more than thirty stores signed up for the cooperative, which would give them enough buying power, but they had to find producers who were willing to sell directly to them. "I'm working on that now," he told Jorge. "I expect to have more information by next week."

"We'll be grateful for anything you can do."

"Well, let's see what I can do."

On Wednesday evening he and Cathy took a taxi to the airport at Ezeiza, a long ride from the center of town. By the time you got there you were on your way out to the *pampa*, the immense plain that extended in every direction except east from Buenos Aires farther than the eye could see or the mind could imagine. You could travel for days across this vast green ocean without seeing a rise or a native tree.

As they approached the airport Stephen was struck by the thought that only six weeks ago he had flown from here to New York still legally married to Leila, and now he was flying from here to Panama with someone he hadn't known then.

It was a long flight. With the stop in Miami it took more than seventeen hours, and they were exhausted by the time they landed in Panama shortly after one in the afternoon the next day. A driver from the bank met them with a roomy, air-conditioned car and drove them to the hotel. By then it was almost three, so the driver left them, saying that he would come back at nine the next morning. In their room they unpacked and rested for a while before going out.

They walked slowly, stretching their legs. The smell of the warm, tropical air was a rich mixture of brine, flowers, ripening fruit, and human effluents.

Cathy inhaled through her nose and sighed as if she recognized the smell.

"Is Cali like this?" he asked her.

"No. Cali is higher above sea level. But down on the coast it's like this. I went there with the families I worked for."

He imagined her in the ocean swimming with the children.

"You know, Panama used to belong to Colombia," she said.

"I know. We took it from you to build the canal."

"We learned that in our history courses. We learned to resent America for taking away part of our country."

"How do you feel about that now?"

"I'm glad it doesn't belong to Colombia. I wouldn't have come here if it did."

He understood. She couldn't take the risk of being identified by the immigration officials in Colombia.

They had dinner at a nearby restaurant and then after walking some more they returned to the hotel and collapsed.

After breakfast he left Cathy in the room, where she planned to spend a few hours doing homework for her course before going out to see the city. The driver was waiting for him in the lobby, and the branch manager was expecting him.

The manager, whose name was Randal, was a rugged American in his mid-fifties. He led Stephen into his office and closed the door.

"I asked our lawyer to join us," he said after they had exchanged preliminaries. They had settled in a meeting area that had a sofa, two chairs, and a coffee table, all in a spare modern style. "He should be here soon. But before he gets here let me explain some things about Panama."

"That would be helpful," Stephen said.

"We have more banks and fewer regulations than just about anywhere in the world. Most of the banks are pieces of paper, which enable people to do things they couldn't do in their own countries. And many of the companies are using Panama to avoid regulations. For example, shipping companies use the Panamanian flag to avoid union rules in their own countries."

"So a Panamanian company can get away with anything."

"Yes. It can. I mean as long as it doesn't run afoul of the government."

"Well, how did your branch get involved in these transfers between the Swiss bank and International Bank & Trust?"

"The business was steered to us by one of your account managers."

"Tito Arias?" he asked, hoping.

"Right. We opened the account with IBT about three years ago, and right away the transfers started coming."

That made sense. It was when the Montoneros began to accumulate ransom money.

"They always came from the Swiss bank with instructions to credit some of the funds to Esmeralda."

"Well, let me tell you what I've found out," Stephen offered. "The transfers are coming from individuals who are clients of Banco Azulay. They want to get their money out of Argentina, so they use the bank they've always trusted."

"But the bank uses them," Randal guessed.

"It uses them to launder the money that goes into the account of Esmeralda."

"Have you figured out how?"

"I think so. The people who want to launder their money deposit cash with the Swiss bank. The Swiss bank combines the cash with a remittance from an individual in Argentina and sends it through your branch to International Bank & Trust, instructing them to credit the amount that represents the cash to Esmeralda and the remainder to the individual, which is the amount he sent from Argentina. So he never knows that his remittance was used as a cover."

Randal nodded as if he recognized the mode of operation. "Is it drug money?"

"I can't tell you. I'm sorry."

"I understand. We see a lot of drug money, and we see a lot of drug people. They use Panama as a banking center. They come here to check on their accounts and to find out what their competitors are doing."

"I assume we're not involved with them."

"Not knowingly," Randal said. "But at times we're used by them, just as we've been used by these people."

"I guess it's hard to avoid here."

"I do my best. I can't wait to be transferred to a nice peaceful place like Beirut."

They both laughed, conscious of the fact that a civil war had driven their bank out of Beirut.

At that moment the phone rang. It was Randal's secretary letting him know that the lawyer had arrived.

The lawyer, whose name was Quintero, had trim gray hair and silver-rimmed glasses that reinforced an image of erudition. He spoke perfect English, with an accent that suggested he had gone to Harvard. He explained the relevant areas of Panamanian law, and then he took a piece of paper out of an inner pocket of his coat, which he held for a long time while he described his research methods, building suspense. When at last he handed over the paper, Stephen was on the edge of his seat.

"Here are the owners of Esmeralda S.A.," Quintero declared.

The paper listed the companies that Stephen immediately recognized from the list that Arias had prepared for him. "They're Argentine companies."

"That's what the registration says. But it doesn't say anything else about them."

"Well, I know something about them."

"What do you know?"

"I know they've been making loans in what we call the *extrabancario* market." Stephen explained how it worked.

"Do they still have loans outstanding?"

"Yes. They have loans coming due."

"Then follow the money," Quintero advised. "When the borrower repays the loan it will lead you to them."

After thanking the lawyer and the branch manager Stephen returned to the hotel and found Cathy back in the room. It was after one, and since they were both hungry, they went out and had lunch at a restaurant that specialized in seafood. While they consumed a platter of shrimp he excitedly shared with her what he had found out.

"The three companies that own Esperanza are the same companies that made unrecorded loans in the *extrabancario* market. So I can tie the two operations together."

"And you think the Montoneros own these companies?"

"I think they do, though they may have a front."

"A front?" she asked with a puzzled look.

"Someone who appears in the records as the owner but really isn't. We say he's fronting for them."

"Who does this kind of thing?"

"Lawyers," he said.

"The lawyers are fronting for the Montoneros," she said, using the new expression in a sentence.

"That's right," he said, smiling.

"Well, please be careful. And please don't let anyone know what you've found out."

"I have to let a few people know."

"You do? Who?"

He had to tell her. "I'm working with two CIA agents who are based at the U.S. Embassy."

"What? Why didn't you tell me about them before?"

"I was sworn to secrecy."

"So why are you breaking your oath now?"

"It wasn't an oath."

"What was it?"

"It was just an agreement not to tell anyone. And now I'm breaking it," he explained, "because I don't want to hold anything back from you."

She looked at him suspiciously. "Is there anything else you haven't told me?"

"There're a lot of things. I haven't told you much about my marriage."

"I don't need to know about that. You know what I mean."

"No. There's nothing else."

"You promise?"

"I promise."

After lunch they walked around the city for a while, and then they went back to their hotel, where they took a siesta.

As he held Cathy, sleeping in his arms, he could feel a breeze wafting through the window, which she had opened earlier in the day. He thought he could smell the ocean, the peaceful ocean that had welcomed Magellan after his rough voyage through the straits. He imagined what it must have been like emerging from the storm and sailing into the warm sunlight. And he felt as if he were on that battered ship with Cathy, approaching the end of the terrible passage.

FIVE

ON THE MONDAY after they returned from Panama he reviewed the list of unrecorded loans from the three companies in the *extrabancario* market, and he organized them by maturity dates: March 31, April 30, and May 31.

Seven of the loans were due on March 31, only two weeks from now. Three of the borrowers were clients of the bank, including a prominent auto dealer who advertised heavily in the daily papers. The account belonged to Eduardo, an amiable young man who would probably go far in banking. Stephen asked him to arrange a meeting with the client to discuss their relationship and to see how they might expand it.

Then he called Ferrer, who by now should have the information about the companies that had made the unrecorded loans. The lawyer wasn't available, but his secretary agreed to schedule a meeting with him that afternoon.

They met in the conference room.

"I have the information," Ferrer said, as usual looking as if he had eaten something that didn't agree with him. Ferrer rummaged through his briefcase and finally took out a piece of paper, which he handed over, saying: "I'm afraid that it won't tell you much. The owners of record are all lawyers."

Stephen unfolded the paper and saw the names of the three companies with the owners listed below each one. The companies all had several owners.

"It's common practice," Ferrer explained, "for lawyers to form companies with themselves as the initial shareholders and then to transfer the shares to the real owners. The transfer is usually recorded, so you can find out who the real owners are. But in some cases the transfer isn't recorded."

"It must be recorded somewhere."

"I should have said there isn't a public record of it."

"If there isn't a public record of a transfer," Stephen said after reflecting, "can we assume that the lawyers are fronting for someone?"

"Not necessarily. They could just be holding the company for someone who may need it."

"Then you really can't tell if they're fronting for someone."

"No. You can't."

Stephen looked down at the paper, wishing that it would tell him something. "Do you know these lawyers?"

"Of course I don't know them," Ferrer said as if he found the idea of his knowing such people highly offensive. "But I know what kind of lawyers they are."

"What kind of lawyers are they?"

"The kind who will do anything for money."

"Are they members of firms?"

"They're sole practitioners. They have an office, a secretary, and a telephone."

"And a bad reputation?"

"They give us all a bad name."

"Well, how can I find out who they're fronting for?"

"You could hire a detective to break into their offices and ransack their files," Ferrer said, evidently trying to be facetious. "Or you could buy the information from them. As I said, they'll do anything for money."

That sounded promising. The embassy guys seemed to have unlimited money that they could use to buy information. They did it all the time.

"Okay," he said. "I have another question."

"Go right ahead," Ferrer said as if he might have an answer to this one.

"When these loans come due, the borrowers have to pay the lenders. And I assume that Arias always handled the payments outside the bank."

"You mean for the unrecorded loans."

"That's right. For the recorded loans the bank handles the payments since both the borrower and the lender have accounts with us. But in these cases the lenders don't have accounts with us, so the borrowers must pay them directly."

"They could pay them through another bank."

"They could," he agreed, guessing which bank. "But now that we know about these loans, I want to have the borrowers pay the lenders through us."

"That shouldn't be a problem. Presumably, the loans are documented by notes saying that the borrowers promise to pay the lenders a certain amount on a certain date. They wouldn't say where the borrowers have to make the payments."

"So I could instruct the borrowers to pay through us."

"I see no reason why you couldn't."

"Then the lenders would have to come to us to collect their money."

"They would. And you would have to pay them."

"Oh, I know. I would have to pay them in any case since we guaranteed the loans."

"Then what do you gain," Ferrer asked, "by having the borrowers pay through you?"

"Information."

The next day he and Eduardo met with the auto dealer. The owner, whose name was Bellini, was a big outgoing man who had made a fortune selling cars, and Stephen immediately recognized him as one of the regular passengers on the Friday afternoon flight to Punta del Este three summers ago.

"We were looking at your line of credit," Stephen said after the usual fifteen minutes of preliminaries. "And it looks like you could use a bigger one. After maximizing use of your line, you borrowed in the *extrabancario* market."

"I do that to build inventory for the fall," Bellini said. "But it's so expensive."

"I see you have a loan coming due on March 31."

"Yes. I can't wait to repay that loan. And maybe the next time I can get all the money from you."

"Maybe. If you're short of money now, we can give you an overdraft to cover the payment."

"*Gracias.* I should be all right. The economy stinks, but people are still buying cars," Bellini said as if he couldn't understand why.

"Since we're guaranteeing the loan," Stephen said, "we'd like you to make the payment through us."

"I usually just give a check to Arias and get a receipt."

"Well, he's no longer with us."

"Really? What happened?"

"He had health problems," Eduardo said, repeating the official line that Carlos had given to all employees.

"I'm sorry to hear that," Bellini said. "So how do you want me to pay now?"

"Just send the check to me," Stephen said.

Bellini nodded. "That's fine."

Back at his desk after the meeting, Stephen decided to have similar meetings with all the borrowers on the list. When a lender contacted Arias looking for the money, Arias would contact the borrower and learn that the payment had been made to the bank, which was holding it for the lender to claim. So the lender would have to come to the bank. Instead of following the money to the lenders, as Quintero had advised, Stephen would make the lenders come to him.

On March 17, as scheduled, the next ship from Panama arrived. This time the cargo was allowed to clear through customs without being inspected, but it was tracked by undercover agents as it was loaded onto a truck and transported out of the city. The agents followed the truck to a small farm, where it was unloaded and the cargo was separated into two lots. When one lot had been loaded back onto the truck, the agents pounced. The lot on the truck was textile equipment while the unloaded lot was arms and supplies, including some crates of automatic weapons. The men were arrested, the truck was impounded, and the farm was cordoned off.

The men admitted that they were working for the Montoneros, but they said they didn't know who was organizing the shipments. They were just following orders, which they received from an anonymous source. The agents were unable to trace either the registration of the truck or the ownership of the farm since the documents had been fabricated.

"By now," John said as they sat in the conference room assessing the situation, "the Montoneros must have figured out that these shipments are being tracked. So they'll look for other shipments to use."

"They'll have to find a source of information about those shipments," Bill said.

"They could find a source in Panama," John said.

"Yeah. They could," Bill said. "Then the military will have to check shipments from Panama."

"If the customs officials were doing their job," Stephen said, "they'd check *all* shipments."

"That won't happen," Bill said, "until the military take over."

"I don't know what they're waiting for," John said.

"They're waiting until they think they'll be welcomed."

"They would have been welcomed months ago."

"Okay," Stephen said, getting back on track. "If the military check shipments from Panama, it'll stop the Montoneros from bringing arms into the country."

"It will until they figure out what's happening," John said. "And then they'll look for another way."

"As long as they have money," Bill said, "they'll find a way."

"So we have to cut off their money," Stephen said.

"Have you made any progress on that front?"

"Yeah. I have." He had their attention. "I found out who owns Esmeralda. It's owned by three Argentine companies, which happen to be the same companies that made the unrecorded loans arranged by Arias."

"That connects the two operations," John said.

"Do you know who owns these companies?" Bill asked.

"The owners of record are all lawyers."

"That's what I figured."

"These shysters are fronting for the Montoneros," John said.

"Well, they'll never tell us," Bill said, "who the real owners of the companies are."

"They might if we paid them enough money," Stephen said.

John and Bill looked at each other, considering this.

"Your idea," Bill said, "is based on the premise that they would do anything for money. Which, I think we agree, is a sound premise. But let's follow the sequence of events. We go to one of them, offer him money for the information, and he says okay, he'll tell us who the owners are. He gives us the information, and we pay him the money. Suppose he's given us false information."

"We've wasted taxpayers' money," John said.

"Since when are you concerned about taxpayers' money?"

"I'm always concerned about it."

Bill resumed. "He goes back to Safadi and tells him that we're on his trail. What do you think Safadi will do?"

"Move the money," Stephen said, deflated.

"And what would happen if the lawyer gave us the right information?"

"Watch out," John said, "that's a trick question."

"Yeah. I know. He wouldn't be dumb enough to do that."

"If he did they'd cut off his *cojones*," Bill said.

"Oh, stop trying to show off your Spanish," John said.

"Okay," Stephen admitted. "It's a bad idea. Do either of you have a better idea?"

"I don't," Bill admitted.

"I do," John said, scowling. "But we have to wait until the military take over."

"I know your idea," Bill said. "You'd have these lawyers arrested, and you'd have the military make them talk."

"I don't like that idea," Stephen said.

"You don't like it?" John said. "What do you think they're doing to those people they caught at the farm?"

"But they were transporting arms for the Montoneros, which is one step away from killing people."

"And you'd draw the line at two steps away?"

"I don't know where I'd draw the line."

"Well, that's the question you have to answer," Bill said. "Where would you draw the line?"

Stephen reflected. You could draw a line that included only people who were directly responsible for the killing, which might not be enough to get the job done. Or you could draw a line that included people who were sympathetic to the issues raised by the Montoneros, which might destroy what you were trying to save. He finally said: "I can't answer that question now. I have to think about it. Anyway, if you arrested the lawyers Safadi would immediately move the money."

"You're right," Bill said. "We were just testing you."

After a long silence John said: "We have to identify the real owners of these companies."

"I think I have a way to flush them out," Stephen said.

They looked at him expectantly.

He explained how he was making the lenders come to the bank to collect their money.

"You'll only meet the lawyers," John told him.

"But I can get to know them," Stephen said, "and maybe they'll reveal something."

"Maybe they will," Bill said as if it weren't a bad idea.

"Well, it's not going to tip them off," John said. "It's what any banker would do in your situation."

"Try it," Bill said, "and see what happens."

On Friday their friends were at the café when he and Cathy got there. They were talking about the imminent *golpe*. Earlier that week a bomb planted by the Montoneros exploded at the army headquarters, killing one person and injuring twenty-nine. It was intended for General Videla, but he wasn't injured. For the army it had to be the last straw.

"It's any day now," Mario said.

"I'm afraid so," Elena said. "I know the military are already running the country, but at least we have the semblance of a civilian government, as bad as it is. When the military take over we'll have a total dictatorship."

"And they'll be brutal."

"Well, they'll have plenty of justification. Last week forty people were killed in the violence."

"How many were killed by terrorists?" Stephen asked.

"Which terrorists?" Elena asked. "The left-wing terrorists or the right-wing terrorists?"

"When the military take over," Mario said, "we'll have government terrorists."

"We already do," Elena said. "But if you want to know how many were killed by the Montoneros, slightly more than half of them were."

"It doesn't matter who killed them," Sofi said.

"It doesn't," Cathy agreed.

"What matters is that they were killed," Teresa said.

"They have to stop the killing," Sofi said.

"Who's going to stop it?" Mario asked.

"The military won't stop it," Elena said. "At least not until they've killed thousands of people."

"What will they do beyond what they're already doing?" Stephen asked her.

"They'll go after people who are more and more remotely associated with the terrorists, people who they suspect are Marxists, the relatives and friends of people who they suspect are Marxists—"

"In other words, everyone," Stephen said.

"If not everyone, then anyone," Elena said. "And they won't stop until they've stamped out all ideas that in their minds threaten our values."

"It sounds like a crusade."

"It is. They believe that only they can save the country."

"They don't know how to save the country," Paco said. "They only know how to kill people. That's what they were trained to do."

"Well, there's absolutely nothing we can do about them," Mario said glumly.

"There is," Paco said with authority. "We can build a church and a school in the *villa*."

"Oh, that's a dream," Mario said.

"It's not a dream," Sofi affirmed. "His bishop has approved the project."

"Tell us about it," Stephen said, interested.

"First of all," Paco said with the light of a vision in his eyes, "the church and the school will be named St. Christopher after our brother."

They listened while Paco described the project, showing them what could be done.

On Saturday at noon he met Cathy at the bookstore, and they walked toward Recoleta going up Avenida Alvear, which was lined with luxury apartment buildings and culminated in the Alvear Palace Hotel.

As an elegantly dressed man and woman strutted out of the hotel and got into a waiting Mercedes, with a liveried driver holding the door and a bodyguard sitting in the front seat, Cathy said: "They probably spend more money on clothes in one week than a poor family spends on everything in one year."

"You sound like a socialist," he kidded her.

"I'm not. I'm not anything political," she insisted. "But it's not right for things to be so unequal."

"It's not right. The problem is, the most effective way to create wealth isn't the most equal way to distribute it."

"Well, things don't have to be equal. But they should be less unequal."

"I agree. And governments should deal with the problem."

"What's the government here doing?"

"Nothing. They're busy building their retirement funds."

"Will you be glad when the military take over?"

"Not at all. I agree with Elena. They'll go too far. They'll end up killing thousands of people to get rid of the terrorists."

"Then what's the solution?"

"Well, as Paco says, the only way to stop the killing is to stop the killing."

"But who's going to stop unless they know that everyone else is going to stop?"

"That's a good question," he said. "Paco's answer is that if we all work and do our part toward creating a just society, then the killing will stop."

"Do you believe it will ever happen?"

"I hope it will. That's not the same as believing it will."

"I understand. I'm hoping for things I don't believe will ever happen."

"Like what?" he asked her.

"I'm hoping to get my degree," she said, "and be a teacher."

"You don't believe it will happen?"

"Well, I guess it will. But it'll take a long time."

"You'll have the time."

She didn't say: "God willing."

From this omission he could tell that she had come a long way from the morning after their first night together when she was afraid that they would never see each other again. Now that he knew what had happened to her in Colombia, he could appreciate the leap of faith she had made in trusting a stranger with her life. And he could understand why she might be reluctant to tempt fate by sharing her hopes with him. Still, he asked: "What other things are you hoping for?"

"Oh, I don't know."

"Tell me," he coaxed her.

She hesitated, and then she blurted out: "I'm hoping to get married and have children."

Though he should have seen this coming, he wasn't prepared for it. Caught off guard, he realized that the possibility had been forming in the back of his mind. An interior voice reminded him that he had finalized his divorce less than two months ago, so he couldn't be ready to get married again. But another voice told him not to listen to such arguments. He finally said: "I'm hoping to get married and have children with you."

She leaned against him happily.

On Monday he and Jorge were driven to the southeast of Buenos Aires Province by Sanchez and Moretti, who had arranged for them to meet with several big potato producers. They left very early in the morning since it was a long trip, and by the time the sun came up the land was flat, perfectly flat, in every direction as far as you could see. Moretti drove, with flair, while Sanchez talked about potatoes, starting with the fact that the area they were going to accounted for almost two-thirds of the country's total production. He told them that the harvest had just ended, and that the potatoes from this area would be sold over the next five months.

Around noon they arrived at the farm of a big producer whom Sanchez had known for a long time. The farmer was very hospitable, and for lunch he served them a *parrillada* with short ribs, chicken, and sausages, which they ate heartily and washed down with red wine.

They talked about the potato crop, which had been good, and the farmer showed them how the potatoes were stored on the field in waist-high piles covered with straw. They looked like a miniature version of the haystacks that Stephen remembered from growing up in Minnesota, and he was amazed that potatoes would keep through the winter with such a simple storage system.

With this farmer and other farmers in the area, they talked about quantities, prices, and payment terms. It became clear that the cooperative would have to buy at least one truck capable of hauling potatoes from the farms to Buenos Aires, and that it would need a line of credit to pay the farmers.

On the trip back Stephen developed a plan with Jorge, who remembered all the details of what they had learned without having taken any notes. Stephen was impressed, and he looked forward to working with Jorge.

The sun was setting in a blaze of red as they approached the city through Lomas de Zamora, and it was dark by the time he got home.

"How was your trip?" Cathy asked.

"It was great," he said. "Would you like to eat at Ligure?"

"Sure. You can tell me about it there."

A waiter, who by now knew them as a couple, led them to a quiet table.

Stephen had eaten enough meat for the day, so he ordered mussels and *tallarines al pesto*, and Cathy ordered an avocado with *salsa golf* and chicken *a la milanesa*.

As they were eating he talked with enthusiasm about the project.

She listened, asked some good questions, and finally said: "You were right when you said there are things you can do here."

On Wednesday morning Elena called him as he was about to leave for work.

"They've done it," she said. "They've taken over."

"When?" he asked.

"Around one this morning. If you can have lunch with me, I'll tell you what I know. By then I'll know more."

They arranged to meet at a restaurant that they could both walk to from their offices. He told Cathy what had happened, and then he left. As he walked toward Plaza San Martín he didn't notice anything unusual on the streets, but when he got to Florida he felt a buzz in the air. The newspaper vendor with the gravelly voice was yelling: "*Nuevo gobierno, nuevo gobierno!*"

He bought a paper, which he tried to read as he walked along. A *junta* of the commanders-in-chief of the armed forces had taken over. There was a photo of the three of them, and one showing tanks on a street, but there wasn't much hard information. He would have to wait to learn more from Elena.

When he got to the bank he went straight to the general manager's office.

"I don't have an appointment," he told Señora Pérez, "but this is urgent."

"He's with Señor Orsini," she said as if this were an insurmountable barrier.

Orsini was the head of personnel, and he was probably updating Carlos on the status of talks with the union, which occupied most of his time. "Please interrupt them and tell him I need to talk with him."

Reluctantly, she picked up her phone and called Carlos.

"He'll see you," she reported, hanging up.

A few moments later Carlos opened the door and beckoned.

Closing the door behind him, Stephen said: "So they've done it. They've taken over."

"Yes," Carlos said, clapping his hands. "And now we can reform this country. We can have a market economy."

Orsini, an ebullient man, was uncharacteristically somber.

"If you want," Stephen offered, "I can work with you on what we communicate to head office."

"*Bueno.* I'll phone them as soon as I know more, but then we have to send them a written report. What can you tell me?"

"Nothing much. But I'm having lunch with a journalist, so I'll find out more."

"All right," Carlos said. "In the meantime, I'll see what I can find out from Colonel Méndez."

"Here we go again," Orsini said gloomily.

When Stephen got to the banking floor the auditors were waiting for him. They had arrived from Brazil the night before and were staying at the Hotel Continental, a few blocks away on Diagonal Norte. He had met them two years ago, and he was surprised that they were still at it, traveling continuously around the world to audit the overseas branches of the bank.

"It's good to be back," said Andy, the senior auditor. He was about the same age as Stephen, and he had a Midwestern accent. He was lanky and lackadaisical, but he had a keen mind and a reputation for never missing anything. "The steaks are still as good as ever."

"Where did you eat?"

"La Estancia. I think you recommended it to us the last time we were here."

"I think I did. You should try their *chivito*."

"What's that?" asked Jeff. He was in his late twenties, short and compact, with a lot of bound-up energy and a Brooklyn accent.

"Baby goat."

Jeff made a face. "Oh, I don't know about eating goat."

"Just try it. You'll like it."

"What's it called?" Andy asked.

"*Chivito*. They roast it over a fire, and it's really delicious."

They went into the conference room, where Andy wrote down the word in the little notebook that he always carried. Then he looked up and said with his usual understatement: "You have an interesting case here."

"We do," Stephen said, wondering how Andy would react if he knew the whole story.

"We've seen rogue traders and rogue cash managers, but we've never seen a rogue guarantor before."

"Where did he get the forms?" Jeff asked.

"From a box in the storeroom."

"Isn't the storeroom locked?"

"Yes, but somehow he got a key to it."

"Well, that's a finding," Andy said, making a note. "You need to have a tighter control of access to the storeroom."

"We already do. We changed the lock, and the only person who has a key is the general manager."

"That's good. Now, what have you done about booking the potential liability?"

"We recorded the amount as soon as we had the information."

"Have you made any special provision for loss?"

"No. Whatever else he is," Stephen explained, "Arias is a good loan officer. The risk on these loans is probably lower than normal."

"Why do you think so?" Jeff asked.

"Because if one of these loans had gone bad, he would have been caught."

"So he used only the strongest borrowers," Andy said, nodding in admiration.

"Then how did you catch him?" Jeff asked.

"A lender demanded payment under our guarantee," Stephen said. He had explained all this in his report, which they must have read, but he figured that they were testing him for consistency. "He had already been paid, but Arias was away, so he tried to get us to pay him again."

"He didn't expect you to talk with the borrower before paying him?" Andy asked.

"He was probably desperate," Stephen said.

"You mean he suddenly needed money to go to Brazil?"

"It happens all the time. People are in trouble, and they try to get away from it by going to Brazil."

"I can think of worse places to go."

"We've been to those places," Jeff said.

"We sure have," Andy agreed as if he were proud of this accomplishment. "So you think these loans are better than average?"

"Yes. I do. Of course you'll want to review them all, and the files are here," Stephen said, gesturing toward the other end of the table, where the credit files of the twenty-three borrowers had been rounded up.

"Are you confident enough to bet on it?"

"I am," Stephen said, smiling. "If you don't agree with my assessment, I'll buy you both lunch at La Estancia."

"You better not mean goat," Jeff said.

"Goat is optional," Andy said.

Stephen left the bank at quarter to one. He expected to hear some news on the street as he walked along Florida, but people were carrying on as if nothing had happened. Some of them might not know about it, and some of them might not care. But most of them were probably relieved, if only because the uncertainty that had paralyzed the country was finally over. It had been ten years since the last *golpe*, and most of these people were alive then. They had endured seven years of military dictatorship and three years of chaos. Their memories of the dictatorship wouldn't have yet faded but must have been filtered by the painful events of the past three years, so you could understand why if given only these two choices they might prefer a dictatorship.

As he passed a construction site he smelled smoke from an outside grill, and he saw the crew at a makeshift table eating lunch. The union rules specified that for all construction crews of a certain size the project manager was required to hire an *asador*, whose only job was to build and tend a fire and to cook lunch for the crew, usually steak.

Approaching the restaurant, he spotted Elena coming toward him from the other direction. She was walking purposefully with long strides.

"Good timing," he said when they converged.

"Perfect," she said.

They found a table in the corner and ordered without looking at a menu.

"Well, now we have a *junta*," she said with disdain. "It's composed of General Videla, the commander of the army, and Admiral Massera, the commander of the navy, and General Agosti, the commander of the air force. Videla is the leader."

"I think you said he's a moderate compared with Massera."

"Anyone's a moderate compared with Massera."

"Since he's the leader, doesn't that mean he has more power than Massera?"

"In theory, yes. But things are still in flux. They say there's already a conflict between them."

"What about?"

"It's not clear. It could be ideological, it could be a power struggle, or it could be personal. They say that Massera doesn't like Videla."

"So it's not a stable government."

"No. But they'll hold it together. As much as they might hate each other, they hate the Montoneros more."

"Unity in hatred," Stephen mused. "It's probably as strong as unity in love."

"It's probably stronger."

"I hope you're not speaking from experience."

"No. I'm speaking from observation."

"So what's their program?"

"They haven't announced it. But we know it's called the Process of National Reorganization."

"What does that mean?"

They stopped talking while the waiter set plates for their salad on the table.

"It means what I was saying last Friday—the complete elimination of Marxist ideas in our country. But that'll come later. Right now the top priority of the *junta* is to eliminate the terrorists."

"You mean the left-wing terrorists."

"The government will take over the activities of the right-wing terrorists. As Mario said, we'll have government terrorists, and they'll go after anyone who questions their values."

"That could include a lot of people."

"It could include everyone we know."

"What about your newspaper?"

"If we keep reporting the truth, they'll go after us. They'll threaten us, they'll censor us, they may even close us."

"Will they harass you?"

"Me personally?"

"Yes, you personally."

She paused as if she hadn't thought about it. "I don't think they will. I'm not high enough in the hierarchy. They'll harass our editor."

The waiter brought their salad in the usual stainless steel bowl, and Stephen reached for the cruet of vinegar. As he poured a little into the bowl he said: "Let me ask you— What if you could stop the Montoneros from killing people, but in order to do that you'd have to report someone to the police who wasn't directly involved in the killing?"

"*Dios*, what a question," she said, staring at him.

He waited while she pondered it.

"When you say that this person isn't directly involved in the killing, what do you mean? He doesn't pull the trigger?"

"No. He doesn't."

"Does he give the gun to the person who does?"

"Not directly, but ultimately."

"Does he buy the gun?"

"He makes it possible to buy the gun."

"Does he provide the money?"

"No. He provides access to the money."

"Is he a banker?"

"No, but he works for a banker."

She frowned in concentration. "Okay. So this person who works for a banker is enabling the Montoneros to buy weapons that they use to kill people. And you want to know if I'd report him to the police?"

"Bearing in mind what the police would do to him, especially now with a military government."

"*Dios,*" she said, struggling with the question. "Whatever I did, I'd be responsible for people getting killed."

"You would be."

"So how could I decide what to do? I couldn't compare the relative value of people's lives."

"It's a tough one, isn't it."

She looked at him, concerned. "I hope you're not in a position where you have to make this kind of decision."

"I'm not," he assured her since he wasn't yet in that position. "It was only a hypothetical question."

She scanned his face as if she didn't quite believe him, but she didn't press him further, evidently respecting his reason for holding back.

Later that afternoon he went down to the general manager's office to work with Carlos on the report to head office. As they had done so many times for the monthly reports, they exchanged information and agreed on what the report should say. By the time they were ready to start writing, Señora Pérez had left for the day, so Stephen used her typewriter to make a first draft, which they reviewed together before he finalized it. When the man who handled interoffice mail had taken the report away for overnight transmittal to New York, they both sat back with the feeling that any two people might have after completing a task together.

"This is a turning point in our history," Carlos declared with satisfaction.

"You really think it's different from the other *golpes?*"

"Oh, yes. This time they mean business."

"What did they mean the other times?"

"The other times?" Carlos waved them aside with the back of his hand. "They didn't have a sound economic program."

He waited for Carlos to continue, ready to hear a lecture on the country's economic history.

"Whenever people write about Argentina, they always make a point of the fact that at the turn of this century we had the same standard of living as you had in America, and that right after World War II we were in a position to continue being one of the richest countries in the world. But from there it was downhill. We turned a country with unlimited potential into a country without a future. Every year we lose educated people who give up and go to America—doctors, scientists, mathematicians, engineers. And I don't blame them."

"But you came back. You could have stayed in America."

"I was offered a job there, a good job. But I wasn't ready to give up on my country. And now it looks like I made the right decision," Carlos said, smiling triumphantly. "This government is going to reverse the policies that set us back—closing the economy, protecting and subsidizing inefficient industries, coddling unproductive labor. Do you know that a car made in Argentina, which has lower quality, costs twice as much as the same car made in America?"

"Yes. I know that," Stephen said. It was one of his reasons for not buying a car.

"You couldn't sell that car anywhere but in this country."

"Not even in Russia?"

"Not even there. They wouldn't let you since they have the same bad economic policies. So now, finally," Carlos continued, "we're going to open the economy and join the world. We're going to make up for lost time."

"It's a lot of time."

"It's only three decades, only three decades since Perón put us on the road to serfdom." Carlos was referring to the title of a book written by the Austrian economist, Friedrich von Hayek, about what inevitably happens when governments interfere with the free market system.

"I guess that's not long in the history of a country."

"It's nothing. Look at what Korea has done in twenty years. You think we can't do what they did?"

"I agree that the country has potential, or I wouldn't have stayed here. But if this is the right economic program, why does it have to be implemented by a military dictatorship?"

"Because our elected governments don't have the will to implement it."

"So it can only be done by force."

"Yes. At least in this country and in countries like us."

"Well, the Montoneros believe that *their* program can only be done by force. So what's the difference?"

"Between the Montoneros and the military?" Carlos smiled as if this were an easy question to answer. "The Montoneros, who started as a group of idealistic Catholic students, believe in socialism."

"And the military, who started as a group of idealistic Catholic soldiers, believe in capitalism," Stephen said. "Is that the only difference?"

Carlos nodded. "It's a big difference. It's the difference between failure and success."

Before going home he sat at his desk on the empty banking floor and thought about what he was doing. His reasons for working with the embassy guys were still clear, and they still seemed valid. Their goals were to cut off the money that the Montoneros had accumulated by kidnapping people and to stop the shipments of arms that they were using to kill people. He wasn't directly involved in supporting the military, and he didn't want to be involved in supporting them since judged by his values they were as bad as the Montoneros, and he worried that at the very least they were going to harass Elena and Mario. But if the Montoneros were unable to pursue the war because they had no money and no arms, then fewer of them would be killed, and fewer innocent people would be killed. The war would end, and the killing would stop.

So he needed to determine the right way to continue working toward this goal, and looking for an answer, he examined the list of lawyers who according to the records owned the companies that owned Esmeralda. He focused on a name that was listed with all three companies: Arnaldo Navarra. This lawyer could be the key to the whole operation, which included both the loans in pesos and the offshore deposits in dollars. He could be Safadi's right-hand man.

At this point Stephen had enough information to have Navarra arrested. In the hands of the military, who would assume the worst and treat him accordingly, Navarra would implicate Safadi, and if Safadi had moved the money, they could make him reveal its location—he certainly wouldn't sacrifice his life for the Montoneros.

But what if the money didn't belong to the Montoneros? What if the operation was simply a way to hide money from the tax authorities? Was he willing to have these men tortured for helping people to evade taxes?

It didn't take him long to decide that the right way was to get enough evidence to have the account frozen in New York.

SIX

THE MILITARY, who must have planned the *golpe* for a long time, immediately began to implement their Process of National Reorganization. On the day they took over they issued a decree that prohibited disseminating information about groups that were involved in subversive activities or terrorism, with a penalty of imprisonment for an indefinite period of time. They also prohibited printing or broadcasting any words or images that might disturb, discredit, or be detrimental to the activities of the armed forces, security, or police.

Within the next few days the government took control of the universities, allowing them to continue operating provided that they met the standards of the military for internal discipline, administrative clarity, and the "regularization" of faculty and students, to be defined.

General Videla was sworn in as president on March 29. Though his government wasn't officially recognized by most other countries, it had been blessed two days earlier by the International Monetary Fund's approval of a credit that had been denied to the previous government. The approval was seen as opening possibilities of further credits, which would require the government to adopt the economic policies that were being promoted by the United States.

Meanwhile, the war had escalated. A former union leader was abducted by a right-wing death squad. A police commissioner was killed by the Montoneros. An army commander announced the creation of war councils to try detainees suspected of involvement in subversion. Another police commissioner was killed. And nine burned bodies were found, presumably victims of right-wing death squads.

During this period Stephen and Carlos sent daily reports to head office, and they talked with the vice president daily. Carlos strongly supported the actions of the military while Stephen had reservations. He was not only concerned for the country, but he was also concerned for his friends, especially for Elena and Mario since their institutions were being attacked.

He got Mario's perspective shortly after the government issued its decree about the universities. He and Mario had begun meeting on Tuesday evenings at a café near the School of Philosophy and Letters, where Cathy's class was meeting. It had turned out that Teresa was taking a postgraduate course there on the same evening.

The café was dingy and poorly lit, which seemed to enhance its appeal to the students and faculty who accounted for most of its clientele. The service was bad, but the food was cheap and the coffee was strong. In addition to coffee they served aperitifs, hard liquor, wine, and cordials, though not many people drank alcoholic beverages. They preferred caffeine.

When Stephen arrived at the café that evening Mario was already there, seated at a table and having a coffee. Stephen went to the bar and got a brandy, which he brought to the table.

"*Hola*," he said, sitting down. "*Qué tal?*"

"*No muy bien*," Mario grumbled.

"I heard about the decree. What does it mean?"

"It means that we no longer have any academic freedom. Not that we had a lot of it. We were just beginning to recover from the last intervention."

"The night of the long sticks," Stephen said, referring to a particularly heinous event. When the last military government decided to take over the university and dismantle its governance system, it was opposed by faculty, students, and alumni who occupied the buildings and refused to leave. On a winter evening the police hurled tear gas into the buildings and ruthlessly beat the people with nightsticks as they staggered out. In the months that followed hundreds of faculty were dismissed, resigned, and left the country.

"That happened in 1966," Mario reminded him, "and we were under their control for the next seven years."

"What were you doing at that time?"

"I was a student. I wasn't present at the attack, but I heard about it from friends and professors. I almost decided against a career at the university."

"What made you decide in favor of it?"

"I saw those professors leaving the country, some of the best minds we had. *Una fuga de cerebros.* I think in English you call it a brain drain."

"That's right."

"I felt that the country needed me, that I could make a contribution as a teacher and as a researcher, so I kept going and finished my doctorate."

"Did the military interfere with you?"

"Oh, yes. They had rules on what you could teach or publish. If I wanted to do a research project, I had to get it approved by an *interventor.*"

"You mean someone appointed by the military?"

"Yes. Some idiot who had a rule book and a list of subjects approved for research."

"You're kidding."

"A little. There wasn't a list."

"So how did the *interventor* decide what to approve?"

"By applying the values of the military."

"That must have been conducive to research."

"Very conducive," Mario said.

"Did you ever think of leaving Argentina?"

"Leaving? No. Never."

"Why not?"

"This is my country. My grandparents came here from Italy. They had nothing there. My father's father worked on a farm here. My father came to the city and worked in a factory in Avellaneda. I'm a professor at the university. This country gave my family an opportunity to move up."

"Are any of your grandparents still alive?"

"Two of them are."

"They must be proud of you."

"They are. They love to talk about their grandson, Dr. Gaetano."

"Where do they live?"

"They live with my parents. Luckily, one of them is my father's father and the other is my mother's mother. So they get along."

"Well, you made it through the last intervention."

"I have experience in surviving."

At that moment Teresa arrived, bringing a soda from the bar.

"How was your class?" Mario asked her.

"Oh, it was fine. But my professor acted like nothing had happened."

"He's smart. What did you expect him to do?"

She shrugged. "I don't know. I thought he might talk about it, just to reassure us. But he went right into his lecture."

"That's what I did. My students didn't seem to mind."

"They understand politics. After all, they're studying political science."

"That doesn't mean they understand politics."

"So can we talk here?" she asked, glancing around uneasily.

"We've been talking."

"They don't have spies here?"

"I haven't noticed any."

"What do they look like?"

"They don't look like the people here."

About ten minutes later Cathy arrived and joined them at the table, bringing a coffee from the bar.

"How was your professor tonight?" Stephen asked her.

"A little strange. There were times when I thought he was speaking in code."

"He was probably trying to tell you what he thinks about the intervention," Mario said, smiling.

"I hope so. I wouldn't want to be tested on it."

"A test on codes. I like that idea."

"Well, it's hard enough to understand the poetry."

"Who are you reading?"

"Rubén Darío."

"I like him," Mario said. "*Yo persigo una forma que no encuentra mi estilo, botón de pensamiento que busca ser la rosa.*"

"I have trouble understanding that," Cathy admitted.

"What does it mean?" Stephen asked.

"I don't know," Mario said. "But it sounds good."

Laughing with them, Stephen believed that they could handle whatever ordeals the intervention might have in store for them.

The next day the bank received payments on the unrecorded loans that were due on March 31. Seven of these loans had been made by the companies of which Navarra was an owner of record. Stephen held the money in a special account, waiting for the lenders to claim it.

Around noon Ignacio, the *ordenanza* at the reception desk, asked him if he could meet with a Doctor Navarra.

"Yes. Please bring him over."

Ignacio returned with a dark-haired man in a khaki suit that looked as if it had come from Brooks Brothers, complete with the blue button-down shirt and the rep tie. The man in the suit could have stepped out of a catalogue, except that he didn't look like a model. He looked like an operator.

"Doctor Navarra," the man proclaimed, extending a hand with a garish ring on the middle finger. The ring didn't go with the outfit.

"A pleasure," Stephen said, shaking the hand.

"Could we talk somewhere in private?"

"Yes. Of course. We can go into the conference room."

Stephen led him there and closed the door behind them. As they sat down he could smell the cologne that emanated from Navarra.

"You're an American, right?"

"Right. I guess you can tell from my accent."

"No. You speak Spanish perfectly. I can tell from the honest look in your eyes."

Stephen wondered if he meant innocent.

"There aren't many Americans left here," Navarra said. "Your bank must have a good reason for keeping you here."

"They don't want me back in New York making trouble."

Navarra smiled. "Are you a troublemaker?"

"Sometimes. When I get bored."

"Well, there are a lot of things happening in this country to keep you from getting bored."

"Yes. There are."

Getting to the point, Navarra said: "I'm the owner of some companies that made loans under your bank's guarantee, and we received notices from you."

Stephen waited while the man reached inside his jacket and pulled out a white envelope. He was struck by the fact that unlike other lawyers he had dealt with this one didn't carry a briefcase.

Navarra opened the envelope and took out the notices, which he unfolded. "They say we need to claim the money for payments on our loans."

"We're holding it for you."

"That's not how we used to get it," Navarra said, frowning. "We got the payments from Señor Arias."

"He used to handle them," Stephen said, "but unfortunately he's no longer with us."

"What happened to him?"

Stephen believed Navarra knew, but he stuck with the company line. "He had health problems."

"Oh, that's a pity," Navarra said indifferently.

"Do you know him well?"

"No, not well. I did business with him."

"What kind of business?"

"Financial business. He invested money for me. And now I don't know what to do with it."

"Well, we could reinvest it for you."

"What rate could you get me?"

"A better rate than you got on this loan. I could probably get you fifty-six percent for ninety days."

Navarra compressed his lips as if he were considering it. "How would we arrange the loan? The same way we did with Arias?"

"Yes." Except that the guarantee will be recorded, Stephen thought.

"All right. If you can get me that rate, it's a deal."

"I'll call and see." Stephen got up and went to the phone and called Salvatori and asked for a rate on a loan for ninety days in the *extrabancario* market. He waited while Salvatori checked. He figured that if he arranged loans for Navarra he could keep his eye on the money, and if he could prove that the Montoneros owned these companies he could have the money taken away from them. Meanwhile, since the money was on loan for ninety days, they couldn't use it to buy arms.

"*Señor?* The rate is fifty-seven percent."

"*Bien. Gracias.*" He hung up the phone and told Navarra: "I can get you fifty-seven percent."

"Excellent," Navarra said happily.

"We can have it done by this afternoon."

"Then I'll leave the money with you," Navarra said, rising. "When should I send someone over to get the papers?"

"Around four," Stephen told him.

"It's a pleasure doing business with you."

He had an appointment with Jorge that afternoon, so he reviewed the documents for the loans he had gotten approved for the cooperative. The bank operated on a credit committee system, which meant that you needed three signatures on any loan with a value of more than ten thousand dollars. He had initiated the credit proposal, and he had gotten Eduardo and another account manager to sign it. They hadn't asked him any questions, which bothered him a little. Was it because they agreed with him that it was a good credit risk? Or was it because he was an American, a representative from head office, who presumably knew what he was doing.

Jorge was early for his appointment, wearing the suit and still looking uncomfortable in it. He read the documents carefully, and unlike Stephen's colleagues he asked questions. He was about to make a major commitment on behalf of more than thirty storeowners, and it was obvious that he took his responsibility seriously.

"So we have five years to repay the loan for the truck," he said, looking for confirmation.

"That's right. Did you find a good truck?"

"Oh, yes. It's used, but it's in good condition."

This meant that the truck had no problems that they couldn't fix themselves. Among the storeowners there had to be men who could fix anything since a lot of people in this country had mechanical skills. Once when his washing machine broke down Stephen asked around the bank to see if anyone knew a repairman, and that evening a teller showed up at his apartment, still in his suit, which he covered with a smock before taking apart the motor.

"And we have up to ninety days to repay the line of credit."

"Right. It's a revolving credit, which means that when you repay any amount you've borrowed, the amount becomes available again."

Jorge nodded, and then he took out a pen and started signing the documents.

"When will you buy the truck?"

"Next week. We have contracts with all but one of the producers, but that was delayed because his daughter was getting married."

Stephen smiled. "He'll have to sign the contract to pay for the wedding."

"Well, he won't get a better price."

Because there were no middlemen, they could afford to pay the farmers a higher price for the potatoes, and they could afford to sell the potatoes at a lower price while making a higher profit than before. In this arrangement the farmers, the storeowners, and the consumers all gained. The only losers were the middlemen.

John and Bill arrived the next day at their usual time and went unnoticed into the conference room since the desks on the banking floor were empty.

Stephen joined them and related what had happened since their last meeting.

"So Navarra looks like our man," John said.

"Yes. He does," Stephen agreed, "but we still don't know if he's fronting for the Montoneros. He could be fronting for someone else."

"Yeah? Who else would have this kind of money?"

"Former politicians," Stephen said.

"He has a point," Bill said. "I heard that Perón stole so much money that he was among the top ten holders of shares on the New York Stock Exchange."

"Still," Stephen said, "we believe that Navarra's fronting for the Montoneros."

"So why did you say he could be fronting for someone else?"

"I wanted to remind you that we don't know."

"Okay. We don't know," John said. "But I think we should have Navarra arrested."

"Suppose we do have him arrested," Stephen said, ready with his arguments. "They'll torture him, and maybe they'll find out that the money belongs to the Montoneros—"

"If it does, they'll find out."

"But what if it doesn't?"

There was a long silence.

"What if it belongs to people who are evading taxes?"

"That could be anyone," John admitted.

"Yeah, everyone in this country evades taxes," Bill agreed.

"So are we willing to have a man tortured for helping people to evade taxes?"

"That's a tough question," John said. "If I knew he was only helping people to evade taxes, I wouldn't have him arrested. But I believe he's helping the Montoneros."

"We all do," Bill said. "But what if we're wrong?"

"I'd feel bad about it."

"Bad enough to wish you hadn't done it?"

"I don't know."

"You don't? Then let's apply the theory of least regret."

"Could you explain what you're talking about?" John asked.

"Sure," Bill said. "You look at the outcomes of different possible actions, and you determine how much you'll regret each outcome if you're wrong. You choose the action that'll make you feel the least regret if you're wrong."

"So if we have Navarra arrested," John said, "then he'll be tortured, and if we're wrong about the money belonging to the Montoneros, we'll feel a certain amount of regret. But if we don't have him arrested, then he won't be tortured, and if we're wrong about the money belonging to tax evaders, we'll feel a certain amount of regret. The question is, which outcome will we regret least?"

"Regret less. We're comparing only two outcomes."

"You said it was the theory of least regret."

"You're both evading the question," Stephen told them.

"We don't have the answer," Bill said.

"Well, then let's go back to our objective, which is to stop the Montoneros by cutting off their money. The only effective way to do that is to freeze their account in New York before they know what's happening."

"You're right," Bill said. "We keep assuming that Safadi controls their money, but they must have the ability to move it. So if we have Navarra arrested, the Montoneros will move the money, and even Safadi won't know where it is."

"Okay," John conceded. "We won't have Navarra arrested. So what's your plan?"

"I build a relationship with him," Stephen said, "by helping him reinvest their pesos."

"That could get you into trouble."

"You mean with the bank?"

"I mean with the government."

"Well, I don't know whose money it is."

"We can always vouch for him," Bill said.

"I build a relationship with him," Stephen resumed, "and I try to find a connection between him and Safadi. Meanwhile, as long as we keep reinvesting their pesos they won't be able to touch that money. And they'll have no reason to move their dollars since they won't know we're after them."

"I don't have a better plan," Bill said.

"I don't either," John said.

On Friday he had lunch at La Estancia with the auditors. They paid for it. They had examined the unrecorded loans arranged by Arias, and they had classified them as normal. Their conclusion was supported by the fact that all seven of the loans due on March 31 had been fully repaid by the borrowers.

"What are you having?" Stephen asked them.

"I'm having goat," Andy said. "What's it called?"

"*Chivito*. You'll like it."

"I'll stick with beef," Jeff said, "but I'll try some of his."

"If you want goat," Andy told him, "order it yourself. I'm not going to share mine with you."

"We'll get two large orders of goat," Stephen suggested, "and one of beef. What kind of beef would you like, Jeff?"

"Steak, please. Medium rare."

When they had ordered, Andy said: "You can read our report after lunch, but there's nothing in it but praise for the way you handled this."

"Thanks," Stephen said. "Maybe I should be paying for lunch."

"No, you won the bet. And that's what we emphasize in the report—your good judgment."

"It looks like the bank won't lose any money on this," Jeff said, lulled by the prospect of a good steak.

"Except for the fees we might have earned," Stephen said.

"That's an opportunity loss," Jeff said. "It's not something you can account for."

"So what did this guy do with the money?" Andy asked.

"I think he invested in real estate."

"That makes sense. When you have such a high rate of inflation, real estate can be a good hedge."

"What's the rate of inflation now?" Jeff asked.

"It's more than four hundred percent," Stephen said.

"So the steak I'm having will cost four times as much a year from now."

"You'll have to eat goat then," Andy said.

"I'll have a hamburger," Jeff said.

After a moment Andy asked: "What can you tell us about the military government's economic policy?"

"They haven't officially announced it yet," Stephen said. "But from what we hear they plan to move the economy to a free market system."

"Will it work?"

"I don't know. It's the only thing they haven't tried yet."

"Why is this country so screwed up?" Jeff asked.

"Well, there's a story," Stephen said. "It was told to me by an Argentine, so it's not my explanation. When God created the world he gave Argentina all the resources a country needs in order to be successful. When St. Peter saw what God had given Argentina he said, it's not fair, you gave this country more than you gave any other country. And God said, don't worry, I'll make it fair. I'll give this country Argentines."

The auditors laughed.

"You said that's not your explanation," Andy pursued, "so then what *is* your explanation?"

"I think this country has had bad leaders."

"But doesn't a country get the leaders it deserves?"

"According to that story, it does. But there are other factors that may determine the leaders it gets. Did the Germans get Hitler because they deserved him?"

"Some people believe they did."

"But you don't believe that, do you?"

"No. As you said, there are other factors, which could be random. If there's a joker in a deck of cards, in theory it'll come up only once in fifty-three draws. But in reality it can come up three times in a row."

"Depending on how you shuffle the cards," Jeff said.

"Or depending on how you deal the cards," Andy said. "The dealer can determine which card comes up."

"That's why I don't play poker," Jeff said.

"So what card came up this time?" Andy asked.

"The ace of spades," Stephen said.

"Well, that can be a good or bad card, depending on the game you're playing."

"They're playing the game of war here."

"I used to play that game."

"You mean with cards."

"Yeah. An ace was a good card in that game."

"In this game," Stephen said, "there are no good cards."

Their food arrived, and after they had begun to eat it they all agreed that there was no better meat anywhere.

Jeff even liked the goat.

When he and Cathy arrived that evening at the café on Avenida de Mayo, only Sofi and Paco were there, evidently having come together from the *villa*.

"How are you doing?" he asked Sofi.

"I'm fine," she said cheerfully, "and the baby's fine."

"The potato project's going well."

"Jorge told me. He said you've arranged financing for them to buy a truck and to pay the farmers."

"Everything's in place."

"I really appreciate your helping them."

"I enjoy doing it."

Meanwhile, Paco had unfolded a large sheet of paper and laid it out on the table, showing it to Cathy.

"Oh, look," Sofi said excitedly. "Paco has the plan for the church."

They joined Paco and Cathy, standing over the plan.

"It's a simple structure," Paco said, "so it won't cost a lot to build. But it'll hold a hundred people."

Stephen looked at the plan, impressed. He had heard Paco talk about the church, but now that there was a plan on paper it was no longer just an idea, it had taken a step toward becoming a reality. "Do you have the land?"

"Oh, yes. We've had it for a while."

"With a deed and everything?"

Paco smiled. "Getting through the red tape was a tribulation, but with God's help we finally did it."

"Without His help you wouldn't have," Stephen said.

"So now we need money to build the church."

"I assume you're getting some money from the diocese."

"My bishop is helping," Paco said, "but we need a lot more than he can give us."

"I got the message," Stephen said.

Cathy was silent, engrossed in the plan.

"Show them the plan for the school," Sofi said.

Paco got it from a chair, unfolded it, and spread it over the plan for the church. "The school is also a simple structure. It's for grades one through five, and it'll hold about two hundred students."

"I'd like to teach there," Cathy said, touching the paper.

"Then hurry up and get your degree," Sofi urged her.

"I have a long way to go. I just started."

"Don't worry. It'll take a while to build the school."

"Well, I hope it doesn't take as long to build the school as it'll take me to get my degree."

"That depends on how long it takes us to raise the money," Paco said.

"I got the message again," Stephen said.

At that moment Mario and Teresa arrived. They joined the others in looking at the plan for the school.

Teresa, who taught fifth grade, asked Paco: "When will you complete it?"

"We haven't started yet."

"When will you start?"

"As soon as we have the money," Paco said.

"You could teach there," Sofi said.

"That's what I was thinking," Teresa said.

"You and Cathy could both teach there."

"Teach where?" Elena asked, looking over their shoulders.

"At Paco's school," Teresa said.

"You have a plan. Oh, let me see it." Elena leaned over to examine the plan. "*Qué maravilla!* Now, when are you going to start building the school?"

"As soon as he has the money," Stephen said before Paco could say it.

"Then what are we waiting for? Let's raise the money."

As he and Cathy were having dinner at Ligure they talked about how they could help Paco raise money for the church and the school.

"I'm going to give him five thousand dollars," Stephen said.

"Well, that should help."

"But he needs a lot more. I might be able to give him more, but we have to find other sources."

"Could the bank lend money to him?"

"No. It couldn't. The bank has a policy against lending to religious organizations."

"It does? Why?"

"I guess because if you lend to one they'll all want loans from you, and if you don't lend to all of them you could be accused of discriminating against some religions."

She thought for a moment, and then she asked: "Could the bank lend money to someone who's not a religious organization, who could then lend it to Paco?"

"It could. But once you start doing that kind of thing you're on a slippery slope."

"Slippery slope? What does that mean?"

"It means you've taken the first step toward perdition."

"I know what that means. It's the same word in Spanish." She took a bite of her chicken *a la milanesa* and chewed thoughtfully. "Are you religious?"

"I believe in God, but I haven't gone to church in a while."

"What religion are you?"

"Catholic. I was raised as an Episcopalian, but I converted when I was eighteen."

"What made you convert?"

"The summer after I graduated from high school I went to Montana to work on an Indian reservation. I met a priest there, who led me through the process."

"What were you doing on the reservation?"

"We were building a school."

"So you know how to build a school."

"I know how to lay cinder blocks."

"Then you can help Paco."

"It's a good idea. We can save money." He sipped his wine. "What about you?"

"I don't know how to build a school," she said. "But I guess I can learn."

"I mean are you religious?"

"Oh, yes. While we were all looking at the plan, I was thinking about how I grew up in a *barrio* like the one where Sofi and Paco work, and how I went to a church like the one Paco wants to build. I wanted to tell him what a big difference it made in my life."

"But you couldn't tell him," Stephen said, "because your father's an American oil engineer."

"They're right about lying. Once you start, you can't stop."

"I hope you don't feel bad about lying in your situation."

"No, but I feel bad about not being able to support Paco with my experience."

"You can support him in other ways."

"Well, I was serious about teaching in his school."

"I know you were. So now you have a goal."

"Yes. I'm going to take more courses next semester."

"Good. Then it won't take long to get your degree."

She smiled in thanks for his support, and then she said: "While you were talking about politics with Mario and Elena, I had a long conversation with Paco."

"Did he ask you if you went to church?"

"He did. How did you guess?"

"I know Paco. What did you say?"

"I said I went to church in Venezuela. You see what I mean? I lied to him. I lied to a priest."

"Everyone does, so don't feel bad about it."

"Anyway, he asked why I don't go to church here, and I said I wasn't a member of a church."

"And he said that's no excuse."

"You do know Paco."

"He's always trying to get me to go to church. I used to go, but I stopped going."

"Why did you stop?"

"I don't know. I just stopped going."

"Was your wife Catholic?"

"No. She didn't believe in God. She believed in evolution."

"Well, I would like to go to church," Cathy told him.

"There's a church right across the street from here, Nuestra Señora del Socorro."

"Our Lady of Help. That's what we need, and if it's that close we have no excuse."

"All right," he said. "But let's go to the noon mass. We'll never make an earlier one."

She smiled. "No. We never will."

He met Cathy at the bookstore the next day at noon. They had lunch at a *confitería*, and then they went to the food market, where they bought what they needed to prepare a new recipe from the cookbook.

It was a beautiful day, so after putting away the groceries they went out again and walked up to the art museum, which had an exhibit of Latin American painters. As they moved slowly around the room, looking at the paintings, he remembered how he met Leila at an exhibit of Latin American paintings. It turned out that this was all they had in common—an interest in Latin America.

"What happened here?" Cathy asked, pointing to an area on the wall where some paintings had obviously been removed.

"Maybe they found out that the painter's a Marxist."

"They did that in my course. They removed the poems by Pablo Neruda."

He took her hand and led her to the next painter. It wouldn't have surprised him if someone was watching and observing the reactions of people who came to that spot. If they weren't already doing that kind of thing, they would soon.

When they got home they started working together on dinner. It was the kind of dish that you could cook in advance and then reheat, which meant that they could relax before eating. They were almost done when they met in the pantry, going in opposite directions, and they were impelled to unite in a long, deep kiss.

As he pulled gently on the string of her apron, undoing the bow, they both had the same thing in mind, so after turning off the stove they headed for the bedroom.

The next morning she reminded him that he had agreed to go to church. She had the hours of the masses at Socorro, and they got up in time to go to the one at noon. She wore a dress that she had bought recently, with a gold cross around her neck that he had never seen before.

Following his eye, she said: "My mother gave this to me before I left Colombia."

"I like it," he said.

"I couldn't wear it at Minas."

"No. It wouldn't have helped you sell champagne."

They walked to Socorro, which was right around the corner on Juncal, and they went in. You could tell right away that it was a wealthy parish, not only from the elegant décor but also from the genteel congregation. They were *gente bien.*

Cathy led the way, selecting a pew toward the rear and leaving a space for him next to the aisle. They both knelt and prayed. He prayed for Vittoria and Sofi. He prayed for all his other friends and for his family. And last but not least he prayed for the safety of the woman at his side.

Sitting back on the pew, he remembered the last time he was here and how he prayed for strength to accept the loss of Leila. Either his prayer had been granted, or it hadn't taken that much strength after all.

He glanced at Cathy, who was still on her knees with her head bowed against her clasped hands. She was perfectly still.

Later, he thought of Paco when the priest said: "Lord Jesus Christ, you said to your apostles: I leave you peace, my peace I give you. Look not on our sins, but on the faith of your Church, and grant us the peace and unity of your kingdom where you live for ever and ever."

When the mass was ended they went out into the bright day and strolled toward Santa Fe, holding hands.

On Monday he met with Carlos to prepare a report for head office on the new government's economic policy. As anticipated, Martínez de Hoz had been appointed minister of economy, and the main features of his program were now known: reduce the deficit by privatizing state enterprises, eliminate trade barriers, and abolish controls on foreign exchange.

"They're applying neoclassical economic theory," Carlos said with enthusiasm. "It'll make our industry more competitive, and it'll make our country more attractive to foreign investors."

"What about the companies that can't compete in the global market?"

"They'll go out of business. But their resources will be reallocated to companies that *can* compete, and the country as a whole will benefit."

"What will they do for the owners and employees of the companies that fail?"

"Nothing. Our governments have already done too much for them. They've subsidized incompetent owners and spoiled unproductive workers. That's why our country has been going backward all these years."

"So this will be a great leap forward."

Carlos snorted, obviously catching the allusion to the disastrous policy of Mao, which set his country back a generation. "It's not like China. In fact, it's the exact opposite of what China did."

"Sometimes," Stephen said, "the exact opposite policies can lead to the same result."

"In politics maybe, but not in economics."

"Well, if this is the right program, I still don't see why you need a dictatorship to implement it."

"Because elected governments represent special interest groups," Carlos said, warming to the subject. "Each group sees the economy as a zero-sum game, meaning that if one group gets something it's at the expense of other groups. So all they do is take from one group and give to the other. They never implement policies that will expand the economy, so that there will be more for everyone."

"You believe that this government doesn't represent a special interest group?"

"It doesn't. In fact, the military are the only institution that represents the whole country."

Though he didn't argue, he wondered if any institution could represent the whole country. "So what are we going to say to head office?"

"We're going to outline the main policies, and we're going to explain how these policies are designed to achieve economic growth and stability."

"Are we going to be optimistic?"

"Yes. We now have a chance to realize the great potential of our country."

By the time they had completed the report Stephen had toned it down to a level of being cautiously optimistic.

The next evening he and Mario were in the café near the university, waiting for Teresa and Cathy, when there was a sudden commotion at the door, beginning with a series of pops that sounded like champagne corks being propelled from their bottles.

"Oh, shit!" Mario cried. "We have to get out of here."

The room was quickly filling with fumes from canisters of tear gas.

People were screaming and rushing out the door in panic, where a gauntlet of police was waiting for them. There were sounds of skulls being cracked by clubs and cries of pain, accompanied by a barrage of curses.

"Follow me," Mario said, heading for the men's room.

Stephen followed him, eyes watering. He took his handkerchief out of his back pocket and covered his mouth and nose with it, filtering the gas.

In the men's room there was a window that evidently faced out into an alley. It was partly open, and Mario pushed it the rest of the way.

"Let's go, my friend," Mario said, offering to help him.

"No, you go first. I'll help you."

Dispensing with politeness, Mario climbed up onto the toilet seat, grabbed the sill of the window, and hoisted himself. Stephen made a sling with his hands for a dangling foot and boosted Mario, who swung his legs out through the window and positioned himself to drop on the other side.

When his friend had disappeared from the window Stephen followed, leaving the sounds of mayhem behind him. He landed hard on the pavement below.

"Are you all right?" Mario asked.

"Yes. I'm fine."

"Follow me."

He followed Mario down the alley, which was illuminated only by the lights from windows in the buildings on either side of it. He could imagine what would happen to them if they encountered the police in this dark alley.

Before leaving it Mario stopped to make sure that no one was waiting to ambush them. Then signaling that the coast was clear, he led Stephen out into a street where normal life was going on. They started walking as if they were ordinary pedestrians, oblivious to what was happening.

"I have a feeling that you've done this before," Stephen said.

"Oh, yes. It happened the last time we had a military government."

"We have to stop the women from going there."

"We should have time to intercept them."

They walked in a roundabout way to the School of Philosophy and Letters, where they didn't see any police, and they waited where Teresa and Cathy would leave the building in which they were taking classes.

Teresa was the first to appear.

"What happened?" she asked, looking concerned.

Mario told her, downplaying it.

"They could have killed you."

"They would have just conked me. And I have a very hard head." As if to prove it he whacked himself on the top of his head. "*Una cabeza durísima.*"

"It's not funny."

"I'm not saying it is. But it happened before, and we lived through it."

"Maybe we were lucky. And maybe this government's worse than that one."

"It's a different situation," Mario admitted. "But don't worry. We won't go to that café again."

"For sure we won't," Teresa said.

As he listened to them Stephen wondered what would have happened if Teresa and Cathy had been with them when the police attacked. At the very least it would have been harder for them to escape through the bathroom window.

SEVEN

RIDING THE TRAIN to Belgrano on Monday, Stephen had time to read the story about the war in Elena's newspaper. Despite the restrictions on the press her paper had continued to report on the violence, tallying the casualties more or less weekly. In the latest count the paper reported that one hundred and one people had been killed since the military took over. And more had been killed by the army, the police, and unidentified death squads than by the Montoneros.

As he walked to Vittoria's house he wondered how many of the people killed by the government were Montoneros, and how many were a step or two removed from them. It came down to the question that Bill had asked: where would you draw the line? How far would you go in order to eliminate the terrorists? How many innocent victims would you sacrifice? Could you justify killing anyone? Clearly, if the vision of the Montoneros didn't justify killing people, then neither did the vision of the military. You had to judge them both by the same standard, and by this standard they were both evil.

He was welcomed at the door by Claudia and Olivia, who had new dolls they wanted to show him, and he sat with them for a while on the sofa being introduced to the dolls and being regaled with information about their hair, their clothes, and their personalities.

As they were having a drink in the kitchen Vittoria said: "The circus is coming to town, and I thought it might be fun for them. They've never been to a circus."

"You mean Claudia and Olivia."

"Yes. Aleja's too young."

He got it. "You want me to take them?"

"Do you want to take them?"

"Sure. Why not? I haven't been to a circus in a long time."

"I'd take them myself, but I couldn't manage it. I mean, I could leave Aleja with my mother, but I'd rather not."

"Is your mother back from Italy?"

"Yes. She says she would have stayed longer, but she was concerned about me."

"And you should appreciate her sacrifice," he said ironically.

"The truth is, she really didn't want to stay."

"Well, I could handle them by myself."

"I think you could," Vittoria said, "but there are two of them and only one of you."

He considered for a moment, and he decided that now was the time. "There's someone who could help me. I have a friend—"

Since they were speaking Spanish she knew right away that the friend was female. "You mean Elena?"

"No. Someone I met a few months ago. Her name is Cathy. We're living together."

Visibly upset, Vittoria asked: "Why didn't you tell me about her before?"

"I don't know," he said, feeling bad about it.

"Did you think I wouldn't like it?"

"No. I thought—" It was hard to explain. "I guess I thought it would somehow affect our relationship."

"You thought I'd feel I no longer had you all to myself?"

"Something like that."

"What does she do while you're with me?"

"She studies. She's taking a course at the university."

"And it's all right with her that you're having dinner with another woman?"

"Yes. She understands."

Vittoria nodded. "She knows you're safe with me since I have three children."

"Whatever the situation, she trusts me."

"Then you must have a serious relationship."

"We do," he said.

"Well, you should have told me about her before."

"I guess I should have."

"I don't like it that you were hiding something so important from me. I don't hide anything from you."

"You're right. I'm sorry."

"Of course it's my fault too," she said after a silence. "All we talk about is me. We never talk about you."

"We talked about my divorce."

"We did. And I *am* happy that you've found someone. Tell me about her."

He gave her the cover story about Cathy's background and then told her, as best he could, how their relationship had evolved.

"You sound like newlyweds," Vittoria said, smiling.

"I wouldn't know. I didn't have the usual experience with my first wife."

"You see? You talk as if she's going to be your second wife."

He nodded, marveling at how women were always ahead of men in these matters.

While they ate dinner they talked about what the government was doing to eliminate the Montoneros. He told her what he had read in the newspaper.

"I know," she said pensively. "I've been following the war. And it looks like my prayers are being answered."

"You don't sound happy about it."

"I don't? Well, I'm not."

He waited for her to explain.

"I prayed for this, and now that it's happening I feel bad."

"It's not happening because of your prayers."

"I know. But I still feel bad."

"For what exactly?"

"For the innocent people they might kill in getting rid of the Montoneros."

"But not for the Montoneros they kill."

"No, not for them. But," she added, "it doesn't give me the satisfaction that I thought it would."

"I understand."

"I've been thinking about what you said last time. I still want vengeance, but not as much as I did before. I'm ready to start wanting something else."

"You already do want something else. You want a good life for your children."

"I do. But how can I give them a good life?"

"You can raise them well."

"That's not enough. I need to do something to make this country a better place for them to live."

He had an idea. "I know a priest. His name is Francisco, but we call him Paco."

"A priest? I don't remember you mentioning him."

"Well, he's more like a social worker than a priest. He doesn't have a parish. He works in a *villa miseria*. He has a project to build a church and a school there."

"Tell me more," Vittoria said as if she might be interested.

The next morning, after reviewing a credit proposal, he left the bank and walked over to Avenida de Mayo, where he entered the subway. He was meeting Sofi at the Caballito train station, near the end of the subway line at Primera Junta. From there they would take a *colectivo* to where she worked. The subway system didn't extend very far from the center of the city, but it covered the areas where traffic was the worst, so it was a quick way to get out of the center.

At the Caballito station he spotted Sofi waiting for him. It was a cool fall day, and she was wearing a leather jacket over her dress. If he hadn't known that she was pregnant, he wouldn't have guessed since the jacket hid the bulge in her abdomen, which he had noticed last Friday.

She greeted him with a bright smile, and then she led him to the *colectivo* stop, where they waited only a few minutes for the next bus. At this time of day the bus wasn't crowded, so they easily got seats together. At other times the buses were packed, with everyone trying to stay as close to the front as possible since there was only one door for climbing on and jumping off. The *colectivo* drivers were notorious for speeding and taking risks as they competed with each other for passengers. It wasn't unusual to see two *colectivos* racing side by side down a one-way street, missing the parked cars by millimeters but occasionally clipping side-view mirrors.

"How long does it take you," Stephen asked, "to get to the *villa* from where you live?"

"About an hour," Sofi replied. She had come by train from her parents' house in Flores, where she was staying for the duration. "With good connections."

"That's a long trip."

"It gives me time to think."

"About what?"

"About my work, my baby, my future."

"Will you go back to work after you have the baby?"

"Yes. I have my mother to help me."

"Does she want you to keep working?"

"Oh, yes. She understands how important it is."

They rode to the end of the line, at which point the street was no longer paved. They walked a few blocks into the *villa* before reaching the grocery store that belonged to Jorge. There was more than a whiff of sewage in the air.

Jorge was standing in front of his store with some other men, whom he introduced as neighbors. They had evidently joined him to welcome the first delivery of potatoes coming directly from the farms. They had the look of people waiting for a plane, a ship, a train, or a bus on which a loved one was arriving.

They heard the truck before they saw it since there were no vehicles on the streets creating a din. By then a number of women and children had joined the men, and they all cheered when the truck came into sight.

It was a big truck, a Mercedes, and it looked as if it had been around the world a few times. But it lurched ahead exultantly and stopped with a shudder in front of them. The driver had another man and a boy with him. He waved to the crowd through the spattered windshield and then jumped down.

Jorge advanced and shook his hand, congratulating him.

Everyone waited and watched as they unloaded two large bags of potatoes, fresh from the farm. You could smell the earth as they lugged the potatoes from the back of the truck and into the store.

The women were already queuing up to buy them.

"This is a great moment," Jorge said buoyantly.

"Thanks to Stephen," Sofi said.

"No, thanks to Chris. It was his project." He put his arm around Sofi, who laid her head against his shoulder. He could see why she didn't mind the long bus trip, and why she wanted to keep working. And he wondered if Vittoria could benefit from such an experience.

That evening, as arranged last Friday, he met Mario at a place near the university that wasn't a hangout for students and faculty. It was a *confitería*, and at this hour the only other customers were a few elderly men having coffee.

"What this place lacks in ambience," Mario remarked, "it compensates with safety."

"That's a good trade-off."

Mario nodded. "But I wouldn't want to give up everything for safety, which is what our country seems to be doing."

"The question is, how safe do people need to feel?"

"Well, they don't need to feel perfectly safe, or they might as well be dead."

"Oh, yeah. But you need to feel safe enough so that you can think about other things."

"You mean instead of always worrying about being killed."

"Yeah. When we were in that alley last week you weren't thinking about political systems."

"I was thinking about saving our asses."

"So in that situation we weren't safe enough."

"No. We weren't," Mario agreed. "In fact, this government makes me feel less safe than before. I never worried about being killed by the Montoneros."

"You have no reason to worry about that."

"But *you* have a reason, my friend."

"I do. But I'm not visible."

"You're not invisible. Doesn't Cathy worry about it?"

"Yes. She does."

"Teresa worries. After what happened last week she shifted into high gear."

"Well, we're not going to that café again."

"She's way beyond what happened there. She worries now about their closing our department."

"Why would they do that?"

"To get rid of Marxists."

"Do you have a lot of them in your department?"

"We did have some, but they were purged by the last military government."

"Then they have no reason to close your department."

"That's what I keep telling Teresa, but she still worries."

"If they did close your department," Stephen said, "you wouldn't have a job."

"Right. And I don't know how to work on a farm." Mario was referring to what happened to university professors in China during the Cultural Revolution: they were condemned to work in the rice paddies.

At that moment Teresa arrived. As she joined them with a soda she scanned their faces. "You were talking about me, weren't you."

"We were," Mario admitted.

"Did he tell you what I'm worrying about?"

"He did," Stephen said. "But he told me they purged his department of Marxists the last time around, so they have no reason to close it."

"That was ten years ago."

"They've been controlling the university most of that time," Mario reminded her.

"Well, even if you don't have any Marxists they'll find them."

Cathy arrived with a young woman that Stephen had never seen before. She had long unruly hair and bold eyes, and she was wearing jeans and a sweatshirt.

"This is Adriana," Cathy said. "She's in my class."

There were introductions, and then Cathy went to the bar with her new friend to get refreshments.

Returning with a coffee, Adriana sat next to Stephen, who was telling Mario and Teresa about the first delivery of potatoes.

"You're an American," Adriana said when he had finished. It was almost as if she were accusing him of something.

"How did you guess?"

"I told her," Cathy said.

"Are you studying to be a teacher?" he asked Adriana before she could pursue the subject of his being an American.

"Yes. I am." She didn't sound thrilled about it. "I wanted to be a psychologist, but last year they closed the program to new students."

"They never recovered from the last intervention," Mario explained. "In fact, things got worse for them under the government of Isabel Perón."

"You mean the government of López Rega," Adriana said. Like a lot of people, she evidently believed that the former minister of welfare was running the country when Perón's widow was nominally the president. His most common nickname was *el Brujo*, the witch, but he was also called the Argentine Rasputin because of his influence over Isabel Perón. "That fascist pig."

"What was his problem with psychology?" Stephen asked.

"It's Jewish and Marxist and everything alien to our culture," Adriana said sardonically.

"But there're a lot of psychologists here." He had read somewhere that in Buenos Aires there were more psychologists per hundred people than in any other city in the world. "What about them?"

"They're being persecuted by the government," Mario said, "especially if they teach."

"So why do you want to be a psychologist?"

"To help people," Adriana said.

"You can do that by being a teacher."

"That's what I keep telling her," Cathy said.

"I'm a teacher," Teresa told her. "I love teaching."

"I'll probably love it too," Adriana said. "But I would have liked to have a choice."

"I understand," Stephen said.

After a moment, following up on his being an American, Adriana asked: "Is it true that the CIA is helping the military government?"

"I don't know," he said, hoping she wasn't as good as Teresa at reading faces. "Where did you hear that?"

"From a professor."

"Whoever he is," Teresa said, "he should know better than to say things like that. He could get into trouble."

"You could get him into trouble by repeating what he said," Mario cautioned her.

"I didn't mention the professor's name," Adriana said as if she felt they were overreacting. "And everyone knows that the CIA was involved in overthrowing Allende and installing a military government in Chile."

"They may have been involved there," Stephen said carefully, "and they may be helping the government here."

"You can't blame him for what his government does," Teresa said, defending him.

"I wasn't blaming him. I was just asking him."

"If we do blame him," Mario told her, "we have to blame ourselves for what our government does."

"You're right," Adriana said. "But if we're not responsible for what they do, then who is?"

"We're all responsible," Stephen said, supporting her.

As they were walking home Cathy asked: "What do you think of Adriana?"

"She's bright and outspoken."

"I didn't expect her to ask you about the CIA. I didn't tell her anything. I just told her you're an American banker."

"I didn't reveal anything to her, did I?"

"No. I don't think so."

"That's what you learn growing up in Minnesota—never reveal anything. Always be deadpan."

"Deadpan?"

"It means *inexpresivo*."

"Always be deadpan," she repeated. "Would you say a person had a deadpan face?"

"You would," he said, impressed by her passion for learning.

They walked in silence for a while, and then Cathy said: "I wish Adriana was happier about being a teacher."

"She'll be a lot better off as a teacher. They have enough psychologists here. And as a teacher she can use whatever she knows about psychology."

"I told her that."

"You should tell her to be more careful about what she says. It's not enough to avoid mentioning people's names."

"I understand," Cathy said. "If they arrest you, they can make you give names."

"And tell her not to talk about the CIA. Even if she's right, it could get her into trouble."

"But she *is* right, isn't she?"

"I think she is. But I really don't know what they do here, other than collect information. I only know that they have contacts with the military."

"I wish you weren't involved with them."

"I won't be much longer," he said, having made a decision. "When we finish this project I'm not going to work with them anymore."

"You promise?"

"I promise."

On Friday after work, as they were hanging out in the café on Avenida de Mayo, he took Paco aside and told him about Vittoria. "She wants to stop wanting vengeance, and I thought you might be able to help her."

"It's very hard to stop wanting vengeance," Paco said as if he were speaking from personal experience.

Curious, Stephen asked: "How do you know?"

"I wanted vengeance. For a long time I wanted vengeance."

He waited, and then he prompted his friend to continue by asking: "What for?"

"My father was killed in the León Suárez Massacre."

"He was? He was a *peronista* leader?"

"He wasn't a leader. He was only high enough to be killed."

"How old were you at the time?

"Ten. An age when a boy needs a father."

"I'm sorry," Stephen said, laying his hand on Paco's shoulder.

"I wanted to kill the military," Paco said. "I wanted to get back at them. But luckily, when I was in high school I met a priest who helped me to stop wanting vengeance. The test was when the Montoneros killed Aramburu. I didn't feel any satisfaction. I felt only revulsion, and I thanked God for sending me that priest."

"So you could have been a Montonero."

"Oh, yes. I could have been."

"You would have had a strong reason for killing people," Stephen pointed out.

"But I wouldn't have had a *good* reason. There's no good reason for killing people."

"Not self-defense?"

"Well, that may be the only exception," Paco admitted. "You may have to kill a person who's trying to kill you. But even in that situation there might be a better way."

"You mean talking him out of it?"

"Yes. That's one way."

But it came down to drawing that line. Should you kill the person as he was about to pull the trigger? Should you kill him as he was raising his gun? Should you kill him as soon as you saw him approaching you with a gun?

"Anyway, going back to your friend—" Paco said. "I think I could help her. At least I understand her problem."

"That would be great. I think she's ready to stop wanting vengeance."

"If more people were, then we could have peace."

Two weeks passed. The government tightened its control of the press. It closed a major newspaper temporarily for breaking a censorship rule. Two reporters were abducted, their fates unknown. Elena's paper reported the discovery of six bodies and then eight more bodies, presumably the victims of right-wing death squads.

On April 22 news about terrorism, subversion, abductions, and the discovery of bodies was banned unless it was based on a public announcement by the government.

That day, during a long lunch at which they both drank too much wine, Elena vented her frustration at not being able to report the political news. She sounded despondent, though at first she didn't blame her editor for complying with the censorship policy. After all, his neck was on the line. But she was obviously disappointed by his failure to stand up to the government. That came out as they were making headway through a second bottle.

"I thought he had *cojones*," she said, disillusioned.

"You want him to be arrested?"

"No."

"And tortured?"

"No."

"Then give him a break. He's probably just waiting for the right opportunity."

"The right opportunity? When will that be? When the streets are littered with dead bodies? When the jails are overflowing with prisoners?"

"I hope it will be sooner than that."

"You hope, you hope. Stop being so hopeful."

"That's how I am."

"Well, you don't have so much at stake. You can always go back to America. But I can't go to England."

"Why not?" he asked, though he knew the answer.

"Because I'm not English. I'm Argentine. When I was in London they could tell I wasn't English."

"They could? How?"

"From my accent. No one there has an accent like ours. We talk the way people in England talked a hundred years ago."

"You mean like Dickens characters?"

"Yes. To them I sound like Little Dorrit."

"To me you don't."

"Who do I sound like?"

"You sound like yourself."

"But who I am? Elena or Helen?"

"Elena," he assured her. "I don't think of you as Helen."

"Then you're confirming what I just said. You think of me as Argentine."

He nodded. "Yes. I can't imagine you as English."

"So I have no choice. I have to stay here. I have to make sure that we don't lose our freedom of the press."

On Wednesday he was awakened in the early morning by the sound of the telephone ringing. As he dragged himself out of bed he checked his watch and saw that it was a little after three. He headed for the family room, where the phone was located, assuming it was a wrong number. His phone was listed in the name of the man who had sold the apartment to the man from whom he was renting. When apartments changed hands the phone would either leave or stay, depending on the deal. If the phone stayed, you never went to the phone company to change the listing. If you did, they would take away the phone, and you might have to wait twenty years to get another.

"*Hola?*" he mumbled.

"Stephen?" said a terrified voice.

"Yes. Teresa? What's wrong?"

"They've arrested Mario."

"What? When?"

"They took him away."

"Where are you?"

"At home."

"I'll come right over. Don't go out, and don't let anyone in. Okay?"

"Okay," she replied, sounding utterly subdued.

As he headed back into the bedroom he almost ran into Cathy, who was standing in the doorway. He told her what had happened.

"Should I go with you?"

"No. Stay here. I'm going to bring her home with me."

"You don't want her to stay in their apartment?"

"They might come back for her."

"Okay. I'll make up a bed."

He had to walk over to Santa Fe to get a taxi. He gave the driver the address in Almagro where Mario and Teresa lived. On the way he thought about how to get Mario released, and by the time he arrived he had a rough plan.

He asked the taxi driver to wait, and then he went into the apartment building. It had no security and no *portero*, so you could walk right in. He took the elevator to the fourth floor and then went down the hall looking for the number that Teresa had given him. Though he had known Mario and Teresa for almost five years, he had never been to their apartment before. It was usual for people who lived in the city not to invite friends to their homes. It was as if friends were outside the bounds of privacy that reserved the home for family.

"Who is it?" Teresa asked after he had rung the bell.

"It's me. Stephen."

As he entered the apartment she flung herself against him and sobbed: "I'm so afraid they're going to hurt him."

"They won't," he said more confidently than he felt. For a

long time he held her in silence, trying to comfort her simply by being there. Then he told her: "Pack some things. I'm going to take you home with me."

"Shouldn't I stay here?" she asked.

"No. They might come back."

"But what if they let him go? What if he comes home and doesn't find me here?"

"Leave him a note. But don't tell him where you are," he added, thinking that the police might find the note and learn where she was hiding from them. "Just tell him you're safe."

"Okay." She packed a small suitcase and then, with a trembling hand, wrote a note for Mario.

Carrying the suitcase, he led her out and down to the taxi. Before they got in he warned her: "Don't tell me anything until we get to my apartment. I don't want the driver to hear what happened."

As they rode in silence he wondered what the driver was thinking. That Teresa had left her husband in the middle of the night and was moving in with her lover? It was a plausible explanation, and it was what a New York taxi driver might have assumed since there wasn't a war going on there.

Cathy was waiting for them, and she hugged Teresa consolingly.

He carried her suitcase into the guestroom, where Cathy had already made up the bed, and then he went to the dining room, where he kept his liquor. He poured a small glass of anisette and brought it to Teresa.

"Here," he said, offering it to her.

She took it. "Thanks."

They sat down in the living room, with Cathy on the sofa next to Teresa, who started telling them what had happened.

"We were both asleep when I heard them knocking on the door. I woke Mario, and he got up and went to the door. I knew who it was. And they came barging into our apartment."

"How many were there?"

"Three," she said.

"Were they in uniforms?"

"No. They were in plain clothes."

"Did they show you any identification?"

"One of them did. It looked like a police badge. But I don't know. I never saw a police badge before."

"What did they say?"

"They said—" Her voice cracked. "They said they were arresting Mario because he was involved in subversive activities."

"Did they say anything specific about these activities?"

"No. They didn't. That's all they said, and they took him away."

"Did they tell you where they were taking him?"

"No." She started sobbing as if she could imagine what they were doing to him.

"Well, I'll find out where they took him," he said, again more confidently than he felt. "But there's nothing we can do tonight. We have to wait until morning."

"So why don't you lie down and rest for a while," Cathy suggested.

"Okay," Teresa sighed.

Cathy helped her up from the sofa and gently led her into the guestroom and stayed with her for a long time.

Returning, she said: "She's resting now."

"I'm sure she won't sleep."

"I won't either. What are you going to do?"

"I'm going to talk with everyone who might be able to help us. Elena, Carlos, the embassy guys—"

"I'm going to pray."

Elena was the first person he called. He had her home phone number, and he waited until he figured someone in her household was up. Her mother answered the phone in English and was very polite when he asked for Elena. He liked her mother, and her mother evidently liked him since she had been disappointed when her daughter's relationship with him didn't go beyond a friendship.

Elena answered in an early morning voice. When she heard what had happened she said: "Oh, God. Do you know where they took him?"

"No. I don't. I was hoping you could help me find out."

"Well, it might be in the police report."

"When would you get it?"

"Later this morning if we're lucky."

"Okay. Will you call me when you get it?"

"Yes. I will. And I'll see if we can get it sooner."

"That would be great."

"How's Teresa?"

"She's absolutely terrified."

"I don't blame her. I would be too."

"She was afraid that something would happen to him."

"But there was no reason. He's never been a Marxist or anything like it. He's more conservative than my father."

"I know. It makes no sense."

"Are they just picking people at random to set an example?"

"They could be. If you want to terrorize people, I guess it doesn't matter who you arrest as long as you pick a member of the group you want to terrorize."

"In the case of university professors it's completely unnecessary. They haven't recovered from the last time they were terrorized."

"Then maybe they won't go too far with him."

"They better not. God damn them."

Cathy called the bookstore and told the owner she couldn't go to work that day because of an emergency. She stayed with Teresa while Stephen went to work, believing he could accomplish more at the bank than at home.

When he got to the bank he went straight to the general manager's office.

"Is he alone?" he asked Señora Pérez.

"Yes, but—"

He walked right by her and into the office.

"*Che, viejo*," Carlos said, looking astonished. "How did you get by her?"

"I walked," he said.

"I should learn your technique. I can't get by her to go to the bathroom."

"*Amigo*, I need your help."

Carlos immediately became serious. "What is it?"

He told Carlos what had happened.

"So he's a professor at the university. In what school? Maybe I know him."

"The School of Law and Social Sciences. He teaches political science. His name is Mario Gaetano."

"Gaetano? I don't know him," Carlos said. "But I think I read a paper he wrote."

"The one about creating a democracy in Argentina?"

"Yes. That was it. The paper had some perceptive insights about the formidable obstacles we face in trying to create and sustain a democracy in this country. But there wasn't anything subversive about it."

"He's not a Marxist."

"Then why did they arrest him?"

"I don't know. Maybe it was time to arrest a professor."

"You mean to keep the others in line?"

"That's the only explanation I can think of."

"And he's a good friend of yours?"

"Yes. He's a very good friend. If it will help," Stephen suggested, "I can swear to them that he's not a Marxist."

"Well, you might have some influence. Your government's supporting them."

"It's not supporting this kind of thing."

"It's supporting the goal of the *junta*—to win the war against terrorism."

"But not by any means," he objected strongly.

"No. Not by any means," Carlos agreed. "And personally, I've never liked these interventions in the university. We're not China, for heaven's sake."

"So will you call your friend?"

"Colonel Méndez? Of course I will. Do you know where they took him?"

"No. I don't. I'm trying to find out."

"Well, I'll have a better chance with Méndez if I can tell him where your friend is. It'll complicate things if Méndez has to go looking for him."

"Okay. I'll get back to you."

He went up to the third floor, where he found a number of phone messages. None was from Elena, so he ignored them.

As he was sitting down the newest account manager, whose name was Lucio, made a beeline for him, looking for help with a deal that he was trying to put together. Stephen asked him to go back to his desk and wait while he attended to something urgent. As he watched the young man slink across the floor he felt bad for having implied that Lucio's deal wasn't urgent.

He called the embassy and got John, whom he asked to come and meet with him as soon as possible. John said he would be there by eleven.

Then he walked over to Lucio's desk and sat down with him. For the moment there was nothing more he could do for Mario, and it made him feel a little better to be helping someone in a situation where his knowledge and experience could be brought to bear on the problem. He showed Lucio how to structure the loan and how to minimize the bank's risk. By the time he had finished, Elena called him.

"I got the report," she said. "And Mario's in it."

"Does it say where they took him?"

"Yes." She told him.

"Good. I have some other things in motion, but I couldn't get anywhere without knowing where they took him."

"I don't want to be overly hopeful, but it's a good sign that he's in the report. In many cases the people who go missing aren't in a report. They just disappear, and they're never seen or heard of again."

"I know," he said.

"Well, good luck. Is there anything more I can do to help?"

"I don't think so, but if there is I'll let you know. You've given me the most valuable information. How did you get the report so soon?"

"I went to the police and demanded it."

"You did? You're crazy."

"I pretended I was English, and they believed it."

"They can't be that gullible."

"They are," she said. "They believe their own bullshit."

"I'll let you know what happens. And thanks for your help."

"*De nada*," she said emphatically.

When he had hung up he called Carlos. He got through Señora Pérez and told Carlos where they had taken Mario, and Carlos said he would call the colonel right away.

Stephen then called home and got Cathy. "How's she doing?"

"Not well. She's imagining what they might do to him."

"Well, I found out where he is. Elena got the information."

"I'll put her on the line so you can tell her directly. But before I do, she wants to go to Quilmes and see his parents."

"I wonder if that's a good idea."

"I wondered too."

"It'll make them worry."

"I know. But she says that if she doesn't tell them, they'll never forgive her."

"All right. At least it'll give her something to do."

"I just don't know how we'll get there."

"I'll see if the bank car's available. Just a second." He put her on hold and called Señora Pérez, who told him the car was available and asked why he wanted to use it. He told her it was for a client. Back on the line with Cathy, he said: "I'll have the driver pick you up in twenty minutes."

"Okay. I'll put her on the line now."

"We know where he is," he told Teresa.

"Is he all right?"

"I think so."

"Can we go and see him?"

"I'm trying to get him released," he said, "so I think it would be better to wait."

"All right. But I'm going crazy."

"Try to hang on for a little longer. I understand you want to go and see his parents."

"I don't want to. I have to."

"I've arranged for our car to take you there. By the time you get back I should have more information."

"*Gracias*. I don't know what I would have done without you."

A half hour later John and Bill appeared at the reception desk. For once they weren't carrying their satchels.

In the conference room he told them what had happened.

"Are you sure this guy didn't do anything?" John asked skeptically.

"I'm absolutely sure he didn't."

"Would you put your hand in the fire for him?"

"I would. He's innocent."

"No one's innocent," Bill said.

"Well, he's not guilty of subversive activities."

"How can you be so sure?" John asked.

"I know him," Stephen said. "I know his wife. I've known them both for five years."

"But maybe you don't know him well enough."

"Stop screwing around. I need your help."

"Okay," John said. "You've helped us. We owe you."

"So tell us what we can do," Bill said.

"You have contacts with the military, right?"

"We do," John said. "But we don't like to talk about them."

"I don't want to talk about them. I want to use them."

"You mean to get your friend released?"

"It's not a lot to ask."

"No. Unless he's done something."

"He hasn't. Believe me."

"Well, let me think about the best way."

"The best way is to put you together with the area chief," Bill said after a moment. "That's the man in charge of the task group that abducted him."

"He's right," John said. "You're this guy's friend, so you have a good reason to petition them. And you're an American, so you have some influence."

"The ambassador would have more influence."

"He would. But let's save him until we need him."

"We'll pave the way for you," Bill said. "By the time you see him, the area chief will have already decided in your favor."

"Okay. I'll try it. But if it doesn't work—"

"If it doesn't work, we'll escalate."

Around five he got a phone call from the office of a police commissioner. He was told that he had an appointment at six.

He took a taxi to the address they gave him. It was a dilapidated public building that until now he would have passed without noticing. Some men in plain clothes were standing around in front of it, talking.

Inside, he was led by a uniformed man to a door at the end of a long corridor.

"Come in," said a voice behind the door.

His guide opened the door for him and then left him.

A man in plain clothes got up from a desk and greeted him, extending a hand. His hair was neatly combed and his mustache was neatly trimmed. His suit looked freshly pressed, and his shirt looked freshly starched.

"Please sit down," the man said smoothly, indicating a chair in front of the desk.

Stephen sat down, on the alert.

"You're an American," the commissioner said but not as Adriana had said it. His tone implied that being an American was something to be proud of.

"That's right," Stephen said as neutrally as possible.

"What are you doing in Argentina?"

"I work for a bank here." He was sure that the commissioner already knew this and probably knew a lot more about him, but he played the game and named the bank. "We finance trade and provide loans to businesses."

"How are they doing?"

"The businesses? They're struggling."

"Well, we're going to reform the economy. We're going to apply ideas from your country."

"So I understand."

"How long have you been here?"

"About five years."

"Do you like it here?"

"Yes. Very much."

"Are you planning to stay?"

"I'm not planning to leave," he replied.

The commissioner smiled. "Where did you learn Spanish?"

"In the army," he said, stretching the point.

"You were in the army? How long?"

"Three years."

"Were you in Vietnam?"

"Yes."

"Then you know about terrorists."

"Yes. I do. And I have two personal reasons for wanting to stop the Montoneros."

"You do? What are they?"

"They killed my assistant at the bank, and they killed a good friend of mine."

"So you support us."

"I support what you're doing directly to stop them. But I don't support your going after innocent people."

"Ah, yes. The professor," the commissioner said as if he had forgotten about him. "Why are you so interested in him?"

"Because he's a friend."

"A good friend?"

"A very good friend."

"How well do you know him?"

"Very well."

"Then you know his political views?"

"Yes. And I know he's not a Marxist or anything like it."

"You do? Hmm." The commissioner studied him for a while, and then he asked: "Do you believe in God?"

"Yes."

"Are you willing to swear to God that you've never heard your friend express a subversive idea?"

Raising his hand, he played the game. "I swear to God that I've never heard Mario Gaetano express a subversive idea."

"All right. We'll release him. You can wait outside, and he'll be with you in a few minutes."

"*Muchas gracias*," Stephen said, getting up.

"*De nada*. We're glad that America supports us."

Outside, he paced the sidewalk, trying to understand what had happened. He was sure that the decision to release Mario had been made before he got there, and that it had not been influenced by anything he had said. But he didn't know whether it had been influenced by the contacts of the embassy guys or by the colonel that Carlos knew. They might have planned from the very beginning to release Mario after holding him a while as a warning to faculty at the university.

When Mario emerged from the building and saw Stephen he stumbled toward him. Though unshaven and bleary-eyed, he looked deliriously happy. "My friend, I don't have words to thank you."

"Don't try. Are you all right?"

"Yes. I'm fine."

They exchanged a long, deep *abrazo*.

They were at his apartment when Cathy and Teresa returned from Quilmes.

Teresa examined Mario closely to make sure that he was all right before she threw her arms around him and cried.

Mario held her, patting her back and saying: "It's all right."

"I was so worried," Teresa sobbed. "I kept imagining what they might do to you."

"They didn't do anything. They didn't touch me."

"It's a miracle," she said.

"Let's go home. You probably didn't get much sleep."

"You probably didn't either."

"No. I didn't."

"You have to call your parents first. Oh, now I wish I hadn't told them."

"It's all right. They didn't have to worry long."

While he called his parents Teresa went and packed her bag.

At the entrance of the building Stephen asked the *portero* to get a taxi.

"Where are they going?" the *portero* asked as if that made any difference.

"Almagro," he said.

When they had left, Cathy murmured: "Poor Teresa."

"That was awful," he agreed.

With wonder she looked into his eyes. "You sounded so confident talking with her, as if you knew that everything would be all right."

"I wasn't confident. I was hoping and praying."

"I was too." She reached for his hand and held it tightly. "You were there for them. But who would I turn to if anything happened to you?"

"Nothing's going to happen to me," he assured her.

EIGHT

ON FRIDAY, April 30, more of the unrecorded loans arranged by Arias came due. Seven of them had been made by the companies of which Navarra was an owner of record. At the current exchange rate the total value of these loans was almost one million eight hundred thousand dollars. That total, added to the amount that Navarra had reinvested on March 31, came to about three million five hundred thousand dollars. If you added to that the value of the remaining loans that were due on May 31, the amount of Montonero money invested in pesos was slightly more than five million dollars.

Since the loans were always for ninety days, the first batch of loans that Stephen had arranged would come due on June 30, and if he could keep getting Navarra to reinvest the pesos as the loans came due, then the Montoneros wouldn't have access to any of this money until then. And meanwhile he would keep trying to get the evidence he needed to freeze their dollar account in New York.

Navarra arrived punctually, and after the formalities they went into the conference room.

"If you can get me another good rate," Navarra said, sitting down at the table, "I'll reinvest this money."

"I can get you fifty-nine percent."

"That's better than the last rate. What's happening in the market?"

"There's more demand, and there's less supply."

"You sound like an economist."

"I'm not, but I can talk like one."

Navarra smiled appreciatively. "You're a smart young man. What are you doing working in a bank?"

"I like it," Stephen said.

"What do you like about it?"

"I like putting deals together."

"I'll bet you're good at it."

"I try to do a good job."

"Are you from New York?"

"No, but I've lived there."

"You talk like you're from New York."

"New Yorkers say I talk like a farmer from the Midwest."

"Midwest? Is that near Chicago?"

"Yes. Chicago's the capital of the Midwest."

"That's where all the gangsters were."

"Not all of them, but Chicago had its share of them."

"We don't have gangsters like that here. I mean guys in hats and striped suits running around with machine guns."

"No. But you have guys without hats running around with machine guns."

"You mean the terrorists? Well, they're not typical. They're crazy," Navarra said, shaking his head disapprovingly. "But don't worry. The military will get rid of them."

"It looks like they will."

Stephen had the forms ready, so he placed them in front of Navarra, who signed them after a cursory examination. It was clear that Navarra trusted him. In the words of the profession, they seemed to have developed a banking relationship.

"All right," Navarra said, putting away his pen as if he had done a good day's work. He looked at Stephen appraisingly. "Do you mind if I ask you a question?"

"No. Not at all."

"Do they pay you well?"

"Yes, well enough."

"But not enough to make you rich."

"Not in my present position."

"Would you like to make some money?"

"It depends," Stephen said noncommittally.

"It always depends," Navarra said. "But this would be legal and above board."

"Then I might be interested."

"All right. I need to think about it, and I need to check with someone, but if he agrees I'll get back to you."

"Okay," Stephen said, hoping that the proposition might lead him to Safadi.

He had lunch that day with Boyd at La Estancia.

"So how's your love life?" Boyd asked as they waited for their food to arrive.

"Fine," he said without offering any details.

"Are you still living with that girl you met at Minas?"

"You mean Cathy? Yes."

"Are you happy with her?"

"Very happy."

"I wish I could meet someone like her."

"You might not be happy with someone like her."

"You have a point," Boyd allowed. "In fact, I can't imagine the kind of woman I would be happy with. They all have their problems. But forgetting my love life, I'm happy with this government. They're really kicking ass, and they're wiping out the Montoneros."

"They're also killing innocent people."

"Collateral damage. You can't avoid it. You know that from Vietnam. You couldn't tell who the enemy was. It could be a little old lady with a plastic bomb in her trousers, or a kid with a hand grenade under his hat."

Involuntarily, Stephen recalled a scene of carnage caused by a waif begging for candy.

"It's the same here," Boyd said. "If you want to wipe out the Montoneros, you have to wipe out their supply base and the people who support them."

"But the military are arresting professors and journalists. *They* aren't supporting the Montoneros."

"They're not supporting the military."

"So if you're not for the military, then you're against them?"

"That's how it is in these situations. You need to win the hearts and minds."

"And you do that by terrorizing people?"

"It's the only way."

"There must be a better way."

"There isn't. If they'd had a government like this in South Vietnam, they could have wiped out the communists."

"That was the problem. They had a government like this."

"Naw. It wasn't like this. Compared with these guys, those guys were pussies."

"Well, I won't argue on that point."

"These guys are tough. And they know what they're doing. When they took over they had a plan and they hit the ground running."

"I won't argue on that either."

"So what don't you like about them?"

"I don't like—" He tried to find the right word. "I don't like their fanaticism."

"What do you mean?"

"They believe that they have all the answers, and that their way is the only way."

"What other way is there to end this fucking war?"

He was sure that Boyd would only laugh at Paco's way, so he didn't suggest it. He only said: "I don't know."

"They tried politics. They even let Perón come back, and look what happened. The terrorists had a field day."

"Some people believe the military knew what would happen when Perón came back and they let it happen just to end the myth about him."

"A conspiracy theory. Do you believe it?"

"I don't think they're that cynical. If they were, they wouldn't be so fanatical."

"You mean they're idealists."

"Yeah. I think so."

"Well, I think they're pragmatists. They have a job to do, and they're doing it."

Their main course arrived, and at least for a while it took precedence.

On Friday at the café on Avenida de Mayo they celebrated the release of Mario, starting with a prayer of thanks by Paco.

"Thanks to Stephen," Mario said, raising his glass.

"I don't deserve the credit. Elena does. She found out where they were holding you, and I just went there."

"You didn't just go there."

"Well, I met with the commissioner, but that was a game. They'd already decided to release you."

"What made them decide that?" Sofi asked.

"I don't know. I think it was all planned in advance."

"You mean they arrested Mario *knowing* they were going to release him?"

"That's what I think."

"Why would they do that?"

"To scare the faculty at the university."

"It worked on me," Mario said, trying to make light of it.

"They won't bother you again," Elena said.

"They've made their point," Stephen agreed. He glanced at

Teresa to see if she was buying this. "And they had no reason to arrest him. Mario's not a Marxist."

"None of us are," Sofi said.

"Does that make us safe?" Teresa asked.

"It makes us safer than Marxists," Elena assured her.

"But how do they know we're not Marxists?"

"We don't have long hair or beards."

"Except for Paco," Sofi qualified.

"And we're not carrying cards," Stephen added.

"What kind of card would we be carrying?" Teresa asked.

"A Communist Party membership card."

"In America, during the McCarthy witch hunts," Mario explained, "they went after people who were members of the Communist Party."

"When did that happen?" Sofi asked.

"During the Fifties," Stephen said. "But there were witch hunts earlier in Salem. That's what the expression refers to."

"What happened in Salem?"

"They arrested women that people accused of being witches. They tortured them and made them confess. And then they killed them."

"Like they're doing here."

"Yes, I'm ashamed to say."

"So we're not unique," Elena said.

"It happens everywhere," Paco said.

"But why does it happen?" Sofi asked.

"It happens because people are afraid," Paco said.

"Afraid of witches, afraid of communists," Mario said.

"And afraid of Montoneros," Stephen said.

"Well, I'm not afraid of them," Sofi said. "And I don't want them to be killed. I only want them to stop killing."

Teresa, who had dropped out of the conversation, peeped around as if she were deathly afraid that someone was watching, listening, and recording every word they said for use in a future action against them.

On Saturday the bank car picked them up at his apartment and drove them to Vittoria's house in Belgrano, where the two older girls were waiting for them, dressed up and ready to go. He introduced Cathy to Vittoria, and they talked for a while. Then they headed back into the city.

The girls were excited, never having been to a circus before. Olivia showed it more than Claudia, who seemed to have already donned the mantle of responsibility that often fell upon the oldest child in a family. She had her mother's gravity while Olivia seemed carefree and open to enjoyment. Claudia was dressed simply, without accessories, while Olivia had a pocketbook that matched her shoes. In the car they sat between Cathy and Stephen, with Olivia next to Cathy and Claudia next to him, and from then on each girl was attached to them accordingly.

At one point as they rolled down Libertador the younger girl whispered something to Cathy, who whispered something back. He later learned that Olivia had asked who the other man in the front seat was, and Cathy had replied that he was a friend of the driver, not wanting to say that he was a bodyguard.

When they got out at Luna Park she took Olivia by the hand and he took Claudia. They were soon caught up in the throng of people, all trying to enter the building at the same time. In the midst of them, like stationary pilings, men were hawking balloons and candy and souvenirs, including glossy programs. Yielding to Olivia, they stopped to buy balloons while the crowd flowed like an incoming tide around them. Cathy knelt down to tie the string of the balloon around Olivia's wrist, using a knot that wouldn't allow the loop to tighten, and he did the same for Claudia.

As they followed the crowd toward the entrance he asked: "Where did you learn to tie a bowline?"

"What's a bowline?"

"The knot you used to tie the balloon."

"Oh, that's what we used to tie up chickens. You need a loop that doesn't tighten, otherwise—" She stopped there, conscious of the girls.

They found their seats, which were in the front row. There were clowns walking around the ring, stopping to perform tricks in front of a section of the audience and then moving on to the next section. Olivia began tracking a clown who was advancing toward them while Claudia kept looking up at her balloon to make sure it was all right.

When the clown stopped in front of them he bowed to the girls, removing his hat and letting a bird fly out. Olivia squealed with delight, and even Claudia was agape while the clown felt the top of his head as if he were trying to find the bird.

"It's there!" Olivia told him, pointing.

The clown looked up, following the direction of her finger, and he saw the bird perched on a wire. He made a gesture, indicating that he must be the dumbest person in the world, and then from nowhere he pulled out a mallet and conked his head as if to punish himself for being so careless. From the spot where he had struck himself a red balloon began to inflate. By then the girls and the people in the section behind them were laughing their heads off.

After the clown came a man dressed like a tramp, selling pink cotton candy. Stephen bought one for each girl, and he noticed the different ways they ate it. Olivia plunged right in and ended up with cotton stuck to her nose and chin while Claudia took careful little bites, as a cat might have done. But they both enjoyed it.

The circus was good from the animal acts to the high-wire performances. When it was over the girls had a hard time saying what they liked best about it, though Claudia leaned toward the animals and Olivia toward the ballerinas on the high wire. They still had their balloons, which joined them in the car, and Olivia still had a little patch of cotton candy on her chin, which Cathy removed with a tissue as the car pulled away from Luna Park. Before they were halfway home Olivia was asleep, curled up against Cathy, while Claudia watched over the balloons.

As they were lying in bed that night Cathy said: "You know, you're very good with those girls. They adore you."

"They'd adore any man old enough to be their father."

"No. It's more than that."

"Well, they've known me a long time. They feel comfortable with me. But they were also comfortable with you, and they just met you."

"I have a lot of experience with children."

"I could see that. You knew exactly what to do with them."

After a pause she said: "I think Claudia has been more affected by what happened to her father."

"I do too. She was four when it happened while Olivia wasn't quite three."

"I don't remember much from being three."

"I don't either. The only thing I remember is moving into the house where I grew up. I was in the dining room, and the movers were bringing in the table. I don't know why I remember that."

"You love to eat. Maybe that's why."

He laughed. "Maybe."

"But even if she didn't remember what had happened, I think Claudia would have been more affected."

"You mean because of the way she is."

"Yes. She's *muy responsable.*"

"From my experience," Stephen said, "there's one child in every family who feels somehow designated to be responsible for the others."

"Designated?"

"Maybe that's not the right word."

"Well, I know what you mean. For sure I'm the one in my family, and you must be the one in your family."

"I am." He had told her enough about his family so that he didn't have to point out that he had been designated even though he wasn't the oldest.

They were silent for a while, and then Cathy said: "I would like to have three children."

"Why three?"

"It feels like the right number."

"Then we'll have three."

"I love you," she said, rolling toward him.

"I love you too," he said, kissing her forehead and inhaling the smell of bath soap.

The next morning he awoke with the vague feeling of dread that came from an unremembered nightmare. In church during the penitential rite he identified the source of his affliction, which must have been aroused by their talk about having children. When he knelt down after communion he prayed for absolution, but the feeling didn't go away. After not bothering him for a long time, it had come back to haunt him.

On the way to the *confitería* where they planned to have lunch he wondered if he should tell Cathy about it. From the moment when he revealed to her his involvement with the embassy guys, he had shared everything with her since they agreed that neither of them would hold back anything from the other. Not holding back was the foundation of their mutual trust. But this was different. This was a part of his life that he was reluctant to share with her, if only because it caused him pain, and Stephen had been raised to believe that pain was something you should keep to yourself.

"What's the matter?" Cathy asked.

"Oh, nothing," he murmured.

She stopped. "I can tell something's bothering you. I could tell from the moment we got up this morning. What is it?"

"It has nothing to do with us," he told her.

"We went through this before," she reminded him. "If it affects you, it affects me."

"Well, it's something that happened a while ago."

"When you were married."

"How did you guess?"

"It's the only thing you told me about that hurt you. And I can tell that whatever this is, it's hurting you."

They resumed walking. "Okay. I'll tell you about it. But let's go to the plaza and find a place where we can sit down."

"Okay," she said.

When they got to the corner, instead of heading for the *confitería* they went the other way toward Plaza San Martín.

They sat on the steps at the base of the statue of the Liberator. The plaza was deserted except for a photographer who gestured to them offering to take their picture. Even the pigeons were somewhere else.

"I told you that Leila was an anthropologist," he began, staring off into the trees. "Well, we took a trip together north, up to Salta—"

They spent a week there, and then he came back to Buenos Aires because he didn't have any more vacation. She kept going, up to Bolivia and into Peru, where she stayed for three months. When she finally came back she made an appointment to see a doctor. She told him she was afraid that she had caught a tropical disease. The doctor did some tests, and they had to wait a few days to get the results. After hearing them in a phone call from the doctor's office she slammed down the receiver and then, with a curse, she hurled the phone across the room.

She told him the results were positive, and it took him a while to pry out of her that she didn't have a tropical disease. She was pregnant, and it wasn't his baby.

Without any discussion she asked him to help her find a doctor who would give her an abortion. It wasn't legal, but there were doctors—good doctors—willing to do the operation under certain circumstances.

He insisted that they talk about it. He said he didn't want her to have an abortion because of him. She said it wasn't because of him, it was because of her. She didn't want to be saddled with a baby. She had her whole life ahead of her, she had her career, and she couldn't live in the jungle with a baby.

He said he would help her raise it. She said he would hate the baby because it wasn't his. He admitted that it would be difficult, but he believed that he could handle it. She said he couldn't, he was just like any other male, who in a natural state would kill a baby if it wasn't his.

They talked back and forth for a long time. His last argument was that it would be wrong to have an abortion, and her response was don't give me that Catholic bullshit, it's my body, and I have a right to do what I want with it.

So he helped her find a doctor, who questioned them thoroughly about their decision. The doctor evidently assumed that the baby was his, and that their reason for having an abortion was that they just weren't ready to start a family. The doctor argued strongly against it, on several grounds, but he finally agreed to do it.

When Stephen brought her home after the procedure she went into the guestroom and stayed there for days. He could hear her wailing in utter misery, but when he went into the room to try to comfort her she cursed him and blamed him for the abortion. She accused him of killing her baby.

"My God," Cathy said, putting her hand on his shoulder.

"You understand why I didn't want to tell you that."

"Oh, yes. But it's good that you did."

"I don't know," he said, still having doubts.

"You must know," she said, "that you're not the one who killed her baby."

"Yeah. I know. And I don't think about it as much as I used to. But when I do I feel like hell."

"I don't ever want to meet that woman, because if I did I would want to kill her."

"Don't worry. You'll never meet her. She lives in Brazil, and most of the time she's in the jungle."

"The selfish bitch. She should have had the baby and taken it with her. She could have lived in the jungle with it. The women she studies live in the jungle with their babies. Who on earth does she think she is?"

He didn't comment, but he was gratified by her reaction. And he felt better.

On Tuesday evening, as they were waiting for Cathy and Teresa at the *confitería* near the university, Mario said: "Teresa wants us to leave the country."

"She's afraid they'll arrest you again?"

"Yes. I tell her they have no reason to arrest me, but she says they had no reason before and they still did it."

"But they didn't hurt you, and they released you."

"I tell her that, but she thinks it was a miracle, and she believes that you don't get more than one miracle in a lifetime."

"It wasn't a miracle. It was planned."

"I agree. They were only trying to scare us. And they succeeded," Mario added. "At least with her."

"You're not afraid?"

"I am afraid, but not enough to leave my country."

"You mean you're more afraid of leaving than you are of staying?"

"That's right. I don't know what would happen to us. She says we could go to Mexico, or France, or even America. But we don't know anyone in those countries, and we don't have family anywhere but here."

"So isn't she afraid of leaving?"

"She is, but she's more afraid of staying."

Stephen nodded, seeing a conflict that would be hard to resolve.

"If her parents were alive, it would be different. But they're both dead, so she has no family ties to this country."

"She has a brother, doesn't she?"

"Yes. But they don't have much of a relationship."

"Well, she must understand," Stephen said, "that if you leave you'll have problems."

"I tell her that. I tell her we'd have problems in France and America because we don't speak the language, and I remind her that in Mexico not long ago the government killed three hundred students who were demonstrating."

He remembered the event—the Tlatelolco Massacre.

"But that doesn't bother her. She says it happened eight years ago, and they have a different government now."

"The same party is still in power."

"I tell her that," Mario said. "And I ask her how she thinks we'll make a living."

"Presumably, you could both teach in Mexico."

"We could. But we'd both have to start over. And there's no guarantee that we could get jobs."

"It might be useful to contact people who went to Mexico the last time there was a military government. They could tell you about their experience."

"That's a good idea. I don't know how to contact them, but one of my colleagues might know."

"Their testimony could help you make a decision."

"You mean to stay."

"To stay or to leave. I mean, it could make her more afraid of leaving, or it could make you less afraid."

At that moment Teresa arrived.

"Yes, we were talking about you," Mario said before she could say it. "Sit down and listen. Our friend, Esteban, has an idea. I told him what we've been discussing."

Teresa sat down and looked at him doubtfully.

"If you're thinking of going to Mexico," Stephen said, "you should find out what it was like for Argentines who went there in exile the last time."

"How would we do that?"

"Mario could contact them."

"And how long would that take?"

"I don't know. A few weeks, a month—"

"That's too long. I don't want to stay here that long."

"But it'll take time for you to get visas."

"We don't need visas. We can just fly there."

"We can't just fly there," Mario said. "They won't let us in."

"They will if we're political refugees."

"But what if they don't let us in? What if they send us back here? We'll really be in trouble then."

"He's right," Stephen told her. "They'll think you have a reason to leave."

"Well, we do have a reason. They arrested Mario."

"They had no particular reason to arrest him. But if you try to escape to Mexico and they send you back here, you'll give them a reason to arrest him."

"Like those people who escaped from Cuba to America and were sent back," Mario argued. "How do you think Castro treated them?"

Teresa was silent, and then she said: "I hear that people are being given refuge in embassies. We could go to the Mexican

Embassy and ask for refuge while they're processing our visas."

"Yes, we could do that. But what if we didn't get visas?"

"I guess they would make us leave the embassy."

"And then we would be in trouble the same as if they sent us back from Mexico."

Teresa glowered. "So you're telling me we have to wait until we either get visas or don't get them?"

"That's right," Stephen said. "If you get visas then you can leave, but meanwhile you can find out what it was like for Argentines who went to Mexico the last time, and based on that you can make a decision."

"I already know what it's going to be. There's nothing that could have happened to them in Mexico that's as bad as what could happen to Mario here."

"Well, you still have to wait to get visas."

"I guess we do," Teresa sighed.

Cathy arrived with Adriana, and they talked about their classes, but it wasn't long before Adriana got into politics. Her target now was the government's economic policy, which she said was transferring wealth from the poor to the rich.

"We have to leave," Teresa said abruptly.

Mario looked puzzled. "We do?"

"Yes. *Buenas noches.*" Teresa got up from the table and headed for the door.

With a helpless gesture Mario got up and followed her.

"What was that about?" Adriana asked.

"It was about Mario being arrested last week," Stephen said.

"Cathy told me about that."

"Then why were you talking like a socialist?"

"I wasn't talking like a socialist. I was only saying—"

"You were saying that the government's economic policy is transferring wealth from the poor to the rich."

"Well, it is."

"I know. But you shouldn't say things like that in public. You could get into trouble. And you scared the shit out of Teresa."

"I didn't mean to. Why would that have scared her?"

"If the wrong people heard it they might assume that Mario hangs out with socialists."

"That's paranoid."

"You can't blame her," Cathy said. "They put her through hell. For her it was as if they had tortured her."

"She imagined what they were doing to Mario," Stephen said.

"I'm sorry," Adriana said contritely.

As they were walking home he said: "I hope I wasn't too hard on Adriana."

"I don't think you were."

"She shouldn't have talked about politics. I mean even if Teresa hadn't been there."

"I guess she felt it was safe with us."

"But someone could have overheard her."

"I'll tell her again to be more careful about what she says."

"Well, I really don't believe that anyone was listening," he said, relenting. "If I did, I wouldn't have had the conversation I had with Mario and Teresa."

"What did you talk about?"

He told her.

"I think you gave them good advice," Cathy said. "I know what it's like to leave your country as a refugee."

"It must have been hard for you."

"It was hard to leave my mother and my brothers and sisters, knowing I would never see them again."

"I can't imagine what that would be like."

"But I had someone who helped me. Mario and Teresa will have to do everything themselves."

"I'll help them if I can."

"You've already helped them a lot."

"I'm only doing what I learned from my father," Stephen said. "To step up to the plate."

"Step up to the plate?"

"It's a baseball expression. It means that if you see a need, you try to meet it."

"But you can't meet every need you see."

"I know I can't, but I can try."

They walked for a while in silence, and then she asked: "Have you always tried to help people?"

He thought about it. "I guess I have, at least since I knew how to do anything. I knew how to read before I started school —my father taught me, reading the comics in the newspaper— and my first grade teacher asked me to try to help three kids who were having problems learning to read. We had these little chairs made of oak, and during the reading period we carried them down to the milk room—"

"The milk room?"

"Yeah. The room where they kept the milk we drank at recess. So we all sat around in our little chairs, and I tried to help them learn to read."

"You should be a teacher."

"I probably will be in my next career."

"Then we could both teach in the school that Paco's going to build." She said this as if it were more than just a dream.

"Well, I don't know how good I'd be with kids that age."

"Why wouldn't you be good with them? That's the age of your first students."

"You're assuming that the kids I taught in the milk room learned to read."

"I know they did."

The next day he got a call from Sofi, who told him that the cooperative's truck had been burned during the night. She urged him to come out to the *villa* right away and talk with Jorge, who was having trouble controlling the storeowners.

He called Señora Pérez and got the bank car, which drove him to the *villa* in less than a half hour. The driver knew the way, but he couldn't understand why Señor Wyatt would want to go there, and more than once he asked: "Are you sure you want to go there? Are you sure you have the right address?"

He found Jorge with a group of men in front of his store. They looked as if they had already degenerated into a mob. They all had clubs or guns, which they looked ready to use.

"Let him through," Jorge told them.

Standing in front of them, Stephen asked: "What happened?"

"They burned our truck, the sons of bitches," a big man with a gun snarled.

"Do you know who did it?"

"Yeah. We know. It was the people who used to sell us potatoes."

He turned to Jorge. "The middlemen that we cut out?"

"It looks that way," Jorge said.

"Do you have evidence?"

"My brother saw them," said a short man with a club. "He recognized them."

"Could he positively identify them?"

"You mean to the police?" the big man asked.

"Forget the police," the short man said. "They won't do anything."

"They work for the rich. They work for the people who burned our truck."

"We'll handle it ourselves."

"So what are you going to do?" Stephen asked them.

"We're going to kill the sons of bitches."

"What will that accomplish?"

"It'll stop them from fucking around with us."

"What will happen if the police catch you?"

"They won't catch us," the big man said.

"How do you know they won't catch you? You caught the people who burned your truck."

"There won't be anyone left to identify us."

"You'll kill them all?"

"We'll kill them all."

"Men, women, and children?"

"We'll kill the men. We won't hurt the women and children."

"What if a woman sees you do it?"

"We'll kill her."

"What if a group of children sees you?"

"They won't see us."

"How do you know?"

There was a long silence, and then Jorge said: "We really don't want to kill anyone. We just want to have our truck back."

"Well, killing people won't bring your truck back."

The men muttered in frustration.

"Look, *amigos*," Stephen said. "It's only a truck. You have insurance on it. You can replace it. But if you go and kill people, you can't replace them."

"Yeah. We know," the big man said.

"So why are you standing around like this?"

"We had to do something," the short man said.

"Let Jorge take care of it. He's your leader. He'll get you another truck."

"But what's to stop them from burning that truck?"

"He'll get you someone to guard the truck."

"Why didn't we do that to start with?"

"I didn't think of it," Stephen admitted.

"You should have thought of it," the big man said with tension-breaking humor. "You dumb *gringo*."

They all laughed.

The next day Elena's newspaper defied the censorship policy by reporting on the front page the disappearance of Haroldo Conti, a left-wing novelist.

When Stephen saw the story he called Elena, and they met for lunch at an obscure restaurant on 25 de Mayo, where only the waiters would recognize them.

"Do you feel better?" he asked her, assuming she did. He could see the elation in her clear blue eyes.

"Much better. And now I understand what he was doing." She was referring to the editor, who had fallen from grace in her eyes two weeks ago.

"What was he doing?"

"He was waiting for the right opportunity. A big story, a story that would get the attention of the international press."

"Well, this should do it."

"Yes. They're carrying the story on all the wire services."

"How has the government reacted?"

"They're not pleased," she said with English understatement. "But they haven't done anything to us yet."

"Do you think they'll close your paper?"

"They might. But if they did, it would be a big story."

"Because you're an English-language paper?"

"That helps. But also because we're owned by an American company."

"I didn't know that. I thought you were owned by Anglos."

"We were, but they sold the paper several years ago."

"Well, that could make a difference."

"It could stop them from closing us," Elena said, "but it won't necessarily stop them from harassing people who work for the paper."

"You mean they figure that as long as they don't hurt the paper economically, they can hurt its people?"

"Exactly. So he stuck out his neck."

"What about *your* neck?"

Raising her chin, she felt her neck. "I think it's too fat."

"You're wrong. It's perfect."

"You're being gallant."

"I'm stating a fact."

"Are you trying to be like that detective in the American television series who always said just give me the facts?"

"The facts, ma'am. Nothing but the facts."

"Was he your role model?" she asked teasingly.

"Yeah. I always wanted to be like him."

"But you're not, are you."

He shrugged. "I guess not. But we were talking about your neck. Could they harass you?"

"You mean to hurt the editor?"

"Yes. I mean, I'm not saying that it wouldn't hurt the paper economically. "

"It would ruin the paper. What would they do without me?"

"You still haven't answered my question."

"That's because I don't know the answer. Yes, they could harass me. And yes, it would hurt the editor because he cares about me. But he cares about all the employees, and he cares about his family."

"Then I hope he knows what he's doing."

"He does. I have faith in him."

He had an appointment at noon the next day with John and Bill, who needed cash for their operations. From the conference room he called the head trader and ordered the amount of Uruguayan pesos they had requested, figuring that they were going to use this money to buy information about the Tupamaros, an urban guerilla movement that was operating across the Rio de la Plata.

While they were waiting for the money Stephen told the embassy guys about his meeting earlier that week with Navarra, concluding: "So he's reinvested the money from all the loans that have come due so far. The last loans come due on May 31, and if he reinvests that money, it'll all be tied up."

"It'll only be tied up," John said, "until the first loans that you rolled over come due."

"Well, that won't happen until June 30."

"Okay. They won't have access to the pesos until June 30, but in the meantime they still have access to the dollars. So we need to focus on the dollars."

"We need to tie Safadi to Navarra." Bill said.

"We may be able to do that," Stephen told them. "Navarra said he might have a proposition for me."

"What kind of proposition?" John asked.

"He asked me if I'd like to make some money."

"Did he say how?"

"He just said it was legal and above board."

"Then it must be a new kind of business for him," Bill said.

"Maybe he wants to buy a banker," John said.

"He already has a banker," Bill said.

"He said he had to check with someone," Stephen said, "and he'd get back to me."

"And you think this person is Safadi," John said.

"Who else could it be?"

"Well, let's assume it is Safadi," Bill said.

"If it is," Stephen said, "then we can tie him to Navarra, which would tie him to the money laundering."

"It would tie him to both operations," John agreed.

"And that would be enough," Bill said, "for the New York banking authorities to intervene."

They were silent for a while, sensing that their goal might finally be within reach.

"You know what?" John said. "I think they wanted Arias to arrange those loans off the books so that no one could track the flow of money and find out who it belonged to."

"I think they did too," Stephen said. "When I caught him I thought it was his idea. But now I think it was their idea. They used him to launder the pesos."

"Well, don't feel sorry for the guy," Bill said. "He walked off with a shitload of fees."

"I think they want me to replace him."

"That makes sense," John said.

"So we're not going to do anything until I hear back from Navarra. Right?"

"Right," Bill said. "We'll wait to see where this leads."

When they met that evening at the café the first thing Sofi did was thank him for preventing the storeowners from doing something they would regret.

"Imagine," Paco said. "They were ready to kill over a truck."

"It makes you realize," Stephen said, "how people will kill for almost nothing."

"You mean how *men* will kill for almost nothing," Cathy said.

"I meant men, not women."

"Why are men like that?" Sofi asked.

"Maybe because of the way we evolved," Stephen said, remembering what he had learned from one of Leila's anthropology books. "While the women were gathering nuts and berries, the men were out hunting."

"But why did they end up killing each other?"

"I don't know. Maybe because the rabbit they killed wasn't enough for all of them."

"Though it's against official doctrine," Paco said, "I believe in evolution, guided by God."

"Then why did God decide that men should kill each other?" Cathy asked.

"He didn't decide that. We did."

"Well, He shouldn't have given us the ability to make that decision," Sofi said.

"If He hadn't, then we wouldn't have the ability to make other decisions."

"He could have given us the ability to make some decisions but not others," Stephen said. "That's how they teach computers to play chess."

"We're not computers," Paco said.

"I know. I was trying to make an analogy."

"I'll give you a better analogy," Cathy said, pursuing the question. "You can take away the ability of a child to do one thing without taking away his ability to do other things. I mean, if you don't want him to play with matches, you put them away where he can't get them."

"So God should have put away our weapons," Sofi said.

"If He had, then we couldn't have killed rabbits," Paco said.

"We didn't have to kill rabbits," Cathy said. "We could have been vegetarians. Though I must admit, that's hard to imagine in Argentina."

They all laughed.

At that moment Elena arrived. "What's so funny?"

"The idea of being a vegetarian in Argentina," Cathy said.

"That *is* funny," Elena said, sitting down. "Where are Mario and Teresa?"

"I think I know why they're not here," Stephen said. He told her about his conversation with Mario and Teresa on Tuesday evening. "So she could be afraid of being seen with people who are on the government's shit list."

"The only one on that list is me."

"You mean because of the story about Conti," Sofi said.

"That's right." Elena looked around at the group. "I don't see anyone else here who would be on that list."

"Well, we all talk freely about things," Stephen said.

"As we should," Paco said. "If we can't talk freely, then we've lost a fundamental right."

"If it would make Teresa feel better, I could stop coming here," Elena said.

"No," Sofi said adamantly. "If we start doing that, then we'll lose each other."

They all agreed with Sofi.

"I'll talk with her," Cathy offered. "I know how she feels. I was with her the night when Mario was in jail."

"If she's willing to listen to any of us," Elena said, "she'll listen to you."

Before they left, Paco took him aside and told him that he had met with Vittoria. "I told her about my own experience, and I think it made an impression on her. The key was, we both lost someone who was vitally important to us, but we didn't lose them to the same side. I lost my father to the military, and she lost her husband to the Montoneros, so we couldn't join forces against either side. We could start at a place where war itself is the enemy."

"I couldn't do that for her," Stephen admitted. "I was on the same side with her against the Montoneros."

"I know you were."

"I still want to stop them from killing people, but now I'm more concerned about the military."

Paco nodded. "Most people were relieved when the military took over. And you can't blame them. With all the kidnapping and killing, they didn't feel safe, and they wanted the military to end the war. But now I think they're beginning to realize that this is not the way to peace."

"It's not the way. But what *is* the way?"

"There is no way to peace. Peace is the way."

"Well, that sounds great, but what does it mean?"

Without hesitation Paco said: "It means valuing human life more than money, power, or ideas."

"But how do we translate that into action?"

"By working to make a better world," Paco said, "instead of fighting wars."

"I can see how if we all did that, we would have peace. But how do we get there?"

"We don't get there. We start here."

"You mean we stop fighting and start working."

"That's right," Paco said. "And we help other people to start working—people like Vittoria. Next week I'm going to take her to see the *villa*."

"That's a good idea," Stephen said, implicitly giving Paco credit for it.

"It wasn't my idea. It was hers."

NINE

CATHY HAD LUNCH with Teresa on Saturday after getting off from work at the bookstore. She didn't return until almost four that afternoon. Meanwhile, Stephen did the food shopping with the plan of making *paella*, using a recipe he had seen a week ago in the Sunday paper. He was in the kitchen peeling shrimp when he heard Cathy come into the apartment.

"I'm home," she said, entering the kitchen.

He turned to her and asked: "How did it go?"

"All right, I guess. I did what I could."

He waited, knowing she wanted to tell him about it.

She leaned back against the counter, folding her arms and staring ahead forlornly. In the stark fluorescent light the look of desolation in her eyes was fully exposed and heartrending. In a low mournful voice she said: "I told her I knew what it was like to be afraid. Without going into details, I told her I had to leave my country as a refugee."

He waited for her to continue.

"She told me she didn't want to leave her country, but she was afraid for Mario."

He could guess what she was going to say next.

"I told her I knew what that was like."

"You shouldn't be afraid for me."

"I shouldn't? Why not?"

"The Montoneros don't know what I'm doing."

"Maybe they don't. But they could find out."

"They won't find out," he assured her.

She shook her head in wonder, asking: "How can you be so confident? Where does it come from?"

He shrugged. "I don't know. I never thought about it."

"Does it come from being an American?"

"What do you mean?"

"I mean from always winning."

"We don't always win. We lost in Vietnam."

"But you're still the most powerful country in the world."

He couldn't deny it. "Yeah. We are."

"So you think you can get away with anything."

"I guess we do."

"But you can't," she said.

"I know," he said. "I told you I'd stop working with those guys when we finish the project."

"Well, when are you going to finish it?"

"Soon. We only need one more piece of information."

"All right," she sighed fatalistically.

"What else did you tell Teresa?"

"I told her how hard it was to leave my country. I told her that the worst things were missing my family and being alone in a strange place."

"The only family she has is a brother."

"Yes. I know."

"And she wouldn't be alone. She'd have Mario."

"Still, it would be hard for them."

"So what do you think they should do?" he asked her.

Cathy reflected. "I think they should do whatever they can live with. And from what I can see, Teresa can't live with her fear for Mario."

"Can you live with your fear for me?"

"Do I have a choice?"

"Yes. You do. We can leave and go to America."

"You would do that for me?"

"I'd do anything for you."

"If we left, you would be giving up a lot."

"I don't care. If you can't live with your fear for me, then I don't want to stay here."

"I never said I couldn't live with it."

"Well, if you can, then what do you want?"

"I want you to be happy. And I know you won't be happy if you don't finish the project."

"How do you know?"

"I just know."

"So where does that leave us?"

"Where we were. Ahead of where we were," she corrected herself. "Now I know how much you care about me."

"How could you have not known?"

"I guess women need a demonstration."

"You mean like bringing home a rabbit?"

"I mean like pulling one out of a hat."

Laughing appreciatively, he asked: "Now, where did you learn that expression?"

"From a book. I couldn't find it in the dictionary, so I had to ask the owner of the bookstore what it meant. I have so much to learn about English," she added, not with a feeling of discouragement but of excitement.

On Monday, when he entered Vittoria's living room, he found the balloons from the circus lying on the floor. They had lost the helium that made them rise, and they had shrunk. But they still had air inside them, and the girls had kept them, prolonging the memory of a good time.

"They thought maybe you could fix them," Vittoria told him.

"I can't fix them, but I'll see what I can do," he said, remembering what his father had done when his balloon had lost its helium. "Do you have a chair that I could climb up on? Not a good one, but a solid one?"

"Sure." She went to the kitchen and brought a wooden chair while the girls stood around him expectantly.

"This might not work," he told them, picking up a balloon. "But let's see."

They watched him as if he were a performer in the circus while he stepped up onto the chair with the balloon. He rubbed the balloon on the top of his head, generating static electricity, and then he held the balloon to the ceiling. Slowly, he let go of the balloon. It stuck to the ceiling.

They all applauded, including Vittoria and little Aleja, who always wanted to do what the others were doing.

Claudia handed him the other balloon, and he was successful with that one too.

"They won't stay up there long," he warned them. "By tomorrow morning they'll probably be down on the floor again."

"That's all right," Claudia told him as if she understood that nothing stays up in the air forever. "*Gracias.*"

The two older girls went into the family room and played while Aleja followed her mother into the kitchen.

As he was making drinks Vittoria said: "I met your friend Francisco, the priest, and I really like him."

"I'm glad," he said.

"He took me to the *villa* where he works. It was quite an experience. I've seen *villas* from a distance but never up close. It made me realize how poor these people are. I mean, I knew but I didn't really know."

"I understand," he said, remembering the first time he had walked into a sharecropper's shack in Mississippi.

"They don't have any of the things we have. They don't have running water, but somehow they manage to dress their children in clean clothes."

"They want a better life for their children. That's what they came for."

"But their children won't have a better life unless they have an education."

He smiled, handing her a drink. "That sounds like Paco."

"He's a wonderful man," Vittoria said with the first enthusiasm he had seen in her since the death of Alejandro. "And his friend Sofi's a wonderful woman."

"You met Sofi?"

"He introduced me to her. I talked with her for more than an hour, and I never would have guessed that she lost her husband the way I did. I learned that from Paco on the way home."

"She's very committed to her work."

"But she still must be hurting."

"She is," he agreed, having sensed and felt it.

"I can't do what she's doing, not with three children, but I can do something."

He waited for her to tell him what, knowing that Paco would have suggested something.

"I can help him raise money for the church and the school," Vittoria said. "I know a lot of people who have money. They're not rich, but they have money that they could spare. And if I show them pictures of how these people live, I know I can get them to give some money."

"I know you can."

"Of course," she said, smiling, "I'll start with my mother. I'll tell her that if she gives some money and gets her friends to give some money, I'll let her take care of my children while I'm raising money from the people I know."

"That sounds like a good deal."

She sipped her drink pensively. "You know, after seeing how these people live I can understand why they would want to overthrow the system."

"Most of them don't want to overthrow it. They want to be part of it."

"Then where did the Montoneros come from?"

"They didn't come from the *villas*," he said. "In fact, they started as a group of Catholic students."

"You mean people like us?"

"Yes. People like us, who wanted to make a better world."

"I don't understand. How could you make a better world by killing people?"

"I don't know. But they believe it's the only way."

"Well, that's insane. If you want to help people in the *villas*, you don't kill Sofi's husband."

"No. You don't."

"God forgive them. I never will."

"I never will either."

"But I'm not going to think about them," Vittoria said resolutely. "I'm going to raise money for Paco."

On Tuesday evening at the *confitería* Mario told him: "We've decided to apply for visas to Mexico."

"I think that's a good decision."

"Would you leave your country if you were in my position?"

"I would if my wife couldn't live with her fear for me."

"Well, that's what it is."

"I know. Cathy told me."

Mario nodded, indicating that Teresa had shared their conversation with him. "But you wouldn't be in my position in your country."

"I guess I wouldn't."

"I'd rather go to America, but at my age I could never learn English well enough to be a professor."

He didn't say that Mario could teach Spanish there, knowing that the suggestion would be an affront to his self-esteem.

"So we're going to Mexico," Mario said, "where at least we know the language."

"I've been to Mexico."

"Were you there on vacation?"

"No. I was there during the year I took off from college. I lived in a *pensión* with students from the university. They were all communists, and they hated America, but they loved baseball. On Sundays we played stickball on the street."

"Stickball?"

"It's a form of baseball."

"But *fútbol* is their main sport, isn't it?"

"Yes. They're crazy about *fútbol,* just like here."

"Is the food spicy?"

"Some of it is, but most of it isn't. They live mainly on beans, rice, and *tortillas.*"

"Beans? How's the steak?"

"Well, it's not as good as here," he said, though he hadn't eaten much steak there.

"That's what he said, the man I was able to contact."

"You found someone there?"

"I just heard from him," Mario said. "He was a professor of sociology here. He's been there almost nine years. He teaches at a high school."

"Is he happy there?"

Mario shrugged as if the question were irrelevant. "He didn't say. But he did say he would never come back."

"Does he have a wife?"

"He married a Mexican. They have two children."

"It sounds like he has adapted."

"Yes. But I don't know if I can adapt. I'm reading Mexican history, and it makes my country look good."

"I know what you mean."

"They have one party, which has been in control for more than fifty years," Mario said critically. "The *peronistas* weren't in control for even ten years."

"Not counting the recent period."

"They weren't in control."

"Well, in Mexico they're not interfering with the university."

"I probably wouldn't be at the university. Like the man I contacted, I'd probably be at a high school. And I could be at a high school here without having to leave my country."

Stephen thought about it. "If you were at a high school here, would they bother you?"

"No. They don't care about high school teachers—unless you wave a hammer and sickle at them."

"So why don't you teach at a high school here?"

"I suggested that, but Teresa wouldn't listen. She has a fixed idea on going to Mexico."

"Well, maybe by the time you get your visas she'll be more open to other ideas."

"I heard what you said," Teresa said from behind him.

"Doesn't that make you feel special?" Mario said lightly. "We're always talking about you."

"You're not going to talk us out of going to Mexico."

"I wasn't trying to. I lived there, and I liked it."

Mario said: "We were talking about the possibility of my staying here and teaching high school."

"You don't want to teach high school," Teresa said, sitting down at the table.

"I'd rather teach at the university. But if I had to choose between teaching at a high school in Mexico and teaching at a high school here, I'd rather be here."

"You only heard from one person. Maybe he didn't have good credentials for teaching at the university."

"Maybe he did. We don't know."

"Well, we know that you have excellent credentials. You'll get a job at the university there."

Mario didn't argue, and Stephen stayed out of it.

Around eleven the next morning Elena called him and asked if he could meet her for lunch. Something had happened, something she couldn't talk about over the phone. They arranged to meet at the obscure restaurant on 25 de Mayo. He got there ahead of her, secured a table, and waited for her anxiously.

When she appeared she was wearing sunglasses with comically large lenses. He noticed that she walked with a limp as she approached the table, smiling as if she were gritting her teeth. She sat down gingerly.

"What happened?" he asked.

Before replying she poured herself a glass of red wine, took a long gulp, and then exhaled through pursed lips, making a barely audible whistle. She finally said: "They retaliated. They did what you were afraid they'd do."

"They hurt you?"

"A little." She removed the sunglasses and revealed two enormous bruises with the deep purple extending halfway down her cheeks. There were broken blood vessels in her eyes.

"Holy shit. How did they do that?"

"They slapped me with their meaty hands."

"God damn them."

"Don't worry. He will."

"What else did they do? I noticed you were limping."

"They whacked me on the backs of my thighs with a curtain rod. They bent me over, lifted my dress, and pulled down my knickers," she told him with controlled fury. "I thought they were going to rape me from behind. They talked about it, they joked about it, but they didn't do it."

"How many were there?"

"There were three big guys. They grabbed me as I was leaving my office, in broad daylight, and pushed me into the back of a car. They covered my face with a cloth that must have been soaked in chloroform. The next thing I knew I was in a room with no windows and these three guys."

"Did they blindfold you?"

"No. They didn't seem to care if I saw their faces."

That usually meant they were going to kill you.

"I know what you're thinking, and the same thing occurred to me. But when they started slapping my face I figured they wanted people to see what they'd done to me. I usually don't show the backs of my thighs."

Stephen laughed as he was supposed to. "Did they break anything?"

"No. I thought they might have broken my nose, but they didn't. Too bad. I might have gotten a free nose job."

They obviously hadn't broken her spirit. "You don't need a nose job."

"I know," she said, mocking him. "My nose is perfect."

"So what did the editor say about this?"

"I wouldn't want to quote him."

"You mean you couldn't print it in your paper?"

"No. If we did, the church would close us down."

"Well, apart from his language, what was his reaction?"

She made a face, which was accentuated by her horrific bruises. "He took me off the political beat. From now on he's doing the political stories himself. He won't even let me do research for them."

"So what'll you be doing?"

"He put me on the business beat," she said as if she had been demoted.

"What's wrong with that? There're a lot of good business stories."

"I don't know anything about business. I took one economics course in college."

"That's all I took."

"Really? I was hoping you could help me."

"I'm sure I can. What do you want to know about business?"

"I need to learn more about foreign exchange. I heard some guys talking about the *bicicleta*. Can you explain it?"

"Well, by definition it has two wheels—"

She picked up a piece of bread as if she were going to throw it at him. "I don't mean that kind of bicycle."

"Oh, you mean the one where you can make a bundle taking advantage of distortions in the foreign exchange market." He explained it to her.

"That's not so complicated. The way those guys were talking, you'd think it was rocket science."

"Guys always talk that way."

They ordered their food, and then she said: "You asked about the editor, but you didn't ask about my father."

"I figured you'd tell me."

"He wants to send me *back* to England."

"Well, he must be afraid for you."

"He is. I guess it's worse being afraid for someone else."

"I guess it is," Stephen said, thinking of Cathy.

"I told my father not to worry," Elena said. "I told him they won't go after me again because I won't be involved in stories about politics."

"How will they know you're not involved?"

"I won't have a byline on them."

"Then they'll go after someone else."

"They'll go after the editor."

"So did you convince your father not to worry?"

"No. I didn't," Elena said. "He says the next time they might kill me. Or worse."

"What could be worse?"

"Remember, he's my father."

"Oh. Well, have you considered going to England?"

"At least you didn't say *back* to England. No, I haven't. And you know why."

"You're not English, you're Argentine."

"*Correcto,*" she told him, putting her sunglasses back on.

Two days later Elena's newspaper reported that the daughter of a former undersecretary of education had been abducted. On the same day a perceptive story about *bicicletas* with Elena's byline appeared in the business section.

As the days passed the paper continued to report abductions, executions, and disappearances, and stories with Elena's byline continued to appear in the business section. She called Stephen with questions, and he was happy to help her. It was like collaborating with Carlos on reports to head office, except that in this situation he was the expert, not the writer.

On the last Tuesday of May, as he was sitting with Mario and Teresa at the *confitería*, Cathy appeared without her friend.

"Where's Adriana?" Stephen asked her.

"I don't know. She wasn't in class."

"She probably has the flu," Mario said. "It's going around, and a lot of students have it."

"Probably," Cathy said. But she looked worried.

The next day Elena's newspaper reported that Adriana had disappeared. He called Elena to see what he could find out. Elena told him that the information had come to the paper from Adriana's mother, who had also reported it to the police. Adriana hadn't come home from class on Monday.

He called John and scheduled a meeting at noon. Then he went out and walked over to the bookstore, where he found Cathy unpacking a box of new books. He told her they needed to talk. She got permission from the owner to take a break, and they went out. It was a narrow street with a lot of people walking by in both directions, and he didn't want anyone to hear him telling her what had happened, so he led her by the hand to 9 de Julio, where they found space on the broad sidewalk in front of a restaurant that still had tables and chairs outside for days when it might be warm enough to sit there. A pigeon was scratching around the table nearest to them.

"Adriana has disappeared," he told her.

"What?" Her face froze in shock. "How do you know?"

"It's in the paper. They reported it this morning."

"What did they say?" she asked in a tiny, heartbroken voice.

"Not much. Her mother said she didn't come home from class on Monday."

After a long silence Cathy said: "I knew there was something wrong. She never missed a class before."

"Elena's trying to get more information. And I'm going to meet with the embassy guys to see if they can help us."

She nodded as tears flowed down her cheeks.

"The problem is," he said, "we don't know where she is. We don't know what happened to her. So it's not like the situation with Mario."

Blindly, she groped for a chair and sank down into it, staring into space without hope.

He pulled a chair close to her and sat down with her. "It would help if we could find out more about her."

"Find out what?"

"If she was involved in anything."

"You mean like subversive activities," she said dully.

"Anything," he said, casting about. "I mean, she could have run away with some guy."

"It's not likely."

"Well, it's possible."

Cathy shook her head. "We know what happened to her."

"But if we knew *why* it could help us find her."

"Assuming she's alive."

"They don't kill prisoners right away."

"No. They torture them first."

He took her hand, wanting to comfort her. "They might just do what they did to Elena—make an example of her as a warning to the other students."

"Please don't try to raise my hopes for her."

"Well, I don't want to give up on her."

"I know. I'm sorry."

At that moment a waiter appeared, thinking they wanted table service. They finally decided to have coffee as long as they were sitting there.

"So what can I do?" she asked more positively.

"You can talk to her friends."

"I don't know who they are. Except for one, a girl in our poetry class. They both wanted to study psychology."

"She might know something, and she might know some other friends."

"Okay. I'll try to find her."

Around noon John and Bill appeared with their satchels. They evidently needed cash, and he wondered if they would have come if they hadn't needed it. He waited for them to get settled in the conference room, and then he joined them.

After placing their order with the head trader he told them about Adriana.

They listened politely.

"So I hope you can help me, as you did before."

"You mean with the professor," John said.

"Whatever you did, it was very effective." Of course he didn't know if whatever they had done was the reason why Mario had been released, but in this situation he was happy to give them full credit.

"What do you know about this kid?"

"I know she's a student at the university."

"Which school?"

"Philosophy and Letters."

"I hear that school's a hotbed."

"No more than any other school. They all have problems."

"She was probably a member of some activist organization that crossed the line."

He noticed that John used the past tense in talking about her.

"How would you classify her politically?" Bill asked.

"I don't know. I guess I'd say she's a socialist. But everyone is at her age."

"Were you a socialist at her age?"

"Of course. Weren't you?"

"That's not in your file. Someone slipped up when they were investigating you for a security clearance."

"Was she a member of a socialist club?" John asked.

"I don't know," Stephen said. "I have someone who's trying to find out more about her."

"You mean your girlfriend?"

In telling them about Adriana he hadn't mentioned Cathy. In fact, he had never mentioned Cathy to them. But he shouldn't have been surprised. "You know about her?"

"We know everything about you."

"Well, that's why I'm interested in Adriana," he told them. "She's a friend of my girlfriend."

"Where's she from?"

"You mean Adriana?"

"No, your girlfriend. She doesn't look like an Argentine."

"Her mother's Venezuelan," he said. He didn't elaborate on the cover story, knowing they could shoot holes in it.

"We saw you with her on Florida. She's a pretty girl."

"She's more than pretty," Bill said.

"Okay. She's beautiful," John said. "How well does she know this missing girl?"

"They're in a class together at the university."

"Does she do things with this girl?"

"She sees her in class, and she brings her after class to a *confitería* where we wait for her and the wife of the professor."

"The professor they arrested?"

"Yes. But there's no connection between them."

"Are you sure?"

"I'm sure. My girlfriend just happened to meet Adriana in class, and the professor's wife just happened to be taking a class at the same time as my girlfriend."

"That's a lot of things that just happened."

"Still, we'll assume there's no connection," Bill said, "other than the fact that they're both at the university."

"But they're not at the same school," Stephen said.

"The schools are probably all the same to the government."

Refocusing them, he asked: "Can you help me find her?"

"We can make inquiries about her," John said. "But this is more difficult than the case of the professor."

"I know it is," Stephen admitted.

"We don't know where she is, and we don't know who took her. We don't even know if they did take her. She could have run away with some guy."

"A lot of them do at that age," Bill said.

"I hope she did," Stephen said, "but I don't believe it."

"You have some reason for not believing it?"

"My girlfriend doesn't believe it."

"That's a good reason," John said. "Women have better instincts than we do."

"What do you know about women?" Bill asked.

"A lot more than you do."

"That isn't much."

"We'll see what we can find out," John said. "Can you bring us up to date on our project?"

Stephen reminded them that the remaining loans that Arias had arranged for Navarra were due on Monday. If all went well,

Navarra would reinvest the money for ninety days, and at that point the pesos belonging to the Montoneros would be tied up. He would let them know what happened on Monday.

On Friday they were all at the café on Avenida de Mayo, including Mario and Teresa. Somehow Mario must have talked her into coming, and maybe the fact that they had applied for visas to Mexico had relieved her anxiety. At least she could anticipate leaving the country and getting to a safe place.

Instead of being late as usual Elena was the first one there. She was still wearing her oversized sunglasses, which drew comments since it was dark outside.

"You look like a jazz musician," Mario remarked when he arrived and saw her.

"That's my new career," Elena said.

"What instrument do you play?"

"Keyboard." It was true. Elena played the piano, which she said was similar to typing newspaper stories.

When they were all there she told them what had happened. She removed her sunglasses just long enough for them to see the extent of her bruises, and she concluded, saying: "Now I report on business."

Teresa, who had listened intently, asked: "Aren't you afraid they'll come after you again?"

"I'm afraid the bankers will come after me for making errors in my stories about the foreign exchange market."

They all laughed, including Teresa who seemed to laugh in spite of herself.

Then seriously Elena said: "But a terrible thing happened this week. A friend of Cathy's disappeared."

"Adriana?" Mario asked, turning to Cathy.

Cathy nodded, looking distraught.

"Remember how she wasn't in class on Tuesday?" Stephen said. "Well, that's why."

"Oh, no," Mario moaned. "She's just a kid. She could be one of my students."

With obvious difficulty Cathy said: "I found out that she was a member of a socialist club."

"But they're just kids playing with ideas," Mario said. "That's what a university is for."

"It looks like she wasn't the only one they took from that club," Elena said. "Another girl and a guy disappeared around the same time."

"And no one knows what happened to them?" Teresa asked.

"The people who took them know."

"Well, who were they?"

"Probably the same people who took me," Mario said.

"Whoever they are, they're assholes," Teresa said with fire in her eyes. "They're fucking assholes."

Surprised by her reaction, Stephen said: "I'm trying to find out who they are, and where they took her."

"What else can we do?" Mario asked.

"We can pray," Paco said, having said nothing until now.

"What good will that do? They say that God is on their side."

"That's what these governments always say," Elena said.

"Well, if He's not on their side, then why is He letting them get away with it?"

"He's not letting them get away with it," Paco said. "And we must remember, it's not for us to punish them. It's for God to punish them."

"Let's pray for Adriana," Sofi said.

Paco raised his hands in supplication. "Lord, hear our prayer for Adriana and the other students who disappeared."

They bowed their heads.

"Grant that they may be returned to their families unharmed, and that they may pursue their education without further interference. We ask this in the name of Jesus Christ, Your only

Son, whom You sacrificed for our salvation."

"Amen," they said.

Stephen and Cathy shared a taxi with Elena, and they got out with her on Juncal. She headed home, and they went to Ligure for dinner. They weren't as hungry as they usually were, but they had established a routine of having dinner at Ligure on Friday, and in such chaotic times it was helpful to stick with routines.

"You know," Cathy said when the waiter had left them after taking their orders, "I didn't expect Teresa to react that way when she heard about Adriana."

"I didn't either. I expected her to turn to Mario and say, you see? This is why we should go to Mexico."

"But she didn't. She was angry."

"She was angry at what they did to someone who could have been one of Mario's students."

"Or one of her students."

"Yeah," he agreed. "Adriana could have been one of her students not that long ago."

"Well, I haven't been a teacher yet, but I know the feeling you can have for other people's children. You can care about them more than their parents seem to care."

"So her feeling for her students might be stronger than her fear of the military."

The waiter brought a carafe of red wine and a bowl of salad, along with cruets of oil and vinegar.

Stephen poured some wine and began to mix the salad.

Watching, Cathy said: "I really admire the way Elena handled what happened to her. I wish I had such courage."

"You do. You've proven it."

"How have I proven it?"

"By the way you handled what happened in Colombia."

"Oh, I just acted out of instinct."

"You did more than that. You used your brain."

"Is that where courage comes from?"

"I don't know. But I don't think it comes from your gut."

"I think it comes from your heart," she said. "From caring about others and not worrying about yourself."

"I never thought of it that way."

"Elena doesn't worry about herself. And when Teresa was cursing the military, she wasn't worrying about herself."

"Well, you don't worry about yourself."

"Why should I worry? They'll never find me."

"I don't see how they could find you, but I still worry."

"You do?" she said, surprised.

"Yeah. I don't think about it, but it's always there at the back of my mind."

"Then you know how I feel worrying about you."

"I can imagine."

She took a small amount of salad and began eating it. Then she asked: "Do you ever worry about yourself?"

"You mean am I ever afraid for myself?"

She nodded. "I mean, are you ever afraid that the Montoneros will find out what you're doing?"

"No, not really. But to answer your question, I've been afraid in situations where my life was in danger. I just don't let my fear overwhelm me, at least until the crisis has passed. I remember the time when I jumped out of an airplane and my parachute didn't open because the lines were tangled. I could have been paralyzed by fear, but instead I very methodically untangled the lines and got the parachute to open. When I landed and knew I was all right, I was scared shitless."

She laughed in recognition. "I never jumped out of an airplane, but I felt that way when we took off from Cali. I was so busy doing what I had to do to escape from the drug lords that I didn't think about being afraid. But as soon as we were in the air, I peed in my pants."

"I'm glad I wasn't sitting next to you."

"Me too. It would have been embarrassing. But somehow I had the presence of mind to have a change of panties in my pocketbook. So you're right," she said, smiling. "I didn't just act out of instinct."

On Monday, as he had told the embassy guys, the remaining unrecorded loans arranged by Arias came due, and as he had expected, Navarra came into the bank and asked what kind of rate he could get if he reinvested the money for ninety days. Stephen got him a good rate, and the deal was done.

After signing the papers Navarra asked: "You remember what we talked about the last time we met?"

"Yes. I do," Stephen replied.

"Well, if you're still interested, we could pursue it."

"I'm still interested. Tell me more."

"It's better if the man I work for tells you." Navarra pulled out a pocket calendar. "Could you have lunch with him on Wednesday?"

"Sure." He didn't know his schedule but if there was a conflict he could always move the other appointment. This one had priority. "Where?"

"In Once. At the bank he owns."

"Which bank is that?"

"Banco Azulay."

"They're a client."

"I know."

"We make a lot of money from our relationship with them."

"Then you should meet the owner."

"Yes. I should. Especially since the man who managed the account is no longer with us."

"Ay, poor Arias." It wasn't clear if Navarra was merely feigning sorrow about the health of Arias or if something else had happened to him.

"What time on Wednesday?"

"How about one?"

"That's fine."

"We could send a car for you," Navarra offered.

"Thanks. I'll use the bank car." With an extra bodyguard, Stephen thought.

Rising from his chair, Navarra said: "Then we'll see you on Wednesday."

"Wednesday, at one."

They shook hands.

That afternoon he met with John and Bill to assess the situation.

"Their pesos are tied up until June 30," John said. "How much is that in dollars?"

"A little more than five million."

"And we figure they have about eighty million in their New York account. So they have about eighty-five million dollars, not counting their petty cash, and we know where it is."

"We do now," Bill said. "But they can move the money out of their New York account at any time."

"I know they can," John allowed, "but they won't unless they have a reason to."

"We won't give them a reason to move it," Stephen said.

"Oh, by the way," Bill said after a moment, "did Navarra get back to you with his proposition?"

"Yeah. He invited me to have lunch with him and Safadi."

"Lunch?" John said, excited. "Where?"

"At Banco Azulay."

"They could be planning to kill you," Bill said without the slightest expression.

"That did occur to me," Stephen said. "But they have no reason to kill me. They don't know what I'm doing. As far as they know, I'm just their banker."

"The guy who replaced Arias," John said.

"Exactly. And I've been giving them good rates."

"So maybe they just want to thank you," Bill suggested.

"I think they want to pay me."

"You mean to watch out for their interests?"

"Something like that."

"Well, now we can tie Safadi to Navarra," John said happily.

"Not yet," Bill said. "He still has to have lunch with them."

"He will. And if they pay him to watch out for their interests, we'll have some additional evidence."

"We don't need it. He only has to see them together."

"Then why are they letting him see them together?"

"They must believe they can buy him."

"Yeah, I can see why they might think he's sharp. What do they call it here?"

"*Vivo*," Stephen said.

"I thought that meant alive."

"It does, but it also means sharp."

"Well, I hope you're *vivo* after you have lunch with this guy," John told him. "And I don't mean sharp."

"Be careful of any package he gives you," Bill said.

"You mean it could be a bomb?"

"It could be. We didn't mention it before, but Safadi knows how to use explosives."

"I'll keep that in mind."

Before they left, John said: "I hate to tell you, but we found out what happened to that student. We picked up her trail, which led to the Naval Mechanics School—"

"Oh, Jesus," Stephen said, his stomach turning. The school was notorious as a place where missing people were tortured and finally killed.

"They held her for a while, and then they transferred her."

"The poor kid," Bill said sadly.

That evening he told Cathy what he had learned about Adriana. She was already prepared for the worst, but she still broke down and cried in his arms. There was nothing he could do but hold her and share her loss.

She grieved through the weekend, and in church he had to touch her shoulder to get her to rise from her knees and stand for the final prayer.

By Tuesday evening, when they met at the *confitería* after class, she was able to tell Teresa what happened. Teresa again reacted with anger, and she cursed the military so vociferously that people out on the street could have heard her.

"Those fucking assholes!" Teresa cried with tears of rage in her dark eyes. "I hope they rot in hell!"

"They will, they will," Mario assured her, trying to calm her.

Clearly, her anger was stronger than her fear, and you could imagine her telling Videla how she felt about him.

On Wednesday he went to Banco Azulay in the bank car with two bodyguards. Carlos had readily agreed to his request for an extra bodyguard, though he did comment that the Montoneros were a declining threat and that maybe in next year's budget he wouldn't have to provide for bodyguards.

After slogging through heavy traffic the car stopped at Banco Azulay, and Stephen got out, accompanied by the bodyguards. One went into the bank with him, and the other stayed outside, positioned as a sentinel. The driver remained in the car, ready to leave at a moment's notice.

A tall *ordenanza* led him to a door in the rear, which opened into a wood-paneled private dining room. The bodyguard stayed outside the door while Stephen went in.

Navarra rose from the table to greet him and quickly introduced him to the other man, who was younger than he expected. The man had theatrical long hair, wrinkle-free skin, and amber eyes that glimmered with a sense of power, along with a hint of impishness.

"Marco Safadi," the man said with a disarming smile. "It's a very great pleasure to meet you."

Stephen reciprocated, shaking his hand.

"Please be seated."

"*Gracias.*"

Safadi sat at the head of the table while Navarra sat across from Stephen. The table was set with expensive china and silverware, with three glasses at each setting. A waiter, who had been standing at attention in the distance, immediately went into motion when Safadi snapped his fingers.

"How would you like your steak?" Safadi asked.

"*A punto,*" Stephen said.

After serving the first course, a half avocado stuffed with shrimp and delicately topped with *salsa golf,* the waiter withdrew.

"I want to thank you," Safadi said, "for taking such good care of our money in the *extrabancario* market. You've done an even better job than Arias did."

"We always take good care of our clients."

"I'm sure you do. I know you're doing a great job with our letters of credit."

Stephen was unable to detect any irony in this statement.

"You know, I own a bank in New York, and I thought maybe we could develop a relationship there. We're a very small bank compared with yours, but we may have some connections that you don't have."

"You may," Stephen said openly.

"So we should explore the possibilities."

"We should. Is there a person in New York we should contact, or are you the person we should work with?"

"I'm the person you should work with."

"I look forward to working with you."

After only the slightest pause Safadi said: "If you don't mind my asking, why have you stayed in Argentina? All the other Americans have left."

"Not all of them have left, but most of them have."

"So why have you stayed?"

"I like it here."

"What do you like about Argentina?"

"It's interesting. I meet people like you here."

Safadi laughed, and then he glanced at Navarra as if to say: "You were right."

Navarra's eyes said: "I told you."

"But aren't you afraid," Safadi asked, "of being kidnapped by the Montoneros?"

"Why would they kidnap me?"

"To get ransom money."

Stephen shook his head. "They wouldn't get one *centavo*. My bank wouldn't pay a ransom for me."

"Why wouldn't it?"

"My bank doesn't pay ransoms. It has branches in more than a hundred countries. If it paid a ransom here, it would have to pay ransoms everywhere, and it would go broke."

"So your bank would let them kill you?"

"They always have three people ready to fill any position."

"It sounds like a tough bank."

"It is," Stephen said. "And it has survived revolutions, civil wars, expropriations—whatever you can think of. So it's not going to yield to a bunch of terrorists."

Safadi nodded approvingly. "It's the kind of bank I want to work with."

The waiter, evidently summoned by a hidden buzzer, returned and removed the plates for the first course. He returned again a few minutes later with the main course, and then he withdrew again.

"You know," Safadi said as they ate their steaks, "I own a finance company in Mexico, and maybe we could develop a relationship with your branch there."

"What kind of loans does your company make?"

"Car loans, personal loans. Nothing longer than five years."

"Do you spend much time in Mexico?"

"When I'm in New York I fly there every weekend. I have my own plane. I bought a house in Mexico, and I plan to move my family there."

"Why would you do that?"

"I don't like this government. They're fanatics."

Stephen could have said that this was his own opinion of the government, which he had expressed in the same words, but he just listened.

"And they're anti-Semites. Sooner or later they'll go after us."

"What do you mean sooner or later?" Navarra said. "They're already after us. Look at the people who are disappearing."

"You have a point," Safadi agreed. "A disproportionate number of them are Jewish."

"So you think you'll be safer in Mexico?"

"Oh, yes. They don't have a problem with Jews there. I mean, like everywhere in the world they have anti-Semitism, but it's not institutionalized."

"There are people at high levels of this government," Navarra said, "who want to have death camps for Jews like they had in Nazi Germany."

"Are a lot of Jews planning to leave?"

"No. Not many," Safadi said. "They're taking their money out, but they're staying here. They're like the Jews who could have left but stayed in Germany."

"It sounds like you think they're stupid to stay."

"Stupid? They're crazy."

Stephen finally took a bite of steak. It was overdone but he ate it anyway.

At the end of the lunch, handing him a portfolio with the name and logo of Banco Azulay embossed on it, Safadi said: "You'll find inside some information on my banks. You'll also find a small token of appreciation."

"*Gracias*," Stephen said, taking the portfolio. It was made of plastic, good quality, but it still smelled of plastic.

"So we'll talk, uh? We'll see what we can do together."

"Yes. I'll get back to you."

As Stephen left the dining room the bodyguard, who evidently hadn't budged the whole time, rejoined him. Remembering what Bill had said, he decided to check the contents of the portfolio before he left the bank. If it contained an explosive, whether on a timer or remotely activated, they wouldn't want it to detonate inside the bank.

He asked the *ordenanza* where the men's room was, a natural request after eating lunch, and he went into it, leaving the bodyguard outside. He locked the door and then slowly unzipped the portfolio, believing but not knowing that if there was an explosive inside, it wasn't likely to be activated by a zipper since out of simple curiosity he might have unzipped the portfolio upon being handed it.

He peered into the portfolio and saw only a few brochures and some packets of what looked like money. He carefully took out the brochures and then the packets, which he dumped into the sink. There was nothing else inside the portfolio.

Relieved, he turned his attention to the packets of money. There were ten packets of one hundred dollar bills. He counted the bills in one packet. There were fifty of them, which meant that if they were all alike there was five thousand dollars in each packet. A total of fifty thousand dollars.

A small token of appreciation? A payment for watching out for their interests? An advance on the money they hoped to make with him? Whatever it was, it seemed to confirm his belief that they didn't know what he was doing and that, having given him this money, they would think they had bought him.

TEN

BACK AT THE BANK, he crammed the money into a safe
deposit box along with a note documenting who had given it to
him, when, and why. He planned to use the money as evidence,
though he couldn't carry it himself to New York, where they
might catch him violating the law on the amount of currency you
could bring into the country or take out. He would have to use
the bank mail pouch.

At home that evening he told Cathy about the money,
knowing it would worry her but keeping his promise to share
everything with her.

"I think you're playing a dangerous game," she told him,
wiping her hands on her apron. They were in the kitchen making
dinner.

"Well, I didn't know he was going to give me money."

"You should have guessed."

"Okay. I should have. But I couldn't have opened the
portfolio in front of him to see what he'd given me."

"Yes, you could have."

"And then what? Give the money back to him? That would
have been worse than taking it. He would have wondered why I
refused to accept it."

"You could have refused because you're honest."

"Yeah. Sure. You think he would have believed that?"

"No." She sighed in frustration.

"And it would be even worse," he argued, "if I returned the
money now."

"Well, you shouldn't have gone there in the first place."

"I had to. And now I have the evidence we need."

"So what are you going to do with it?"

"Take it to New York."

"Really? When?"

"We could leave on Friday."

She brightened at the thought of going to New York but she still looked concerned.

"Don't worry," he told her. "They think they've bought me."

"What will they do when they find out they haven't?"

"By then it'll be over."

"I hope so."

The next morning Randal called him from Panama. He had to go down to the general manager's office to take the call, and he had to get by Señora Pérez.

"There's been a development," Randal told him. "We got a transfer yesterday from International Bank & Trust. The money was coming from Esmeralda and going to another Panamanian company, which has an account with our Swiss friends."

"Oh, shit," Stephen said, afraid that they had gotten a jump on him. "How much was the transfer?"

"Ten million. But here's the funny thing. An hour later we got two transfers from the Swiss for five million each, coming from a third Panamanian company and going to Esmeralda's account with International Bank & Trust."

"So the ten million is back in Esmeralda's account?"

"Yeah. It looks like they just round-tripped the money. And guess what. These other Panamanian companies have the same owners as Esmeralda."

"Well, thanks for letting me know about this."

"Any time. I'll call you if it happens again."

Sitting by the phone, he tried to imagine what they were up

to. They weren't taking the money out of International Bank & Trust, so maybe they were simply building another layer in the process of hiding the source of the money. Or maybe they were preparing to move it. In any case there was nothing more to be gained by waiting. It was time to act.

"I need to go to New York," he told Carlos, "and meet with the banking authorities."

"About the money laundering?"

"Yeah. I'd like to leave tomorrow."

"That's fine. How long will you be there?"

"I'll need about a week."

"Fine. You haven't had a vacation in a while, so why don't you take an extra week as long as you're there. You could see your family."

"Yes. I could." He could introduce Cathy to his parents.

"I assume your *novia* is going with you," Carlos said as if he had read his mind. "And since it's for vacation, the bank will pay for her plane ticket."

"I thought it only paid for wives or children."

"It did. But in keeping with the times, I just made the policy more flexible."

"*Gracias, amigo.*"

That afternoon he met with John and Bill. He told them about his lunch with Safadi and about what Randal had reported.

"You should go to New York right away," John said.

"I'm leaving tomorrow."

"You'll have to prepare a report for the banking authorities," Bill said, "with documentation."

"I'll do that in New York while I'm waiting to see them. I'll take the evidence with me."

"Don't take the money. You don't need it."

"Are you sure it won't be useful?"

"Yeah. And it might only complicate things. I mean, people might wonder why you accepted it."

"I accepted it to collect evidence."

"That's what they all say."

"Okay," Stephen said. "You think I have enough to tie Safadi to the money laundering?"

"You have enough," Bill assured him.

"Just make sure they don't find out that you've gone to New York," John advised him.

"How would they find out?"

"Someone at the bank might tell them."

"You mean if they call the bank and ask for me." He thought for a moment. "Then I'll have a cover story. I've gone skiing in Bariloche."

"Do you ski?" John asked.

"No. But they don't know that."

"You're from Minnesota. Don't they ski there?"

"They do, but it's not good skiing. There're no mountains. But even if there were, I couldn't have skied. I played hockey, and if you were on the team you weren't allowed to ski."

"Why not?"

"If you broke an arm or a leg skiing, you wouldn't be much use to the team."

"That's fascinating," Bill said.

"I think it's a good cover," John said. "There's no way they can find out if you're in Bariloche."

"Okay. So that's where I've gone."

He gave the cover story to Carlos, who passed it on to Señora Pérez, who told her friend in personnel, who spread it all around the bank in less than an hour. So the only two people in the bank who knew where he was going were Carlos and Señora Pérez, who booked the flight.

They took the only direct flight to New York, which left at

nine on Friday evening and arrived at ten on Saturday morning. It was the bank's policy to fly its officers first class, so they enjoyed the first few hours of the flight, eating and drinking sumptuously, but after that it was only hour after hour of flying, and when they finally got off the plane they were utterly exhausted, not having gotten any sleep.

They took a taxi to the hotel, which was near the bank, and as soon as they had hung up their clothes they crashed into bed.

They didn't awake until it was beginning to get dark.

By now they were hungry, so they went out to find a place to eat. It was Saturday night, but in that area of Park Avenue there was nothing but office buildings, so there wasn't much activity. Still, it felt good to be walking again, and Cathy looked as if she was thrilled to be in New York.

They found a small French restaurant in the Forties off Lexington Avenue where the food was excellent, though Cathy was appalled by the prices.

"How can people afford to pay so much for a meal?"

"They make more money here."

"Does everything cost more here?"

"No. Not everything. Cars cost less, and so do vacuum cleaners."

"Vacuum cleaners? How do you know that?"

"They told me to bring a vacuum cleaner to Argentina. They said it cost a lot more there, and they were right. It cost almost four times as much in Argentina."

"Did you bring one?"

"No. I thought it was ridiculous to bring our own vacuum cleaner to a country that made them."

"What did your wife think?"

"She thought we should bring one. It was the subject of our first argument in Argentina. And things went downhill after that," he added ruefully.

"If she was never there with you, why did she care about a vacuum cleaner?"

"Good question. She didn't use it. The maid did. But for her it was a matter of principle."

"For you it was too, wasn't it?"

"Yeah. We never agreed on principles."

After dinner they walked up Lexington and then over to Third Avenue. They passed bars and restaurants from which people were spilling out onto the sidewalks, where some of the restaurants had set up tables. It was a perfect evening in early June, when eating outside was still a novelty after the winter and the air was still relatively fresh. The noise of the traffic didn't seem to bother people.

As they strolled, holding hands and not letting the people walking toward them separate them, Cathy asked: "How long did you live here?"

"Well, I lived here as a student for two years when I was at Columbia, and I lived here as a banker for a year after I got out of the army. So I lived here for three years."

"Did you like it?"

"Oh, yeah. I loved it."

"Then why did you leave?"

"I wanted to live in a foreign country. I can't explain why. Maybe because I grew up in Minnesota, as far as you could get from a foreign country."

"I thought Minnesota was near Canada."

"You're right. It is. But the part of Canada over the border is exactly like Minnesota. You can paddle a canoe across the border and not even know you're in a different country."

"That sounds nice. So now that you've lived in a foreign country, how do you feel?"

"I'm glad I did it," Stephen told her. "I met people I wouldn't have met if I'd stayed in New York."

"Sometimes I wonder what would have happened if the club owner in Cali had picked another country for me to escape to."

"Sometimes I wonder what would have happened if I hadn't gone to Minas that night."

"Well, you still would have had all those women."

"Women? What women?"

"Elena, Sofi, Vittoria, and Teresa."

"They're friends."

"I know. But if you hadn't met me," Cathy said, walking more slowly, "you could have had another kind of relationship with one of them."

"No, I couldn't have. One is married," Stephen reminded her, "and two are widows who still love their husbands. So you can rule them out three of them."

"That leaves Elena."

"A client fixed us up, believing we'd make a perfect couple, but neither of us wanted to be more than friends."

"You *would* make a perfect couple."

"No, we wouldn't. We're too much alike."

"So our relationship works because we're different?"

"It works because—" He stopped and got her to face him on the sidewalk with people streaming by, with taxis and buses hurtling up the avenue, with a siren wailing in the distance. "It works because we love each other, and because we know that at any moment we could be killed."

Without blinking Cathy asked: "Aren't all people who love each other in that situation?"

"I guess they are. They just don't know it."

On Monday he met with the vice president, the man who hired him seven years ago. He had just been discharged from the army, and he still had a regulation army haircut. The vice president, whose name was Frank, was a veteran of World War II, a marine who fought in the epic battles of the Pacific, and Stephen believed that Frank hired him at least in part because of his haircut. After his interview he overheard Frank talking on the phone to the vice president in personnel, telling him it was good to see a clean-cut young man for a change. The year was 1969, when men under the age of thirty flaunted a profusion of hair from the top of their heads to the bottom of their chins as well as on the sides of their faces.

Frank was a plainspoken man with an uncanny ability to see through excuses and demolish them with a few pithy words. His desk was in the last row of the desks that ran from the windows to the central aisle, and the people who worked for him were all lined up in front of him in rank order, starting with assistant vice presidents and ending with trainees in the front rows. As a trainee Stephen heard him dictating a telex to the branch manager in Paraguay, who for weeks had been saying that the reason a client still hadn't repaid his loan was that the rains still hadn't come, so the river was still too low for the client to float his logs down to market. Frank, making each word count because they charged by the word for a telex, told the manager that he had heard enough about the rains and that next time before making such a loan, instead of analyzing the numbers, he should get a long-range weather forecast.

Frank had spent ten years in Argentina. He was assigned there back in the days when you had to be single to go overseas, and you got a home leave every three years with a round-trip steamer ticket. You had two months of leave, and if during that time you could find a woman willing to marry you, and if you could get the woman approved by the vice president, then you could go back as a married man.

"It's good to see you," Frank said, getting up and shaking his hand. "Sit down and tell me about Argentina."

Stephen sat down in the chair at the side of Frank's desk.

"Before you do, though, I want to tell you how much I appreciate your staying there and keeping an eye on things."

"Thanks. I'm having an interesting time there."

"It sounds like you are. And you're making a lot of money for us."

"So far we've had a good year."

"That business of Arias gave me a scare, but the auditors had nothing but praise for the way you handled it."

"I just wish I'd caught him sooner."

"Fraud is a tough thing to detect," Frank said. "I remember a loan I made when I was your age. It was secured by government bonds, and the borrower was one of the most respected men in his community. It turned out that he pledged those bonds to three different banks, and we all ended up on the same tit. Needless to say, there wasn't enough milk for all of us."

"Well, I was lucky to catch him."

"The important thing is that you did catch him, and you handled it well." Frank found a piece of paper on his desk. "I was looking to see how much of our profits we get from the *extrabancario* market. You know, last quarter it accounted for more than half of our profits in Argentina."

"It's a good business," Stephen said. "We get the fees from both sides, and we have no assets on our books, so that increases our return on assets."

"How do you think this market will be affected by the new economic program?"

"If they stick to the program, it will disappear. But if we can pay market rates for deposits, and if we can charge market rates for loans, we won't be affected. The people who are making loans in the *extrabancario* market will put their money into the bank, and the people who are borrowing in this market will borrow from the bank."

"So it should be a wash."

"It should be," Stephen said.

"I just wonder if the government will stick to its program."

"So far it has. But you never know."

Frank nodded, and then he moved on to his next question. "How do you think the program will affect our local clients?"

"Some will have problems, especially the ones who've been protected all these years." Like the company that made vacuum cleaners. "They haven't had any competition from imports. Their costs are high, and their quality is low. So if they don't adapt to the new situation, they're not going to make it."

"What's our exposure?"

That was the question you were always asked, and Stephen was ready for it. "We don't have a lot. We have about a million in loans that could be affected, but we're secured in all cases. With property, not government bonds."

Frank laughed. "You better watch out. They might find a way to pledge property to three different banks."

"After the problem with Arias we checked everything—our guarantees, our security, our policies and procedures—and we put everything in order."

Looking satisfied, Frank leaned back with his hands clasped behind his head. "So tell me about this business that brings you to New York. I understand that you think people are using our Panama branch to launder money."

He gave Frank the sanitized version, without mentioning the Montoneros, and in this area Frank didn't push for more information since he knew about the special arrangement between Stephen and the bank's chairman.

"Well, I hope you nail the sons of bitches. I always wondered if we should have a branch in Panama. It's not our kind of market."

Later that morning he met with the man in the bank who handled its relations with the state banking department. His name was Flaherty, and he was efficient as well as personable. He had already scheduled a meeting with the department at ten the next morning, and they arranged to meet at nine-thirty so that they could take the subway downtown.

After his meeting with Flaherty he returned to the hotel, where he picked up the portable typewriter that he had requested earlier that morning. He had taken some paper from the typing pool that served the international division, so he had what he needed to write his report.

He had arranged to meet Cathy at five, which gave him the whole afternoon to work. She had gone out to explore the city and maybe do some shopping. He had suggested that she go to Bloomingdale's.

He got the information he had brought from Argentina, and he cleared the desk. Before sitting down, he transferred a bra from the back of the desk chair to the back of another chair, where other female garments were lying.

With a pencil he made an outline on a piece of paper, which he placed to the left of the typewriter, and then he began to type. He produced a first draft in about two hours, took a break to eat a sandwich that he had ordered from room service, and then spent another hour revising his work. By four he was done, and at that point he undressed and got into bed to take a nap since he was still feeling the effects of the sleepless night on the plane. As he rolled over and faced the side of the bed that Cathy had slept in, he smelled her in the sheets, and as he drifted off to sleep he was infused with her.

He awoke feeling her lips on his ear.

"Hey," she said softly. "It's five o'clock."

He looked up at her groggily.

"I bought a dress, and I want you to see if it's all right."

"You're not wearing it, are you?"

"No. I'll put it on."

He sat up and watched as she unzipped the dress she was wearing and hung it up and removed the new dress from its Bloomingdale's box. The color was a light, delicate blue, and when she put it on she looked adorable.

"Do you like it?" she asked, gracefully modeling it.

"I love it," he said.

"I needed something to wear in Minnesota."

"It's perfect for Minnesota. It's the color of sky-blue water."

She looked perplexed.

"That's what the name of the state means—the land of sky-blue water."

She smiled. "So I did well. And it was on sale."

She took off the dress and carefully hung it up. Then, as if it were a natural continuation, she undid her bra and draped it over the back of the chair where the other bra had been. And finally, in a fluid motion, she stepped out of her panties and dropped them on the seat of the chair.

Turning, she faced him in her full glory.

The next morning he and Flaherty met with two officials of the state banking department in a conference room that had a view of the harbor. Their names were Perrone and Makowski, and they came equipped with notepads and pens.

Perrone was older and evidently senior since he took the lead in asking questions. He was a short man with an impassive face and eyes that looked as if they had seen everything. His accent sounded like Brooklyn as he said: "I assume you have a write-up of what you're going to tell us."

"Yes," Stephen said, taking out the copies of his report that he had made on the bank's machine. He handed a copy to each of the officials and one to Flaherty.

"Do you have an extra copy?" Makowski asked. He was a big man with a placid manner.

"Sure. Take two."

"I appreciate it. They charge us for copies."

"Tell us," Perrone said, leaning forward, "what you think is happening at International Bank & Trust."

Prepared, he said: "Money laundering. It starts with a group of terrorists in Argentina who kidnap business executives and hold them for ransom."

"So we're talking about ransom money, not drug money."

"Right. From what's been reported, I figure they've collected more than eighty million dollars."

"Eighty million?" Makowski said, his eyes widening.

"More than eighty million," Stephen said, "but they've spent some of it. Eighty million is the net amount that I figure they have with International Bank & Trust."

"What would they have spent it on?" Perrone asked.

"Arms and supplies. They're fighting a war."

"I read about that," Makowski said.

"Okay," Perrone said, making a note. "So how do they get this money out of Argentina?"

"In bags of cash, which they take by plane to Panama."

"They have their own plane?"

"No. They take the bags on regular flights of Argentine and Brazilian airlines. When they get to Panama they deposit the cash in a Swiss bank, which combines it with remittances from individuals in Argentina. The combined money is transferred through our Panama branch to International Bank & Trust, with instructions to credit the laundered money to the account of a company called Esmeralda S.A."

"Is this company owned by the terrorists?"

"It's owned by three Argentine companies, which have a common owner of record. His name is Arnaldo Navarra."

The name was evidently unfamiliar to the officials.

"Navarra works for the owner of International Bank & Trust, Marco Safadi."

The two officials exchanged a look that indicated that the name was not only familiar to them but also of current interest to them.

"You say Navarra works for Safadi," Perrone said after making another note. "How do you know?"

"I had lunch with both of them last Wednesday."

"Okay. So what does Navarra do for him?"

"Navarra acts as a front for the terrorists," Stephen said, "and he handles their operations in pesos."

"How do you know he's fronting for the terrorists?"

"He's fronting for someone, and Safadi's laundering money for someone. Do you care who it is?"

"No. We don't. How do you know he's laundering money?"

"I have evidence. It's in my report."

"You have the details of the transactions?"

"I have them all," Stephen replied, "for the past three years."

Perrone leaned back, looking satisfied. "We've been hearing rumors about Safadi, but they were only rumors. Things you hear from brokers and consultants."

"We didn't have any evidence," Makowski said.

"But we've been watching this bank since he took it over. We had a feeling he was up to something."

"We're so glad we could help you," Flaherty said amiably.

"Before you go, I have a question," Perrone said. "How did you get involved in this?"

"We had a problem with one of our account managers, who was operating in the *extrabancario* market." Stephen explained how this market worked. "The account manager was arranging loans off the books and keeping the fees. When I caught him my investigation led me to Navarra, who according to the records was an owner of the three companies that had made the unrecorded loans. I later found out that these same companies owned Esmeralda, which had been receiving transfers through our Panama branch that looked like laundered money. So I had evidence that Navarra was involved in both operations. I worked with Navarra, rolling over the loans and gaining his confidence. And he finally led me to Safadi."

"Did you have any reason to suspect Safadi?"

"Yes. There were rumors about him."

"Things you heard from brokers and consultants," Perrone said shrewdly.

"That's right." They exchanged a look of recognition.

Outside the building Flaherty complimented him and said: "From the way they talked, it looks like they're going to act quickly. They could intervene by Monday."

"I hope it doesn't take them longer than that."

"I don't think it will. I think they were looking for a reason to act, and you gave it to them."

Though he would have liked them to act more quickly, he figured that nothing would happen to the money between now and Monday. It was less than a week. And he hadn't given Safadi any reason to act.

Since he couldn't do anything more for now, he booked a flight to Minneapolis-St. Paul for the next day. He was able to get a direct flight on Northwest Airlines that arrived in the early afternoon. There was an earlier flight, but that would have meant getting up earlier and going in rush-hour traffic to the airport, so he happily settled for the later flight.

Cathy was nervous about meeting his parents, and he did his best to reassure her, telling her that they would be glad he had found someone to love, especially after what had happened with his first marriage. He was sure of his father but he had doubts about his mother, who had always been impressed by the fact that Leila came from a family with deep roots in the horse country of northern Virginia. Though his mother came from a

Pennsylvania family that predated the Rockefellers in the oil industry, she was easily impressed by aristocratic credentials, and she was all too willing to forgive the sins of people who presented such credentials.

As they walked through the terminal on their way to the baggage claim, Cathy said: "I don't look like these people."

"Thank God. They're overweight."

"They have blond hair and white skin."

"A lot of them probably bleach their hair."

"Do they bleach their skin?"

He laughed. "I don't know. They should have tans by now, but in Minnesota it's not yet summer."

"When's summer?"

"July."

"Oh. Well, maybe I look like I just have a tan."

"A perfect tan. They'd give anything to look like you."

His parents were waiting for them at the baggage claim. His father was wearing a suit and tie as he always did during the week, and his mother was perfectly dressed as always. He noticed that she had a tan, and he wondered how she had achieved it. Maybe she had maintained her tan from the four months they spent in Delray every winter. He remembered how during the summer she used to lie out in the sun on a lawn chair in her bathing suit, having coated her skin with Johnson's Baby Oil. Explaining within the family why she got so dark, she said it was because of her Spanish grandmother. Unlike most of the women around them she still had her figure, and she probably still looked good in a bathing suit.

When he introduced Cathy his father shook her hand in a friendly way and his mother gave her a tentative hug. They made conversation while they waited for the conveyor belt to start moving with the baggage.

"How long are you staying?" his mother asked.

"Until Sunday," he said.

"I wish you could stay longer."

"Maybe next time. I have to get back to New York."

"Be glad they're here," his father said.

He noticed that his father was already using a pronoun that included Cathy.

They waited at the curb with their suitcases while his father went and got the car.

"That's a pretty dress," his mother said to Cathy.

"Thank you," Cathy said, smiling brightly.

"Did you buy that in New York?"

"No. I bought it in Buenos Aires. But I did buy a dress in New York. I'll wear it tonight."

As they drove out of the airport his mother looked around at Cathy, who was in the back seat behind his father. "Stephen told us you're from Venezuela."

He had told them about her in the weekly letters he sent them, though he hadn't revealed that she was living with him. That would have shocked even his father.

"Yes," Cathy said in a small voice.

"Where in Venezuela?"

"Caracas."

"Oh," his mother said as if that were a happy coincidence. "Stephen's older brother lived there for a while."

"I know. He told me."

"Her father's an American oil man," Stephen said, knowing that his mother would be favorably impressed. He had decided that it would be better if he did all the lying for Cathy. That way only one of them would feel guilty.

"Really? My grandfather was an oil man."

"He met her mother in Caracas."

"Do they still live there?"

"Yes," Stephen said, watching for pitfalls. "They decided to stay there since all the children live there, except Cathy."

"How many children are there?"

"Six," Cathy said, telling the truth.

"My, what a big family."

He waited for his mother's next question.

"What do you do in Argentina?"

"I work in a bookstore."

"You do? That's nice," his mother said approvingly.

"And I'm a student at the university."

"What are you studying?"

"I'm studying to be a teacher."

"Stephen was going to be a teacher. He almost completed his doctorate. But then he decided he had to go to war."

"I admire him for that," his father said. One of the things his father regretted was not having seen action in World War II. They had given him a desk job.

"Well, he should have completed his doctorate first."

"The war would have been over by then," his father said.

They drove through St. Paul and out to White Bear Lake, where they had their summer home. It was on the Peninsula in a family compound that his grandfather had built in the Twenties. There were four houses: one for his grandparents, one for his father's sister, one for his father, and one for Stephen and his older brother. They were summerhouses with screen porches, nothing fancy. They drew their water from the lake. His father's house was under the trees, facing the extensive lawn that while the grandchildren were growing up had served as a playing field for a variety of games including softball, horseshoes, badminton, croquet, and touch football.

"We thought you'd like to sleep in your house," his mother said as they got out of the car, meaning the house that he had shared with his older brother. "And Cathy can have the guestroom."

Cathy gave him a plaintive look, which he returned with a mum signal. There was no way that his parents would let them sleep together. But as he carried her suitcase into his father's house he was already thinking of how they could get around that. He would tell her later when he had a chance.

After they had unpacked in their separate accommodations they joined his parents on the front porch. Cathy had put on the dress from Bloomingdale's, which drew compliments from both his parents. He helped his father get drinks, and Cathy helped his mother bring hors d'oeuvres.

As they sat on the porch his father asked him about his job, and his mother asked Cathy about her background. Though he was paying attention to his father, he couldn't help overhearing the questions his mother was asking, and he couldn't help admiring the way Cathy kept steering her away from areas where she would have to lie. When his mother found out where Cathy had bought her dress, they were off and running on the subject of clothes: what they liked, what they could wear, and what they could never wear.

His mother, who had learned to cook only recently since she could no longer find any acceptable domestic help, served a Minnesota dinner, with pheasant that his father had shot on a hunting trip the previous fall and that she had saved in the freezer for a special occasion, accompanied by wild rice and little green peas from Le Sueur.

During dinner his mother expressed concern about the situation in Argentina, saying: "I read in the paper that the country's having a civil war."

"Oh, that's an exaggeration," he told her.

"Well, it doesn't sound like a safe place to live."

"I feel safe there," Cathy said.

"If the young lady feels safe there," his father said, "it must be all right."

Before going to bed he told Cathy that he would join her in the guestroom after his parents were asleep. The guestroom was on the opposite side of the house from where his parents slept, so his parents would never hear them.

Around midnight he left his house and stealthily entered his father's house, remembering the night when he and his sister, then in college, came home drunk from a party undetected by their parents and were later aroused by one of her boyfriends, who entered the house and blundered into what was now the guestroom but then had been their grandmother's bedroom. Their father wanted to kill the boy, but until the day she died their grandmother talked about her brush with the intruder as if it were the high point of her life.

Unlike his grandmother Cathy was expecting this intruder, and as he slipped into the bed she gave him a warm welcome.

The next day, while his mother took Cathy shopping in the village, his father took him to a place in Willernie, where they stood at the bar and drank his father's favorite beer, Old Milwaukee.

"You can tell me what it's really like there," his father said.

"It's safe for Cathy," he said.

"Is it safe for you?"

"It's safer than being in Vietnam."

"I've read about the kidnappings and assassinations of business executives. Is that still going on?"

"Yeah. But less than before."

"So it's getting safer."

"I think it is." He thought for a moment, and then he decided to tell his father what he was doing to stop the terrorists.

His father listened with fascination.

Though he downplayed his exploits, it felt good to share them with his father.

"I'm proud of you," his father said when he had finished. "You've done things I wish I'd done."

"But without you I couldn't have done them."

"What did I have to do with it?"

"You taught me to step up to the plate."

"I did? Well, I guess I did. But you know," his father said, "you were a lousy hitter."

He laughed. "Yeah. That's why I ended up playing tennis."

"You were good at tennis. I never could understand it. You could hit a tennis ball but not a baseball."

"Maybe a baseball's faster."

"It's not. When those guys serve a tennis ball it's much faster than a pitcher throws a baseball."

"Maybe it's easier to see a tennis ball. Who knows?"

They swigged their beer.

"I like this girl," his father said after a silence. "Compared with your first wife, it's like night and day."

"It sounds like you expect me to marry her."

"Why do you say that?"

Stephen smiled. "You compared her with my *first* wife."

"Well, you'd better marry her," his father said. "You'd be a damned fool if you didn't."

He put his arm around his father, thanking him.

When they got home his mother's car was in the parking area and his mother was sitting on the porch, but he didn't see Cathy.

"She's down at the lake," his mother told him before he could ask.

As he crossed the lawn he saw Cathy in the distance, standing out at the end of the dock. She must have felt his footsteps on the dock, but she didn't turn to greet him, and approaching her, he could tell from the slump of her shoulders that something was wrong. He stopped beside her, putting his arm around her back.

"I was thinking," she said, "about how my mother must feel not knowing where I am or what I'm doing."

He drew her toward him.

"It must feel like losing a child, and I can't imagine anything worse."

By now he had learned not to offer her any hope of ever seeing her mother again. The people who wanted to kill her would be watching for her to make contact, waiting for the opportunity.

"All she knows is that I'm alive."

Her mother knew this from the money transfers, and he imagined her mother waiting each month for the next transfer, wondering if it would come.

"I wish I could tell her where I am and what I'm doing, but if I did, they could find me."

They wouldn't get the information from her mother, who would never tell them, but they could intercept a letter or any other form of communication.

"I talk to my mother in my prayers," Cathy said. "Do you think she can hear me?"

"I'm sure she can," Stephen said, at last finding something he could honestly say.

She put her arm around his waist and leaned against him.

They gazed together out at the lake, where a few sailboats glided in the wind. Their white sails looked like the wings of angels.

On Thursday they had lunch with his parents at the University Club, and after they were done eating he led Cathy down to the barroom and showed her where F. Scott Fitzgerald had carved his name in the oak bar, along with hundreds of less famous people. Later, as they toured Summit Avenue, he pointed out the house where Fitzgerald had lived. His mother was surprised that a Venezuelan would have heard of Fitzgerald, and his father muttered his usual judgment that Fitzgerald was a drunk—a great writer, but still a drunk.

They stopped on Grand Avenue at the studio of Stephen's sister, who showed them her latest paintings. She apologized for the fact that her husband wasn't there. He was down at the state legislature trying to organize opposition to a bill the governor wanted to pass.

At the family party the next evening Cathy met his sister's husband as well as his brother, his brother's wife, and his brother's four children—two girls from his first wife and two boys from his current wife. His brother tried to impress Cathy with his knowledge of Caracas, but she kept saying no, she didn't know the people he was talking about.

Together he and Cathy cooked *paella*, and it was a hit with everyone, including the children, who could pick out what they liked from the pans on the table.

After they had cleaned up, his mother found him alone in the kitchen wiping the counter.

"You cooked an excellent dinner," she told him.

"Thanks," he said. "We're learning together how to cook."

"Are you serious about her?"

"If I wasn't, I wouldn't have brought her home with me."

"I like her, but I wonder if you're ready to get married again. It's only five months since you were divorced."

"It's three years since we separated."

"Is it that long? It doesn't seem that long."

"It does to me. So I'm not exactly rushing from one marriage to another."

"I suppose not." His mother was silent for a while. "But we really don't know much about her."

"I do. I know everything about her."

"We've never met her family."

"You don't have to meet her family. You already have two

sets of in-laws. And you still keep up with Leila's parents."

"How do you know?"

"I know you."

"Well, at our age," his mother said, "it's very hard to let people go."

"I understand. And I don't mind. But you don't have to meet her family to know what Cathy's like."

"I suppose not. And we can meet them at the wedding."

"You can," he said, realizing that he would have to kill them off before then.

His mother sighed. "To be perfectly honest, I didn't think you knew what you were doing when you married Leila. But what could I say?"

"You couldn't have said anything to stop me."

"I know. And if you'll allow me, I'd like to say—" She paused as if she were trying to find the right words. "I think you know what you're doing now."

"Thanks, Mom," he said, hugging her.

On Saturday, the last night of their visit, they took his parents out to dinner at a restaurant in North Oaks that his mother liked. They had a good time, and both his parents were already treating Cathy as if she were a member of the family.

"I just wish you could stay longer," his mother said before going to bed.

"Next time we will," Stephen promised.

He and Cathy remained in the living room for a while. Cathy turned on the television, still entranced by the novelty of hearing the programs in English. She was idly switching from channel to channel when they caught the tail end of a story: "There were no survivors. The only passengers were the pilot and an Argentinean banker named Marco Safadi. The private plane was flying to

Guadalajara from New Orleans, where it had stopped on its way from New York."

"Isn't that the man you were after?"

"Right. See if you can find the story on another channel."

While she tried to find it he wondered what had happened. It was clear that Safadi had been killed, but had it been an accident? Had the government discovered what he was doing? Had they captured a Montonero and made him talk? Whatever had happened, it was now certain that the banking department would intervene and that they would move quickly.

"Forget it," he told Cathy after she had tried a number of channels. "We'll find out tomorrow what happened."

She turned off the television and faced him, asking hopefully: "Does this mean you've finished the project?"

"It does. We just have to tie up the loose ends."

She came into his arms and pressed her face against his chest, saying: "*Gracias a Dios.*"

ELEVEN

ON MONDAY, back in New York, he went into the bank at nine and called the office of Navarra wondering if something had happened to him. From a story in the newspaper that the hotel delivered to their room that morning, he learned that the plane had exploded in midair, which suggested that it had been sabotaged.

Buenos Aires, normally two hours ahead of New York, was an hour ahead with daylight savings, so it was ten there, and someone should have been at Navarra's office. But there was no answer. He tried again, but there was still no answer.

He called Elena and got her at the office, where she was working on an article about the effects of a free market on Argentine manufacturing companies. She had a lot of questions and couldn't wait for him to return.

He told her he had been calling a lawyer named Arnaldo Navarra, wondering if something had happened to him, but there was no answer at his office.

Elena said: "It sounds like you have reason to believe that something did happen to him."

"He was working for Marco Safadi."

"The man who was killed in the plane?"

"Yeah. Whoever killed Safadi may have killed him."

"I'll see if he appears in any reports, and I'll get back to you."

"I'll be moving around, so I'll call you. Say, in an hour?"

"Fine. I'll be here."

While he was waiting to call her back he contacted Flaherty

and told him what had happened and asked him to find out what the banking department was doing.

He waited more than an hour to call Elena, wanting to give her more time to get information, and once again she came through for him.

"He didn't appear in any reports," she told him, "so I went to his office, and I found it locked. As I was standing in the hall the *portero* approached me and told me that Navarra had cleaned out his office, that he owed a month's rent, and that the landlord would never rent to a lawyer again."

"So what do you think?"

"I think he went away. The *portero* told me that the police came looking for Navarra earlier this morning, so he must have been one step ahead of them."

"I wonder where the hell he went."

"Could he have been in the plane with Safadi?"

"If he had been, they would have identified his body."

"I guess they would have."

"It's too much of a coincidence that they both disappeared the same weekend. It must have been planned."

"Are you suggesting," Elena asked him after a moment, "that Safadi wasn't in the plane?"

"I'm beginning to wonder."

He had to wait until Thursday morning to meet with Perrone and Makowski. By then he had learned from the newspapers that International Bank & Trust had been taken over by the state and declared insolvent. Almost eighty million dollars in cash was missing, so the bank was unable to meet the claims of its depositors. Though federal insurance would cover deposits for up to forty thousand dollars per account, above that amount the bank's depositors would lose everything.

"You were right," Perrone said when they finally met. "They

were laundering money big time. They were also embezzling it from the depositors."

"What happened to the money that was in the account of Esmeralda?"

"They moved it to another account, and then they withdrew it. All in cash."

"What did they do with it?" Stephen asked.

"I don't know. Safadi must have taken it somewhere."

"I wonder if they found out what he was doing."

"You mean the terrorists? Well, they know now, but they haven't come forward to make a claim."

"The lawyer who fronted for them skipped town."

"Now, that's a coincidence," Perrone said.

"I think it was planned."

"You do? Including the accident?"

Stephen nodded, believing that Safadi had given him the fifty thousand to buy just a little more time.

"You'll be interested to know," Perrone said, "that Safadi's brother flew to the scene of the plane crash and made a positive identification of the body."

"If the plane exploded, there couldn't have been much left of the passengers."

"That's what I was thinking, but the police in Mexico confirmed that there was enough left for the brother to identify. Of course we can't verify that because the brother had the body cremated."

"The papers said the plane stopped in New Orleans."

"That's right," Perrone said. "It always stopped there to be serviced and refueled."

"Was Safadi observed reboarding the plane?"

"Three witnesses saw someone who looked like him get back into the plane."

"I wonder who it could have been."

"I have a theory," Perrone said. "You don't take eighty million dollars in cash out of a bank without someone noticing. From what we can see, it looks like the bank's controller covered up for him. And guess what?"

"What?" Stephen said.

"The controller's missing, and so is his car."

"His car?"

"Yeah. Instead of flying to New Orleans, which would have left a trail, he could have driven there and ditched his car. He could have been planning to join Safadi in Mexico, and he could have boarded the plane in New Orleans."

"He could have. But how would Safadi have explained why he wasn't going with him?"

"The plane could take only one passenger. Safadi says politely, you go first, and I'll come on the next trip."

"A nice boss," Makowski said.

"Yeah. You're lucky."

"So that leaves Safadi in New Orleans," Stephen said.

"Not for long," Perrone said. "He boards a plane with a fake passport and flies to Brazil, where they have the best plastic surgeons in the world."

"I wonder where the money is."

"It's probably in Panama being laundered."

"Would you like to try to find it?" Makowski asked.

"No, I'm done," Stephen said. "As long as the terrorists don't have it, I don't care who has it."

"I've seen a lot of cases," Perrone said, shaking his head, "but this one takes the prize. Imagine having the balls to steal from terrorists."

"Imagine how the terrorists feel," Makowski said.

To celebrate, he took Cathy to a highly rated French restaurant that evening, and they drank a bottle of champagne.

The next day, Friday, they took the overnight flight back to Buenos Aires. They were exhausted when they got home, but they were glad to be back. They had been away for two weeks, and they had missed their routines.

They slept through the afternoon on Saturday and had dinner at Ligure. After dinner they took a walk, stretching their legs. It was more than thirty degrees colder than in New York, but it felt good. They walked up Santa Fe as far as Callao and then came back on the other side of the street. A new restaurant had opened in their absence, a Chinese restaurant. They stopped to look at the menu, which not surprisingly featured steak along with moo-shoo pork and shrimp with black bean sauce.

After church the next day they walked over to San Telmo, where they browsed around the flea market that was held there every Sunday. They had lunch in a café where tango music was playing, and they decided to come back there on a Saturday night and watch a tango show.

"Do you know how to tango?" Cathy asked him.

"No. I never even tried it," Stephen said, shaking his head. "It looks so difficult."

"I think you have to practice a lot with the same partner."

"Well, maybe we could learn it together."

"You're not a bad dancer."

"How do you know? The only time we ever danced was the night we met. And we didn't do anything fancy."

"Still, I liked the way you held me."

"How did I hold you?"

"Like I was someone special."

"That's how I felt."

"You felt that right away?"

"Yes, right away."

"I felt that too," she confessed, gazing at him tenderly. "This may sound corny, but I felt like the girl in the fairy tale who gets rescued by the prince."

"That does sound corny."

"But it's how I felt."

"Then it's not corny. A prince?"

"Yes. Girls are entitled to their fantasies."

"Are guys entitled to *their* fantasies?"

"Well, that depends," she said with a knowing smile.

"You mean it's all right if we fantasize about princesses."

She nodded. "Or about girls from the *barrio*."

"Speaking of guys," he said, taking her hand, "tomorrow I'm going to meet with the embassy guys, and I'm going to end our relationship."

"I'm glad. Then I can stop worrying about that situation."

"What other situations will you worry about?"

"The situations of our friends."

"Yeah. I worry a lot about them."

They fell into a silence.

"Oh, look at that couple," Cathy said. She pointed through the window to a man in a slouch hat and a striped suit bending over a woman in a slit skirt, who kicked up a spiked heel as they danced to the music that flowed out into the street.

"You think we could do that?"

"I think we could try."

When he arrived at the bank on Monday he found his desk piled with proposals. In a voice loud enough for all the account managers to hear, he said: "I see that you guys were really busy while I was away."

They all turned and looked at him as if to make sure they were being addressed.

"You could have taken these proposals to Carlos."

"Carlos told us to save them for you," one of them said. "He said you'd only be gone a week."

"Well, I'll get to them as soon as I can."

He spent the rest of the morning reviewing the proposals, approving most of them without any changes but modifying some of them and making suggestions on how to improve them. They were getting better, he was happy to see.

He had made an appointment with the embassy guys, and after the account managers had gone to lunch he looked up and saw them following Ignacio to the conference room. They didn't have their satchels, so at least today they didn't need cash. If they needed cash in the future they would have to find someone else with a security clearance. He had done his part with them, and he believed that the Montoneros weren't the main problem now, the military were.

"How was New York?" John asked when he joined the agents in the conference room.

"It was great," Stephen said. "But I'm glad to be back."

"Well, it didn't end the way we expected, but we achieved our goal. And we should be grateful to Safadi for helping us."

"We should give him a medal," Bill said.

"Yeah, good luck on finding him," John said.

"So you don't believe he was killed in the accident?" Stephen asked, anxious to hear their opinions.

"Accident?" John scoffed. "How often does a private plane explode in midair?"

"I don't know. I guess not very often."

"Once in a million," Bill said as if he had checked the statistics on this.

"Navarra disappeared the same weekend," Stephen said.

"We knew that," John said. "How did you know?"

"I have my sources."

"I hope you're not planning to compete with us," Bill said.

"Don't worry. I'm not."

"They're probably both in Brazil," John said, sounding envious, "ogling the girls in their bikinis."

"I wish we could get assigned there," Bill said. "I hate this cold weather."

"It could be worse. We could be in Canada."

"Why would we be in Canada?"

"They have terrorists there."

"You mean the separatists? Oh, they don't need us to deal with that."

"Is it fair to say," Stephen asked, returning to the subject, "that the Montoneros are out of business?"

"It's fair to say that," John said. "They lost their big pot of money, and even if they still have some money they can't use it to bring arms into the country. The government opens every carton that arrives by ship, by plane, by train—"

"By mule," Bill added.

"Then we can disband our operation?"

"Yeah. Sure," John said. "Operation Safadi is *terminado*."

"*Terminada*," Bill said. "Operation is feminine."

"Why is it feminine?"

"I don't know, but it is."

"I have a loose end," Stephen told them.

"What's that?" John asked.

"The money Safadi gave me. What should I do with it?"

"Give it to charity. But don't tell anyone about it."

"That would complicate things," Bill agreed.

"And we don't know about it, do we."

"No. We never heard about it."

"Okay," Stephen said, knowing what he would do with the money. "I have one last question. Are you going to need cash in the future?"

"It's hard to say," John said as if he were surprised by the question. "These governments are working together now, so they don't need us as much anymore."

"But we hope you'll be available in case we need you," Bill said, looking at him expectantly.

"I won't be. It's nothing personal—"

"That's what the mob says before they kill you," John said.

"He's taking over our territory," Bill said.

"No. I'm leaving it."

"Can you give us a reason?" John asked.

"I promised my wife."

"That's a good reason."

"The best reason," Bill said.

"Except that you don't have a wife," John pointed out.

"I should have said my fiancée."

"Are you going to marry that girl?"

"Yes." He wished they didn't know so much about him, and he wondered if they would ever drop his security clearance.

"Well, I hope you invite us to the wedding."

"I will. The guest list wouldn't be complete," he told them, "without a trade specialist and an agricultural attaché."

That night, as they were lying in bed, he shared with Cathy his idea about what to do with the money.

"I'd like to give it to Paco," he told her. "With that money and the other money he's raised, he may have enough to build the church and the school."

"That's a great idea," she agreed. "But what will you tell him when he asks where it came from?"

"I'll say I got it from an anonymous donor."

"All right. But where *did* it come from? I know you got it from Safadi, but where did he get it?"

"He got it from his business."

"You mean from pretending to help the Montoneros?"

"Or from pretending to help his people. Or even from his normal banking operations. You can't always tell where money came from. It's fungible."

"Fungible?"

"That means it's interchangeable. You can substitute one pot of money for another, and it makes no difference. That's why you can launder it."

"Money is fungible," Cathy said, using the new word in a sentence. "Unlike people."

"Yeah. We're not fungible."

"So you could say truthfully that you don't know where that money came from."

"That's right," he said. "And you know what? Wherever it came from, if I give it to Paco for a church and a school, I believe that God will look the other way."

On Tuesday evening at the *confitería* after welcoming him back, Mario said: "We got our visas for Mexico."

"That's good. Have you set a date?"

"No, not yet. We'll probably leave at the end of the semester."

"What do you mean probably? You sound like you have doubts about it."

Marie sighed. "I always had doubts. But now Teresa is having doubts."

"She is? Why?"

"I don't know. I think it started when Adriana disappeared. I've never seen her so angry. I've seen her lose her temper, but this is different."

"We noticed that the last time we saw her."

"You did? Then you know what I'm talking about."

"Is it because Adriana was a student?"

"That's basically it. But there's something else. Remember that evening when Adriana was talking politics and Teresa just got up and left?"

"Yes, I remember."

"Well, I think she feels guilty about it. Like she abandoned Adriana."

"Abandoned her?"

"It was the last time she saw Adriana."

"So she feels guilty about the way she acted the last time she saw someone who disappeared. I can understand that. But what's it got to do with her doubts about leaving Argentina?"

"I think she feels," Mario said haltingly, "that if she leaves she'll be abandoning her students."

"Well, she *will* be abandoning them."

"I know. And I'll be abandoning my students."

"So you might not leave after all?"

"We might not. But then again we might. One day she's adamant about leaving, and the next day she has doubts."

At that moment Teresa appeared with her usual bag of books and her usual bottle of soda.

Stephen got up and hugged her.

"Welcome back," she said warmly.

"Thanks," he said. "It's good to be with friends again."

"Don't you have friends in New York?"

"Yes, but I really haven't kept up with them."

He pulled out a chair for her, and she sat down at the table. She looked at Mario as if she knew that they had been talking about her, and she said to Stephen: "I guess you know we got our visas."

"Mario told me."

"Well, I've been reading about Mexico, and I don't know if I'm going to like it."

He waited for her to elaborate.

"For one thing," Teresa said, "I read that Mexico City is two thousand two hundred and fifty meters above sea level. So we could have trouble breathing there."

"The altitude isn't the only problem," Mario said. "There's also the pollution."

"Oh, yes. The pollution. I read that the city is surrounded by mountains, so all the pollution from the industry and the vehicles is trapped inside a natural bowl, and the air is never cleared by wind. It just sits there."

"When I was in Mexico City," Stephen said, "it wasn't so bad. At least you could still see the volcanoes."

"Volcanoes?" Teresa said. "Do they erupt?"

"They haven't for a long time."

"I still don't like the idea of living near volcanoes."

"What volcanoes?" Cathy asked, arriving from her class.

Teresa got up, and the two women joined in a long *abrazo*.

"I've missed you," Teresa said.

"I've missed you too."

When they had sat down at the table Teresa asked her: "Did you like New York?"

"I loved it. I also loved Minnesota."

"Minnesota? So you met his parents? *Dios mío*," Teresa said, looking happily from one of them to the other. "It sounds like things are moving along."

"You're making him blush," Mario said.

"I'm not blushing," Stephen said.

"How can you tell with Americans? They always look pink."

"I'm not pink."

"Well, you could never pass for an Italian."

"I couldn't either," Cathy said.

They all laughed.

Then changing the mood, Teresa said: "While you were away some more students disappeared."

"Oh, no," Cathy said softly.

"There's no sign of them," Mario said.

"I hate the assholes who are doing this," Teresa said fiercely. "I want to kill them."

"God will punish them," Cathy said, taking her hand.

Around ten the next morning Sofi called him at the bank, and he could tell that something was wrong before she told him: "They've taken Paco."

"What?" he said, dismayed. "Who?"

"Three men in a big car. They grabbed him and drove away."

"Were they in uniforms?"

"No. They were in plain clothes."

"When did it happen?"

"A half hour ago."

"Where are you now?"

"I'm in a café. It was the nearest phone."

"Well, tell me how to get there."

She did. "I think we should go and see his bishop."

"Do you know where he is?"

"Yes. I went to see him once with Paco about the church and the school."

"I'll come and get you right away."

"I'll wait for you here."

"Are you all right?"

"I'm fine. They didn't bother me."

He called Señora Pérez and tried to get the bank car, but it wasn't available, so he rushed out to find a taxi.

Walking fast, he went to Diagonal Norte, where he got a taxi within a few minutes. He gave the driver the address and asked him to hurry.

"Hurry? In this traffic?" the driver said, meeting his eyes in the rearview mirror.

"Try to get around it. I don't care if you take a longer way."

The driver did his best, and it took him only about twenty minutes to get to the café where Sofi was waiting. She had spotted the taxi and was heading toward it before they came to a complete stop.

She got into the taxi and told the driver where to go next.

When they were under way she said: "Thanks for coming. I couldn't have handled this myself."

"So they're going after priests who they think are Marxists?"

"Oh, yes. While you were away they killed two priests who work in the *villas*."

"And the church let them get away with it?"

"The church is divided," Sofi said. "The hierarchy supports the military, but most of the priests oppose them."

He knew that the hierarchy had welcomed the *golpe* and supported the military's crusade against communism, but he hadn't expected the church to turn a blind eye to what they were doing. "Where does Paco's bishop stand?"

"He opposes the military, and he supports what priests like Paco are doing to help the poor."

"Then the military might kill him."

"They might. They already tried to kill a bishop."

"That was the Triple A," he said, remembering the incident.

"It's all the same," Sofi sighed.

"Well, I hope this bishop is a tough man."

"He is. Wait until you meet him."

"Should I wait for you?" the driver asked when they arrived at their destination.

"No. Thanks. We'll be here a while," Stephen said, paying him and giving him a big tip. "You did a good job."

"*Gracias.*"

A nun, who reminded him of Señora Pérez, went to great lengths to prevent them from having access to the bishop, but they finally made her realize that this was an emergency, that the life of a priest was in danger.

The bishop received them in his office. He was a wiry man who looked as if he had spent his life doing manual labor instead of sitting in an office. When they shook hands Stephen felt calluses.

Sensing their urgency, the bishop asked: "What did they do to Father Francisco?"

Sofi told him, recounting how the three men had come to the *villa* in a big car and grabbed Paco and driven away.

"Do you know if the car was a Ford Falcon?"

"I don't know cars," Sofi said.

"Does it make a difference?" Stephen asked respectfully.

"It could tell us which group of thugs has him. If it's the police, then there's a good chance I can get him out before they do a lot of damage. But if it's the navy," the bishop said grimly, "then God help us."

"Well, assume it's the police. Do you know where they'd be holding him?"

"I think I know. I've been there before."

Without further discussion the bishop got up and told them to come with him.

They followed him past the nun, who for a moment looked as if she were going to stop them, and out to a car.

"Wake up!" the bishop said to the driver, who was dozing in the front seat.

The driver jumped and got out and opened a door.

"You get in first," the bishop told them.

They did as he said, and after the driver had returned to the front seat the bishop instructed him where to go.

The bishop said nothing until they stopped in front of a nondescript building. Then he told them: "Stay here. I may need you as witnesses."

When the bishop had gone into the building the driver answered their unasked question. "He means in case he doesn't come back."

The driver kept the engine running, ready to go.

They waited tensely, not talking.

After what seemed like a very long time the bishop emerged

from the building supporting Paco, who looked as if he could barely stand up.

Stephen jumped out and helped the bishop.

The driver got out and opened the passenger door in the front, and they eased Paco into the car.

"Should we take him to the hospital?" Stephen asked.

"It's not necessary," Paco said hoarsely.

"Are you sure?"

"Yes. It's only bruises."

As they rode away, no longer in a hurry, Stephen asked the bishop what he had said to the police.

"I told them that if they didn't release Father Francisco immediately, they would have to arrest me," the bishop said with complete composure. "And I repeated what we said in our pastoral letter last month—that it was an error, a grievous error, for them to confuse terrorists with Christians who are working to help the poor."

"Do you think that'll stop them from doing this again?"

"No. It won't stop them. But it might make them think twice. And the Vatican has sent them a strong message by the appointment of Cardinal Pironio."

That was the bishop they had tried to kill. The assassins had narrowly missed him and killed a florist standing near him. "He was made a cardinal?"

"Yes. A month ago. And those thugs won't kill a cardinal," the bishop assured them.

Early the next morning Stephen took the subway to Primera Junta and met Sofi at the Caballito station, where they got on a *colectivo* to where she worked.

"How's the baby?" he asked her on the way.

"Growing," she said, "and moving."

Her face was filling out, making her look even softer. "I can't imagine what it's like, but it must be a good feeling."

"It's not a comfortable feeling, but it's a good one."

"What are you going to name it?"

"If it's a boy, Christopher. If it's a girl, Christina."

"Would you rather have a girl or a boy?"

"I'll be happy with either."

They rode in silence for a while, and then Stephen said: "I was really impressed by Paco's bishop."

"He was magnificent. He risked his life for Paco."

"With bishops like him maybe the church can end this war."

"At this point they're our best hope."

"Is the Greek Orthodox Church involved?"

"Yes. But there aren't many of us," she said. "I depend more on the Catholic Church to support what I'm doing."

"Have you ever thought of converting?"

"I have. But my parents wouldn't be happy about it."

"My parents weren't happy when I converted, but now they're okay with it."

"Still, I might do it for Chris. I think he'd want his son or daughter raised as a Catholic. What do you think?"

"We didn't talk about religion."

"We didn't either. Except about which church we should get married in, and he went along with my church to make my parents happy."

"Well, I know a priest who would love to convert you."

"I know one too," Sofi said, smiling.

When they arrived at the *villa* he checked with Jorge to see how the cooperative was going. Jorge told him it was going well. They hadn't had any further problems with the middleman, and they had expanded from potatoes to several other products that they were now buying directly from the farms. They would soon need another truck.

He walked around the *villa* with Sofi looking for Paco, whom they found with a group of children. The children ranged from about eight to ten in age, and two of them had obviously just been fighting. Paco was explaining to them, in terms that they could understand, that fighting was not the way to solve problems, it only made things worse. The two children whose faces showed evidence of blows were resisting the message, but the other children seemed open to it. Paco finally convinced the fighters to shake hands as a sign of peace.

When the children had dispersed, Stephen asked: "How are you feeling?"

"Fine," Paco said. "Thank you again for rescuing me."

"Your bishop was the one who rescued you."

"But you went and got him."

They walked to the hut where Paco lived, and they went inside. It had one room with a bed, a table, and two wooden chairs. It could have been a monk's cell. On the wall over the bed hung a framed quotation which Stephen recognized as the manifesto of liberation theology: "The Lord sent me to bring glad tidings to the poor, to proclaim liberty to captives."

Turning to Paco, Stephen said: "I have something for you."

"You do? What?"

He took an envelope out of the inside pocket of his jacket and offered it to Paco. "Another donation."

"From you?"

"No. From someone else."

Paco looked intrigued. He took the envelope and opened it, pulling out a check. Gaping, he said: "Fifty thousand dollars? Where did this come from?"

"It came from an anonymous donor."

"But you must know who it is."

"I don't. I didn't get it directly from the donor."

"Well, this is very mysterious," Paco said, gazing at the check. "Very mysterious."

"Isn't that what faith is about? Accepting mysteries?"

"Are you telling me that I should accept this donation and not question it?"

"Yes. Accept it as a gift from God."

"All right," Paco said, his voice changing from doubt to excitement. "Do you know what this means?"

"I hope it means you can build your church."

"And the school too," Sofi said.

"With the money I've raised and the money raised by your friend Vittoria and this money," Paco said, waving the check, "we have what we need."

"Then let's start building."

Paco embraced him, saying: *"Mil gracias!"*

On Friday evening, after they had all arrived at the café, Paco announced that his project was fully funded.

"Qué maravilla!" Elena said.

"How did you raise the money so fast?" Mario asked.

"We had help from Stephen's friend Vittoria—"

"The wife of your assistant?" Elena asked Stephen. "How's she doing?"

"Better," he told her.

"—and yesterday we received a major contribution from an anonymous donor."

"An anonymous donor?" Mario said. "Who could it be?"

"It could be someone in the military," Sofi suggested, "with a guilty conscience."

"Do you think they have consciences?"

"Well, they must feel guilty now and then."

"I wonder. Do people who think they're God feel guilty?"

"They usually don't," Paco said.

"I think it's an American," Teresa said.

"Why do you think that?" Sofi asked.

"It's the kind of thing an American would do."

"How many Americans have you known?" Mario asked.

"Only two. Chris and Stephen."

"That's a very small sample."

"It's big enough for me."

"It's only big enough for you to know that this is the kind of thing that Chris or Stephen would do."

"Are you saying," Elena asked, "that you think this money came from Stephen?"

"No, not exactly," Teresa said.

"It didn't come from me," Stephen insisted.

"Who gave it to Paco?" Mario asked.

"I gave it to him. But I was only a messenger."

"You were an angel," Paco said thankfully, "bringing me a gift from God."

"He's not an angel," Cathy assured them.

"She ought to know," Teresa said.

"Well, I agree with Paco," Elena said. "Not about Stephen being an angel, but about where it came from."

That ended the speculation.

Two days before the first loans that Stephen had arranged for Navarra came due, the government impounded all the loans that had been made by the three companies that they believed were owned by the Montoneros. So as a result of embezzlement by Safadi and confiscation by the government, the Montoneros lost the money they had accumulated by kidnapping people and holding them for ransom. At least they lost about eighty-five million dollars.

Meanwhile, the war continued. On Friday, July 2, a bomb exploded in the Buenos Aires police headquarters, killing twenty-one and wounding sixty-three. Two days later three Irish priests and two seminarians were shot in a building next to their church in Belgrano. The story about the killing made the front page of

Elena's newspaper, which reported an inscription presumably left by the assassins that said: "For our dynamited police comrades."

The next day Stephen had lunch with Elena, who told him that the government had threatened to close her paper for accusing the police of killing in vengeance.

Stephen was returning from lunch when they grabbed him.

"The guy behind you has a gun pointed straight at your back," said the guy who had taken his right arm. "So you better do what I tell you."

Another guy took his left arm.

They led him to a car that was waiting at the curb with its doors open.

"Get in," the guy on his right told him.

Seeing no good alternative, he got into the car.

The other guy went around the car, and Stephen ended up sitting between them. The guy behind him with the gun jumped into the front.

The driver edged the car forward, respecting the traffic and behaving like any other driver returning a car full of bankers from lunch.

Stephen said nothing, waiting for them to reveal their intentions, but they said nothing as the car left the financial district and headed south on Paseo Colón. In fact, they said nothing until the car stopped in a neighborhood that looked like the Boca, with its bright-colored buildings.

"Get out," the guy on his right told him.

He got out and did what they said, going with them into a building and up a flight of stairs. The guy who had been sitting at his left opened the door, and the other one pushed him into an apartment that looked as if its inhabitants were in the process of moving either in or out.

They led him into a bedroom that looked out onto a patio where laundry was hanging out to dry, and they locked the door, leaving him alone.

The room had a bed, a table with a lamp on it, and three wooden chairs.

He paced around for a while thinking. The three guys were all under thirty, and they didn't act like police or military. They must be Montoneros, and they must be planning to hold him for ransom.

The door was unlocked, and two of them came into the room, one with a gun and the other with a clothesline.

"Turn around," the one with the gun told him.

He turned around and stood still while the one with the clothesline tied his hands behind his back, wrapping the cord several times around his wrists.

"I'm sorry if it's tight," the rope-tier said.

"Don't apologize to him," the gun-holder said. "He's a capitalist pig."

They weren't police or military.

When his hands were securely tied behind his back they left him alone again, and he started pacing around again, remembering how he had told Safadi and Navarra that his bank had a policy of not paying ransom money. He had said that in the hope that if they ever talked about him to the Montoneros they would mention it, and that it would remove any possible motivation for kidnapping him. But either they hadn't talked about him or these guys didn't believe it.

They weren't wearing masks, so they didn't care if he saw their faces. If they were police or military, that would mean they planned to kill him. But maybe it wouldn't. The police who had beaten Elena had let her see their faces. So maybe these guys were planning to use him to send a message, just as the police had used Elena to send a message.

No, it was about money. They might have found out that he had done business with Navarra and Safadi. They might have found out that he had tried to get the state banking department to freeze their dollars. They might have found out that the information he had collected helped the government to confiscate their pesos. Whatever they had found out about him, they blamed him for the loss of their money, and now they planned to use him to recover it.

TWELVE

IT WAS AFTER DARK when two of his captors, the one who had taken his right arm and the guy with the gun, came back into the room. The former, who had curly hair and stone blue eyes, straddled a chair and confronted him, saying: "We want our money."

"What money?"

"The money you and that asshole Safadi stole from us."

"I have no idea what you're talking about," he told them blankly. "Could you explain?"

"We kept our money in Safadi's bank, and he embezzled it."

"What's that got to do with me?"

"You were working with him."

"Who told you that?"

"Tito Arias."

"Well, he's lying. I fired him for stealing, and now he's trying to get back at me."

"We want our money."

"I don't have it."

"Your bank has it."

"How much do you want?"

"Eighty million dollars."

"Eighty-five million," the guy with the gun said.

"You think my bank would pay that much for me?"

"They better, or you're dead."

He breathed deeply. "What can I do?"

"You can write a note to them."

292

"I can't write a note with my hands tied behind my back."

"You can write the note tomorrow," the guy with the curly hair said, rising.

They left him, closing the door behind them but not locking it. A few minutes later the guy who had tied his hands brought him an *empanada* and a glass of red wine.

"I'm sorry it's not warm," he said, referring to the *empanada*.

"That's okay. Thanks." Stephen wondered how he was supposed to eat the food or drink the wine with his hands tied behind his back.

Evidently becoming aware of the problem, the guy said: "I'd untie your hands, but that would complicate things. Do you mind if I feed you?"

"No. I don't mind." He wasn't hungry, but incongruously he didn't want to hurt the guy's feelings.

"My hands are clean."

Stephen took bites of *empanada* and sips of wine as the guy brought them to his mouth. The *empanada* wasn't bad, but the wine was bitter. From the darkness in the back of his mind crept the thought that this might be his last meal.

When they were done the guy left him, not taking the plate or the glass but locking the door.

During the night, unable to sleep, Stephen imagined what would happen to Cathy if they killed him.

The next morning the guy with curly hair untied his hands and dictated a note, which Stephen wrote with the pen and paper provided to him.

At one point he said: "This doesn't sound like me."

"Then make it sound like you."

"Okay." He changed the wording.

When the guy was satisfied with the note he tied Stephen's hands again. He didn't apologize for it being tight.

He heard them lock the door, and he heard them talking as they left the apartment. It sounded like two of them had gone, presumably the one with the curly hair and one of the others, which meant there was only one guard. He hoped it was the one who had tied his hands the first time, the one who had fed him.

Looking around, he spotted the empty glass on the table. He backed up to the table and picked up the glass with his tied hands, being very careful not to drop it. He carried the glass over to the bed, where he sat down, releasing the glass onto the blanket. He got the pillow and set it on the floor. After placing the glass on the pillow he folded the pillow and then got up and stood on it, muffling the sound as he broke the glass with his weight. He sat down on the bed again, opened the pillow, and selected the most useful looking shard.

It took him a while to cut through the clothesline using the piece of broken glass, but he finally felt the loose ends, which he unwound from his wrists.

With his hands free, he unplugged the cord of the lamp from the outlet and then unscrewed the nut that fastened the shade. He set the shade down on the table and coiled the cord so it wouldn't be in the way.

Then he walked over to the window and swung the lamp, breaking the glass with a loud noise.

He quickly hid behind the door and waited for the guard, holding the lamp by its neck in a raised position.

When he heard the key unlock the door he readied himself, and when the guard rushed in he struck him on the head with the lamp. The guard went sprawling onto the floor, with the gun sliding out of his hand.

Stephen dropped the lamp and picked up the gun, but he could have taken his time since the guard was unconscious or possibly dead.

Checking the gun, he noticed that it was still on safety.

With the safety off he stooped and felt the guy's neck. When he found a pulse he was relieved. He hadn't wanted to kill the one who had been considerate.

As he stood up it occurred to him that this guy, who for some reason had joined the Montoneros, could have been one of Mario's students.

He left the room, locking the door and pocketing the key. He held the gun ready in case there was someone else in the apartment. But he didn't see anyone, and he went out into the hall and down the stairs without running into anyone.

Outside, he kept the gun off safety until he had looked around and made sure that neither of the other guys was anywhere in sight. Then he stuck the gun into his belt and buttoned his jacket to cover it.

Keeping an eye out for the guys, he walked quickly toward a busy street, and when he got there he boarded the first *colectivo* that came along. He didn't care where it was going, he just wanted to get out of the neighborhood.

As the bus lurched forward, its engine blatting, he remembered his conversation with Cathy about fear, and only then did he succumb to it.

The bus took him north on Paseo Colón, and when it reached Córdoba he got off and took a taxi home from there.

"It's me," he said as Cathy hesitated to open the door.

"Oh, God," she cried, seeing him.

"I'm all right," he said, hugging her.

Evidently feeling the gun that he had stuck into his belt, she asked: "What's that?"

"A gun," he said. "It's a long story. But first I have to call Carlos, and then I'll tell you. Okay?"

"Okay." She stayed close to him as he went to the phone and dialed the bank.

Señora Pérez, who must have known that he was missing, still wanted to know why he was calling before she put him through to Carlos.

"Are you all right?" Carlos asked.

"I'm fine. Did you get a note from me?"

"You mean the one asking for eighty-five million dollars?"

"That's the only note I wrote."

"It didn't sound like you."

"It wasn't my idea. Did you pay it?"

"Are you kidding? The bank has a strict policy not to pay ransom money."

"I know, but—"

"You thought we would make an exception for you?"

"I was hoping you would. But I wasn't counting on it," he added lightly.

"Seriously," Carlos said, "we were in the process of getting the money, so I'm glad you called."

"It would have blown your budget."

"I would have paid anything for you."

"*Gracias*," he said appreciatively.

"Where are you?"

"At home."

"Well, I'm sending the car with a bodyguard—two bodyguards—and I'm going to leave them in front of your building. You will not go anywhere without them," Carlos told him. "Not for a walk, not out for dinner, not anywhere. Do you understand?"

"I understand."

"I'm calling head office as soon as we get off the phone. After what just happened, they'll want to transfer you back to New York."

"Will you recommend that?"

"No. I won't. I know you want to stay. But other people have a stake in your safety."

"I know," he said, thinking of Cathy.

After hanging up he set the gun on the coffee table and sank into the sofa.

"Can I get you anything?" Cathy asked.

"How about a brandy? Just bring the bottle and a glass."

When she had done this she sat down beside him.

He told her what had happened, and she listened without comment. She didn't have to tell him that this was exactly what she had been afraid would happen.

"Carlos is sending bodyguards," he told her. "They'll stay in front of the building."

"Good." She waited for him to tell her more.

"Head office will want to transfer me back to New York."

"Do you still want to stay?"

"Yeah. I do. But things are different now. The Montoneros know who I am, and they think I had something to do with the loss of their money."

"You did have something to do with it."

"Well, it doesn't matter what I did. What matters is what they think I did. So they might come after me again." He paused, remembering his worst fear. "You know, as I was lying in bed last night I imagined what would happen to you if they killed me. That's why I had to escape."

"While you were imagining that," she said in a strained voice, "I was imagining what they might do to you."

"I know," he said, abashed. "I don't want to put you through that again."

There was a knock on the door, which startled them.

"Señor," a familiar voice called from the hall. "I wanted to let you know we're here."

"Thanks," he shouted, getting up and going to the door. When he opened it he saw the driver, who was breathing heavily. "Are you all right?"

"The power's off," the driver explained. "So I had to climb the stairs."

"Well, take it easy going down."

"I will, señor. If you want to go anywhere, I'm parked in front of the building."

"*Bien. Gracias.*"

Before rejoining Cathy on the sofa he called Elena to let her know he was all right. He figured that his kidnapping had made the newspapers and that his friends had been worried about him. He gave Elena a shortened version of what had happened, and then he asked her to let the others know he was all right.

Cathy welcomed him back to the sofa with a warm place to lay his head.

They stayed in the apartment for the rest of the day, not wanting to stretch their luck even with bodyguards.

The next morning they left in the car, which dropped Cathy off at the bookstore with one of the bodyguards and then continued to the bank. On his way up to the third floor he stopped at the general manager's office, where he found Carlos standing by the desk of Señora Pérez.

"Come in," Carlos said in a heavy voice. He closed the door behind them and sank into a chair, saying: "They want to transfer you back to New York."

"I figured they would."

"I argued with them, but I didn't get anywhere."

"Did you talk with Frank?"

"I talked with Frank, and I talked with the head of personnel. They have a job for you in New York."

"That's good." He hadn't thought about it.

"They want you to leave without delay."

"What does that mean?"

"No later than this weekend."

"I have a lot of things to pack."

"We'll pack them for you."

"I have to say goodbye to my friends."

"You'll have time to do that."

"Okay. We'll leave on Sunday."

"I think I heard a plural."

"You did. I'm taking Cathy with me."

"She'll need a visa," Carlos pointed out, "and I don't know if you can get one that fast."

"I can. I have connections at the embassy."

Carlos smiled. "You mean the trade specialist and the agricultural attaché?"

"They owe me," Stephen said.

"I'll ask Señora Pérez to book the flight. Would you like to stay at the same hotel?"

"Yes. It was fine."

Before he left the office Carlos said: "No one in the bank will know you're leaving, except for Señora Pérez and me. I'll make an announcement after you've gone."

He understood. If it leaked out then the Montoneros would know they had only four more days to kidnap him again. "What will you say?"

"I'll say you've been promoted."

"Will they believe that?"

"Yes. It's true. You *have* been promoted."

For many reasons Stephen wasn't as pleased as he should have been.

When he got to the third floor he called the embassy and told John he needed a visa by the next day.

"For your fiancée?" John asked.

"For my wife," he said, making a decision.

"When did you marry her?"

"I didn't yet. But I'm going to."

"Before you leave?"

"Yes," he said. "I'll let you know the time and place."

"Then I'll start the ball rolling on her visa."

"Don't you need to know her name?"

"It's Catalina Linton, and she has an Argentine passport."

"That's right." He wondered what else they knew about her.

"I'll use her married name in the documents, which I assume will be Catherine Linton Wyatt."

"Yes. It will be."

After hanging up he left the third floor and took the elevator down to the entrance of the bank, where his bodyguard was waiting for him. He got into the car, followed by the bodyguard, and he told the driver to go to the bookstore. There they picked up Cathy and her bodyguard, and then he gave the driver directions to the *villa*.

As the car moved forward he told Cathy: "They've decided to transfer me back to New York."

"Then you have to leave Argentina."

"I have no choice." He could have found another job there, but after what had happened he couldn't expect her to live with her fear for him.

"I'm sorry," she said, understanding how he felt.

"We're leaving this Sunday. You need a visa since this time you're not going as a tourist. I have one of the embassy guys working on it." He paused, and then he said: "I asked him to issue you the visa as my wife."

"Your wife?"

"Yeah. I should have asked you first, but we have so little time. Will you marry me?"

"Before we leave?"

"It'll simplify the visa process."

"But what about your parents? Wouldn't they want to be at your wedding?"

"They'll understand," he assured her. "They wouldn't want us to live together without being married."

"No. They wouldn't," she agreed, evidently remembering the separate sleeping arrangements.

"You still haven't answered my question."

She looked at him with a tumult of feeling in her eyes. "Yes, I'll marry you. I love you. I want to have your children."

"Well, I just wanted to make sure before we talk to Paco."

"Is that where we're going?"

"We need a priest to marry us."

"You mean right now?"

"On Saturday."

"Oh." She smiled in relief. "At least that gives me time to wash my hair and change my clothes."

"We'll have a regular wedding," he told her.

"I have no idea what that is. I've never been to one."

"Your relatives and friends didn't have weddings?"

"They didn't get married. The women just had babies."

"Where were the men?"

"Making babies with other women."

At the *villa* they found Sofi, who had heard from Elena that he was all right.

She led them to Paco, who was teaching some children how to play *fútbol* on a dusty street. Paco left them, telling them to play for a while by themselves.

"Thank God you're all right," Paco said.

"We need a favor," Stephen said. As they stood there he was conscious of the bodyguards who were positioned on both sides of the street.

"Anything. Just name it."

"Cathy and I would like to get married."

"That's wonderful," Sofi said, putting her arm around Cathy.

Paco looked at Cathy and then back at him. "And you need a priest?"

Stephen nodded. "We'd like to have the wedding this Saturday."

"What's the rush?" Paco asked, scrutinizing him.

"It's not what you think. The bank's transferring me back to New York, and we want to get married before we leave."

"You're leaving Argentina?" Sofi asked, dismayed.

"I have to," he told her. "I have no choice."

"You mean because of what happened," Paco said as if he understood.

"The bank doesn't want to have the exposure."

"It won't be the same without you," Sofi said with tears forming in her eyes.

"I'll still be here in spirit."

"We don't have much time to find a church," Paco said.

"Could we get married in Socorro?" Cathy asked.

"Socorro? I don't know. With all those society people it's probably booked for the next two years."

"There might have been a cancellation," Stephen said.

"Well, I'll see what I can do. Maybe my bishop can help us."

While the women were talking about preparations Paco took him aside and said: "I know you're divorced. I hope you weren't married in a Catholic church."

"I wasn't."

"Good. Then it doesn't count."

The next morning he heard from Paco that with the bishop's help they had scheduled the wedding in a chapel at Socorro for Saturday morning.

That afternoon he and Cathy went to the embassy and concluded the process of getting her visa. He told John the time and place of the wedding, which John had already backdated for the paperwork.

Before they left, John asked: "Are you inviting anyone else from the embassy?"

"No. Just you and Bill."

"That's good. And I won't tell anyone else about it. We don't want the Montoneros to attend."

"You have them in the embassy?"

"Not that I know of, but they could have sources here."

"I'll ask Carlos to put on some extra bodyguards."

"I assume you haven't told many people about the wedding."

"We've just told our friends."

"How many people in the bank know?"

"Carlos and his secretary."

"Do you trust them?"

"Completely."

"You wouldn't have made a good agent," John said almost as a compliment. "It's a good thing you went into banking."

"Good for both of us," Stephen said.

When he returned to the bank he had a phone message from Boyd, who was in town for a weekend of rest and relaxation. As usual Boyd was staying at the Plaza Hotel, and he picked up his phone immediately.

"Could you have lunch today?" Boyd asked.

"I'd like to, but—" He explained what was happening.

"I never thought you'd leave Argentina," Boyd said as if he were in shock.

"I have no choice."

"I understand. But still, after all these years. I'm beginning to feel like the last American in Saigon."

"If you can get yourself out of bed this Saturday morning," Stephen said, "I'd like you to come to our wedding."

"Wedding? You're marrying that girl?"

"Yes. I'm marrying her." He gave Boyd the place and time of the wedding.

"Well, you don't mess around," Boyd said admiringly. "But even I could tell it was love at first sight. Congratulations."

"Thanks," he said. "I hope you can make it."

They were all at the wedding on Saturday: Elena and Sofi and Mario and Teresa and Vittoria and Carlos as well as John and Bill and even Boyd, who looked hung over. Cathy wore a navy blue suit with a white lace camisole that she had bought the day before, shopping with Elena, and he wore what he referred to as his banker's uniform, with a white shirt and a new tie that Cathy had bought for him.

Paco conducted the wedding mass with dignity, and Cathy responded with a clear, unwavering voice. As Stephen slipped the ring onto her finger he remembered what his mother had said to him in the kitchen, and he felt that her words applied to Cathy as well as him—they both knew what they were doing.

As they left the church he saw the bodyguards, and he was reminded of why they were leaving.

They had reserved enough tables for everyone at Ligure, where they spent the next few hours celebrating and saying goodbye. It was both a happy and sad occasion, though it felt as if the happiness of their wedding outweighed the sadness of their departure, even for a cynic like Boyd.

On Sunday they packed and then, accompanied by the bodyguards, they made a last visit to Plaza San Martín. It was a cold day, and the two women walking ahead of them both wore nutria fur coats.

They stopped and gazed up at the statue of the Liberator, who was still pointing toward the Andes with the usual pigeon perched on his finger.

Cathy clapped her gloved hands and made the pigeon fly away.

"That's better," he agreed. "They never should have brought pigeons here."

They were taking the overnight flight to New York, and they arrived at the airport with plenty of time since there was relatively little traffic.

He was tipping the driver when he heard a thud where Cathy was standing.

She dropped as if her legs had turned to rubber.

Not knowing what had happened, he knelt down beside her. She was lying on her back, and there was an ugly hole in her jacket over her heart.

"Get a doctor!" he yelled to the bodyguards, who were looking around to see who had fired the shot.

He attended to Cathy, who gazed up at him with a mixture of pain and sadness in her eyes.

He found one of her hands and held it.

"*Te amo,*" she said.

"*Te amo también. No te ve.*"

"*Bésame—*" she whispered. She tried to say another word that sounded like "*mucho.*"

He kissed her softly.

Her eyes glazed.

"Get a doctor!" he cried, though he could tell it was too late.

He laid his head on her, realizing that she had been trying to say "*Bésame mucho,*" the song they were playing at Minas when she asked him to dance.

The words echoed in his head dolefully: "Kiss me, kiss me a lot, as if tonight were the last time."

He rode with her body in the ambulance to the morgue, where he was questioned by two weary detectives who kept implying that he knew something that he wasn't telling them. They were at a stalemate when the commissioner, the man who had released Mario, joined them.

"We meet again," the commissioner said.

"Yes," Stephen murmured, feeling as if his insides had been ripped out.

"I know it won't make you feel better," the commissioner said, sitting down in one of the chairs, "but I have some information for you."

He waited, saying nothing.

"We found the weapon at the airport. It's a rifle that professional snipers use, with a silencer and a telescopic sight. It even has an infrared feature."

He didn't care what kind of rifle had killed her.

"The sniper dropped it right on the spot, and he went back to wherever he came from, probably on the next flight."

"So it was a contract killing," one of the detectives said.

"No doubt about it," the commissioner said. "This wasn't done by a terrorist or by one of our comrades."

Stephen had already figured that out.

"And she was the target, not you."

"I know," he finally said.

"Then maybe you can tell us why she was killed."

"She witnessed the murder of a man, his wife, and his three children."

"Where?"

"In Colombia. She changed her name and came here to hide from the people who did it."

"Who were they?"

"Drug lords."

"I wonder how they found her."

"I don't know," Stephen said, but he could guess. They followed the money she was sending to her mother, and they got someone in Panama to tell them where it was coming from. If he could track money, so could they.

"We'll do our best," the commissioner said, "but I don't think we'll ever catch the heartless fucker who did this."

"I don't expect you to."

"I'm so sorry. I have a daughter her age."

It was after two in the morning when the driver, who had followed him to the hospital with the bodyguards, took him back to his apartment. He wandered around aimlessly, going from one room to another, unable to bear the anguish of knowing that he would never see Cathy again.

He opened the door of the closet she had used, but it was empty. Then he went back into the living room, where the driver had left their luggage. He knelt on the floor and unzipped the suitcase in which Cathy had packed her clothes. On top was a dress, the one she had bought at Bloomingdale's and worn in Minnesota. He gently lifted it out of the suitcase and held it to his face, inhaling.

The next morning around nine someone knocked on the door of his apartment. Unable to sleep, he was lying on the sofa.

"Stephen? Are you there? It's Elena."

He pulled himself up from the sofa and went to the door.

When he saw her he lost it. He let go a reserve of tears that he must have still been holding back.

Elena took him into her arms.

After a while they sat down on the sofa, where she told him that she had heard about it from a news report.

At that point he decided to tell her the whole story.

When he had finished she said: "I didn't think it was the Montoneros."

"They're amateurs. The kid who was guarding me didn't even know enough to take his gun off safety."

They sat for a long time in silence.

"I don't know what to do," he said, feeling helpless. "I don't know whether to leave or stay. I mean, now there's no reason for me to leave."

"I thought they were transferring you back to New York."

"They were. But I could have found another job here. I was leaving because I didn't want Cathy to live with the fear that the Montoneros would kill me."

"So you were leaving because of her."

"Yeah. And now I feel like I should stay because of her."

Elena nodded as if she understood, and then she said: "If you stay, you'll have friends to support you."

He gave her a look that rejected the whole idea of his needing support.

"Stephen, don't look at me that way. You've supported us, and now it's our turn to support you. And don't tell me you don't need it."

"I never needed it before."

"Yes, you did. You just didn't know it."

"Well, maybe you're right," he finally said.

They held the funeral on Wednesday, July 14, at a church in Caballito, with Paco conducting the funeral mass only four days after he had married them. The same people attended the funeral, including the embassy guys and Boyd, who flew back up from Comodoro Rivadavia.

Paco had convinced him that he should do a reading. He didn't see how he would be able to control himself, but for Cathy and their friends he forced himself to go up to the pulpit and read from the First Epistle of John.

"Beloved, let us love one another, because love is of God; everyone who loves is begotten by God and knows God. Whoever is without love does not know God, for God is love. In this way the love of God was revealed to us: God sent his only Son into the world so that we might have life through him. In this is love: not that we have loved God, but that he loved us and sent his Son as expiation for our sins. Beloved, if God so loved us, we also must love one another. No one has ever seen God. Yet, if we love one another, God remains in us, and his love is brought to perfection in us."

Blinded by tears, he almost tripped going down from the pulpit, but Paco was there for him, taking his arm and guiding him in the right direction, toward the front pew where he had been sitting next to Elena.

After the Gospel, standing down with the congregation, Paco talked about Cathy and her short life. He ended by saying: "Our sister Catherine was a loving daughter, a loving wife, and a loving friend. She wanted to be a teacher, so that she could help children be what God imagined they could be when He created them. She was taken from us at the age of twenty-two, before she had a chance to give the world all the things she had to give. She was a victim of war, which arises from the fatal error of valuing money, power, or ideas more than human life. She is now with God, where war can never touch her again. May she rest in peace."

They buried her in Chacarita, and as Stephen trudged away from the cemetery he resolved to stay in Argentina.

Though the bank was sympathetic and gave him time to recover from his loss, the people at head office still didn't want him to stay there, and even with strong support from Carlos he lost the argument.

The day he got the bank's final decision he asked the driver to take him out to the *villa*. He still had two bodyguards, and they accompanied him through the dusty streets on high alert. Both had expressed their regrets for his loss of Cathy, and both still acted as if they had somehow failed at their job, though he had assured them that there was nothing they could have done to prevent what happened.

He found Sofi talking with an old woman who was missing

one of her front teeth. He listened as Sofi patiently explained the value of getting a medical check-up, which her organization would pay for. The woman resisted on principle but finally agreed to go to the clinic the next day.

"How are you doing?" Sofi asked when they were alone.

"Not well. You know what it's like."

She nodded. "You never get over it, but you have to keep going."

"That's why I'm here," he told her. "I want to stay in Argentina, but the bank won't keep me here, so I need a job. And if I remember correctly, the organization that Chris worked for never replaced him."

"They never did," Sofi said, brightening. "You want his job?"

"I've been doing it part time, so I have experience."

"I know they'll be happy to give it to you."

"So how do I contact them?"

She told him.

The bank gave him two weeks of vacation, which he used to go to Minnesota and see his family. He hadn't told his parents about the wedding or about what had happened to Cathy. There hadn't been time.

It was hard telling them, and he almost wished they hadn't met Cathy or known about her so that they could be spared the feeling of loss.

On the long flight back to Buenos Aires he thought about his family and about his friends, and he realized how lucky he was at a time like this to have a family and to have friends. Elena was right: he needed them.

He started his new job on Monday, August 2. His new employers understood that a necessary resource for economic development was education, so they were happy to let him work on building the church and the school while he looked for opportunities to help people start businesses.

On Friday evenings he met with his friends at the café on Avenida de Mayo, and on the second Monday of every month he went to Belgrano and had dinner with Vittoria, who was busy raising money for Sofi's organization and was now willing to let her mother help her with the children, within limits.

Mario and Teresa decided to stay, not out of fear of what might happen to them in Mexico but out of commitment to their students. The government continued to interfere with the university, and at times the situation got worse, but they stuck it out, hoping for a better future.

Sofi had her baby early in the morning of September 14. It was a boy, and she named him Christopher. The baby was baptized by Paco at the church in Caballito where they had held Cathy's funeral.

Elena remained on the business beat of her newspaper, and while her editor didn't let her write about the war, he did let her write about the economy, where instead of performing the miracle that Carlos expected, the military government was making things worse, especially for working people.

The church in the *villa* was completed in January, and the school was completed a month later in time for the next school year. To help organize the school, Paco found two Sisters of Mercy who had years of experience in administering schools that their order had founded for the Irish-Argentine community. The ceremony to inaugurate the school was attended by Paco's bishop, who praised the work that Christians were doing to help the poor and challenged the military government to follow their example, instead of making war.

Teresa started teaching at the school, leaving her job at a school that was closer to her home and taking the *colectivo* to work. She had never looked so happy. And she presided at the ceremony to dedicate the addition they made to the school, financed with money that they had raised—the Catherine Linton

Wyatt Library, which had books for people of all ages in the community.

Stephen kept going, trying to do his part, but every day he thought about Cathy, every day he remembered being with her, walking with her, talking with her, eating with her, sleeping with her, and waking with her.

Every month he sent money to her mother. There was no reason to use the method that Cathy had used since the people who killed her knew where to find him, so he transferred the money directly to the bank in Cali. Not wanting to delude her mother, who would see the money transfers as evidence that Cathy was alive, he included a letter with the first transfer, relating what had happened and telling her mother how happy Cathy and he had been during their short time together.

He didn't hear back from her mother, but six months later he heard from the bank that no one had ever picked up the money, so they were returning it.

BOOK CLUB GUIDE TO

No Way to Peace

Tom Milton

An introduction to *No Way to Peace*

Stephen Wyatt, an American banker in his early thirties, has volunteered to stay in Argentina and keep an eye on things after his American colleagues and their families have been evacuated for their safety. It is a time when foreign business managers as well as local managers who work for foreign companies are being kidnapped and held for ransom or simply killed by terrorists at the rate of more than one per week.

Stephen has just returned from New York, where he has finalized his divorce after a three-year separation from his wife, when he agrees to help a pair of CIA agents track the money that the terrorists have collected from their kidnappings. Evidently, they are laundering this money through his bank's branch in Panama and using it to bring arms into the country. Though Stephen supports their goal of social justice, he opposes the methods used by the terrorists, who have murdered many innocent people, including his assistant, who left behind a wife and three children under the age of five. So his motive for helping the CIA is to stop the killing.

That evening he meets a young woman who has fled her country and is living under a false identity for reasons that he will eventually learn. She has taken the name of Cathy Linton, the heroine in *Wuthering Heights*, which she was encouraged to read by an American teacher assigned to the school in the slum where she grew up. Inspired by him, Cathy pursued her education to the university, where she was studying to be a teacher when her life was shattered by a terrifying event.

Having lived in Buenos Aires for five years, Stephen has a group of friends who share his values: Chris, an American who works for a nonprofit organization committed to helping unemployed people start businesses; his wife Sofi, a social worker; Elena, a reporter for an English-language newspaper; Mario, a professor of political science at the university; his wife Teresa, a school teacher; and Francisco ("Paco"), a young priest who has dedicated his life to helping the poor in the slums (*villas miseria*) that surround the city of Buenos Aires. Outside this group of friends, Stephen also has an ongoing relationship with Vittoria, the young widow of his assistant, whom he tries to help in coping with her loss.

In love with each other, always in danger, and often needing bodyguards to protect them, Stephen and Cathy try to build a life together, but when the military take over the government the war of terror escalates and Stephen's friends become targets for their "subversive" activities. As he tries to save them from being tortured and killed by the military, Stephen gains a new perspective on the war, and from the women who deal with its havoc he learns the true meaning of courage.

A conversation with Tom Milton

Your novel shows how five women deal with a war of terror waged by men. Why did you use the point of view of a male character to tell the story?

I wanted distance, and I wanted to show all these women from a single point of view instead of jumping from one point of view to another. In some stories that can work well, but I didn't think it would work in this one. So I decided to use a male character who has some kind of relationship with each of the women.

Most novels set in a war focus on the courage displayed by men. Why were you interested in the courage of women?

In times of war, as in most times, women hold the world together. Males are all too willing to kill for money, power, or ideas, and without women to keep things going there wouldn't be anything left of the world.

You're referring to the constructive actions taken by the women in your novel, as opposed to the destructive actions taken by the men.

That's right. The women work for a better world while the men destroy it.

But your narrator, Stephen, and his male friends are working for a better world.

They are, but they're not typical. And it takes Stephen quite a while to understand that what he has been doing to stop the war will not lead to peace.

At the core of the novel is a love story involving Stephen, an American banker, and Cathy, a refugee from another Latin American country who is living in Argentina under a false identity. What was your interest in the love story?

Love is always heightened in a state of war since death is always imminent. I wanted to show two people, who have common values, falling in love and trying to build a life together under extremely stressful conditions. I wanted to show how love can triumph even under such conditions.

In one of their dialogues they talk about living with the fear that something will happen to the other person. Does this fear heighten their love for each other?

It does. We should always live in fear that something will happen to the people we love. I don't mean to the point where the fear incapacitates us, but to the point where we never stop appreciating them.

Discussion questions

1. Compare the five major female characters (Cathy, Elena, Vittoria, Sofi, and Teresa) with respect to the types of courage they show in their different situations.

2. What are the values that drive Cathy? How is her fate determined by a strict adherence to her values?

3. Describe the relationship between Elena and Stephen. Can you imagine it evolving into something else?

4. Compare the responses of Vittoria and Sofi to the loss of their husbands. How do they evolve as characters?

5. Teresa emerges relatively late as a character in the novel. How do her motivations change from the time Mario is arrested to the end of the story? Why do they change?

6. Adriana, though a minor character, plays a role in advancing the emotional awareness of some characters. What effects does she have on Cathy, Stephen, and Teresa?

7. Are Stephen's actions motivated by ideology? If not, what drives him?

8. If Stephen's friends knew that he was helping the CIA, how would they react? How would he justify his actions?

9. Discuss the issue raised by Stephen in his conversations with John and Bill about where to draw the line in dealing with terrorists.

10. Do John and Bill conform to your image of CIA agents? How does the author humanize them?

11. Carlos and Boyd have definite ideas of what should be done economically and politically to create stability in Argentina. What do you think of their ideas?

12. Which characters take advantage of opportunities presented by the war of terror, and how do they exploit the suffering of other people?

13. In the background of the novel is the rise of "liberation theology" in Latin America, an attempt by some clerical and lay members of the Catholic Church to redirect its focus toward helping the poor, freeing the oppressed, and achieving social justice. Where do you see its influence in the novel?

14. Explain what Paco means when he says: "The only way to stop the killing is to stop the killing." How does this idea relate to the book's title?

15. How do Stephen's perceptions of the Montoneros evolve during the course of the novel?

16. Does Stephen achieve redemption by the end of the novel?